T0012857

Praise for *The Woman from Lydia*

"*The Woman from Lydia* is a terrific story. I love the way Hunt weaves history throughout to bring readers into ancient times. The book is rich in detail, and the characters are fully rendered. Lessons and Scripture are smoothly woven into the story. And I love a happy ending."

Francine Rivers, *New York Times* bestselling author of the MARK OF THE LION series

"I couldn't stop reading. A long-proven, gifted storyteller, Angela Hunt takes her craft to new heights—and depths—as she fully immerses us in the lives and struggles of first-century followers of Yeshua. I *had* to learn the truth about what happens to Euodia and those she loves—and those who may wish her harm. Hunt's vast biblical knowledge shines through on every page while never overshadowing her master storytelling. Pure pleasure!"

Tamera Alexander, bestselling author of *Colors of Truth*

"I completely lost my heart to Euodia, Ariston, and Sabina. Hunt doesn't shrink from the harsh reality of life in the first-century Roman world. Life was cheap. But Messiah Yeshua taught His followers to love others, and we see that in the actions of the main characters of this story. A beautiful beginning to a new series."

Robin Lee Hatcher, bestselling author of *All She Ever Dreamed* and *To Enchant a Lady's Heart*

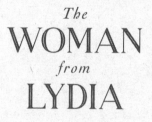

The
WOMAN
from
LYDIA

The WOMAN from LYDIA

ANGELA HUNT

BETHANYHOUSE

a division of Baker Publishing Group
Minneapolis, Minnesota

© 2023 by Angela Hunt Communications, Inc.

Published by Bethany House Publishers
Minneapolis, Minnesota
www.bethanyhouse.com

Bethany House Publishers is a division of
Baker Publishing Group, Grand Rapids, Michigan

Printed in the United States of America

All rights reserved. No part of this publication may be reproduced, stored in a retrieval system, or transmitted in any form or by any means—for example, electronic, photocopy, recording—without the prior written permission of the publisher. The only exception is brief quotations in printed reviews.

Library of Congress Cataloging-in-Publication Data
Names: Hunt, Angela Elwell, author.
Title: The woman from Lydia / Angela Hunt.
Description: Minneapolis, Minnesota : Bethany House, a division of Baker Publishing Group, 2023. | Series: The emissaries ; book 1 | Includes bibliographical references.
Identifiers: LCCN 2022061904 | ISBN 9780764241840 (casebound) | ISBN 9780764241567 (paperback) | ISBN 9781493442157 (ebook)
Subjects: LCSH: Lydia (Biblical figure)—Fiction. | Philippi (Extinct city)—Fiction. | LCGFT: Bible fiction. | Christian fiction. | Historical fiction. | Novels.
Classification: LCC PS3558.U46747 W66 2023 | DDC 813/.54—dc23/eng/20230103
LC record available at https://lccn.loc.gov/2022061904

Scripture quotations are from the Tree of Life Version. © 2015 by the Messianic Jewish Family Bible Society. Used by permission of the Messianic Jewish Family Bible Society.

This is a work of historical reconstruction; the appearances of certain historical figures are therefore inevitable. All other characters, however, are products of the author's imagination, and any resemblance to actual persons, living or dead, is coincidental.

Map is copyright © Baker Publishing Group.

Cover design by LOOK Design Studio
Cover model photography by Mike Habermann Photography, LLC

Author is represented by Browne & Miller Literary Associates.

Baker Publishing Group publications use paper produced from sustainable forestry practices and post-consumer waste whenever possible.

23 24 25 26 27 28 29   7 6 5 4 3 2 1

The Emissaries

The New Testament's book of Acts gives us brief outlines of Paul's missionary journeys. In his subsequent letters to the churches he founded, we can see Paul's love and concern in the way he praises, encourages, and admonishes the Gentile converts. But although the Scriptures paint an overall picture of the age in which they lived, the modern reader may find it difficult to fully appreciate the pressures facing the fledgling believers.

THE EMISSARIES series features the stories of men and women who came to faith through Paul's church-planting efforts in Gentile cities. Our own society—which grows ever more saturated with unbiblical worldviews—is not so different from that of ancient Rome. May we be challenged by the first-century believers' vision, courage, and commitment to Messiah Yeshua.

Since reading involves "hearing" words in your head, you might find it helpful to know the pronunciation of several names of people and places in this story. *Euodia* is pronounced U-oh-dee-ah, *Syntyche* is pronounced Sin-tee-chee (or -key), and *Magaere* is pronounced Meh-JEER-ah.

The Roman greeting *salve* is pronounced SAL-vey.

The early church was the *ecclēsia* (ek-la-SEE-ah), and our heroine, from *Thyatira* (Thy-ah-tire-ah) and *Philippi* (Fil-ip-pie), visits several cities: *Thessalonica* (Thess-ah-lo-ni-kah), *Amphipolis* (Am-fip-o-liss), and *Lychnidos* (Leek-nee-dose) as she travels the *Via Egnatia* (VEE-ah Egg-NOT-tee-ah). Some of these pronunciations may vary according to the source.

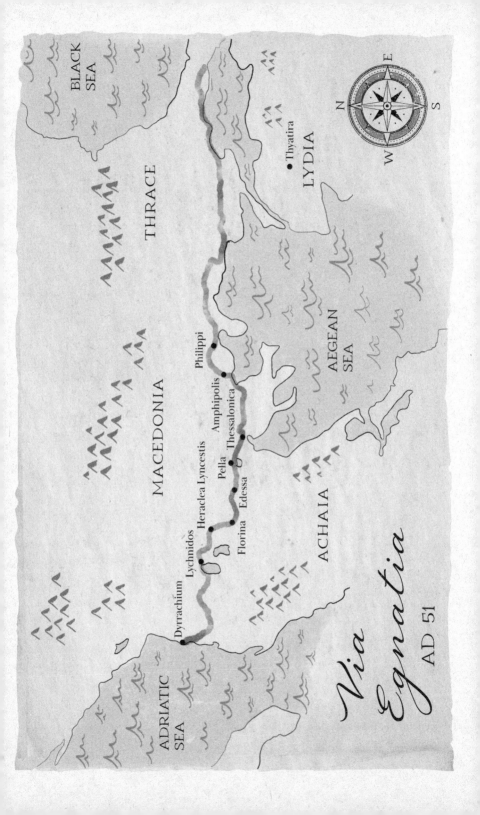

If a man gets lost in the mountains, hundreds will search and often two or three searchers are killed. But the next time somebody gets lost just as many volunteers turn out. Poor arithmetic, but very human. It runs through all our folklore, all human religions, all our literature—a racial conviction that when one human needs rescue, others should not count the price.

Robert A. Heinlein

One

APRIL AD 51

I stood in the river shallows, my smile tightening as Syntyche's little daughter splashed in the rippling water. "Adonai gave—" I whispered, pushing past the lump in my throat— "and Adonai has taken away, blessed be the Name of Adonai."

I looked away and bent to pick up a gray shape on the sand. Another snail of the right shape and size.

"I found another one!" A woman emerged from the middle of the river, her hair wet and her smile exultant. She waved a gray shell. "I thought I had found every snail in this spot, but the little beasts are good at hiding."

"You are blessed to be such a good diver," I called. "Not everyone can swim so well."

Behind me, an older woman complained, "My toes are as wrinkled as my face."

"I cannot feel my feet," another worker called, flashing a wide grin. "But I have nearly filled my basket. My children will eat well tonight!"

Syntyche watched us from the shore. "Fill your basket

completely and your husband will eat well tonight, too," she yelled, her voice reaching even the edge of our group. "Be sure to stop by the chicken keeper's booth at the market. My neighbor is selling a group of fat hens."

Syntyche's comment was unusually encouraging for a woman with a generally dour temperament, but she was doing exactly what I had hired her to do. Pleased with her efforts, I continued searching the shallows.

The valuable snails blended easily into the sand, but experience had taught me to spot them even when hidden among the rocks. I squinted yet found it difficult to focus with Syntyche's little daughter scampering at the river's edge. How could I spot anything through a veil of tears?

I blinked the wetness away and lifted my head. The sun hovered just above a bank of approaching clouds, so only two or three hours of daylight remained.

"Ladies!" I lifted my voice. "We have gathered enough for today. Now let us count the result of our efforts."

"And do not forget," Syntyche shouted, "tomorrow you will receive a bonus if you bring another woman to join us."

The women waded toward shore, the younger ones playfully splashing their friends. Syntyche moved behind the table and pulled the purse from her tunic, preparing to count the snails in each woman's basket.

I remained in the water, my eyes fixed on the sky. Behind me, Syntyche's daughter began to count the incoming waves of high tide, her childish treble rising above the softer chorus of women's voices. "*One, two, three . . .*"

"'You have changed my lament into dancing,'" I whispered, closing my eyes. "'You undid my sackcloth and girded me with gladness. You redeemed my soul from the battles that were upon me, for the sake of the multitudes who were with me . . .'"

Paulos had taught me those words, and they never failed to calm my mind. I could not honestly say I felt like dancing, but at least I was no longer mourning.

When I was certain my smile would not wobble, I turned and studied the women who stood in line to have their baskets examined. Nearly a dozen joined us today—young and old, married and widowed, and one as yet unmarried. A good group, but we could always use more willing hands. To complete my latest commission, I would need twice as many helpers.

The sun was within a hand's breadth of touching the horizon by the time I reached the table. "How did we do?" I asked, lowering my basket.

"We did well." Syntyche scrutinized my catch. "Have you counted yours?"

"Sixty-four."

"Good." She jotted the number on a parchment while I looked beneath the table and found her daughter sitting cross-legged on the sand. "Hello, Lena. What are you doing under there?"

"Waiting." The girl's lower lip edged forward in a pout. "I am hungry."

"Your mama will have dinner ready soon enough."

"Four hundred thirty," Syntyche announced, her voice dripping with disappointment. "Added to the count from prior days, we have four thousand six hundred snails. We are still a long way from ten thousand."

"But we are nearly halfway to our goal," I answered, determined to remain positive. "Tomorrow these women will

15

bring their friends, and then we will have enough hands to begin the extraction. We will send half to the water and put the others to work on the table."

"We will need wool. Do you have enough to begin?"

"I am going to the market now. Do not worry, dear friend." I nodded with a confidence I did not feel. "I will have everything ready."

Two

Hector stood in the doorway of his house and clenched his hands. One of the Nabatean's servants had arrived late last night, promising the mare would be delivered this morning. But though Hector looked up and down the street, he saw neither man nor horse.

He stepped onto the flagstone road and glanced left and right again, eager to see the horse that had cost him more than a common man would earn in two years. Since the Nabateans were famous for their fast, courageous horses, Hector had dared to spend a sizable chunk of his pension for a mare that should bear superlative foals. He would race some of them and breed those with no gift for racing. After twenty years of caring for the beasts of Rome's army, he knew how to spot an excellent broodmare—

He turned at the sound of iron-rimmed wheels grating against flagstone. A cloth-covered *cursus clabalaris* approached, driven by a man in Bedouin garb. The man met Hector's gaze and nodded, then pulled a pair of mules to a stop.

Hector felt an internal shiver as he approached the

conveyance. A good idea, hiding the magnificent beast from would-be thieves. Even better to have the clabalaris drawn by ordinary mules.

"How did she manage the journey?" he asked the driver. "Is she calm?"

The man dropped from the wagon and dipped his head in a show of respect. "A horse senses the mood of its handler," he said, smiling. "I am calm, and so is she." He gestured toward the back of the conveyance. "Come, I will show you."

Hector walked to the back of the clabalaris, where the driver lifted the bar from the double doors. They swung open, releasing the familiar scent of manure. Inside, Hector saw another Bedouin and his purchase, the Kohl-ani mare.

He sighed. "Magnificent."

"She is." The driver gestured to the servant, who had traveled with the horse. The man led the mare forward, tilting the wagon bed as the mare stepped onto the flagstones.

Smiling, Hector placed his hands on her head and took inventory. The mare's large, bulging forehead was a sign of intelligence and a blessing from the gods. Her muzzle was perfect, delicate and small. The flaring nostrils would allow her to inhale more air than other horses, and her wide rib cage would enable her to outrun any steed from Rome. The mare's blue-black skin was the color of kohl, the mineral wealthy women generously applied to their eyelids and lashes, hence the name *Kohl-ani* for this magnificent breed.

Hector ran his hands down the horse's forelegs, noting the fine bones and strong muscles. This animal had been bred for speed and stamina in the desert, enabling it to survive on dates and camel's milk. Its strong hooves could gallop over sharp rocks and hot sand. Though the mare appeared as delicate as a flower, Hector knew she could carry heavy loads over great distances.

"Age?" he asked.

"Three years," the driver answered. "And she is well trained."

Hector looked into the mare's eyes. Few animals had been able to withstand his gaze; most looked away after a moment, if they looked at him at all. But this mare . . . her wide brown eyes took him in, then she blew out a breath and lowered her head as if acknowledging his ownership.

"Amazing beasts," he murmured.

"Yes," the driver agreed, "and quite affectionate with humans. Like many others, my family invites our horses into our tent, and we raise their young with our own. I have found that the Kohl-ani's desire to please is as strong as a dog's."

Now, thanks be to the gods, this mare belonged to him.

The driver cleared his throat. "Would you like to examine her gait?"

"Of course."

The driver nodded to the servant, who walked the mare down the street, then turned and brought her back.

"Stop." Hector peered at the right foreleg, then glared at the driver. "Did you know this horse was lame?"

"I do not believe she—"

"Watch her. When she walks, her head bobs and her stride is short. There is a problem with her right foreleg."

The Bedouin frowned but bade the servant walk the mare forward and back again. "It is not a serious problem," he said. "You must remember that she has been locked inside the clabalaris for many days."

"She should have been exercised."

"She was, when time allowed. We could not bring her out

when strangers were present. I would sooner die than have your horse stolen."

"I did not pay nine hundred denarii for a lame mare."

The Bedouin squinted. "How can you know so much about horses? You were a soldier, yes?"

"A soldier in the Roman cavalry. Twenty years of riding in an *alae quingenariae* will teach a man a thing or two about four-legged beasts."

"Ah." The Bedouin folded his hands. "I do not doubt your expertise, but I believe you will find this mare is sound. A little tired perhaps, but if she is rested, she will be worth every denarius."

"And if the problem worsens?"

The man lifted his hands. "She would still be suitable for breeding. A mare does not have to run."

"She has to stand. She has to bear the weight of the stallion." Hector shook his head. "I will not accept a lame horse."

Lines of concentration deepened along the driver's brows. "How can I return the horse to my master? She was sound when he put her in the wagon."

Hector shook his head, stunned by the man's blindness. "If she was sound and now is lame, then the problem must have arisen on her journey to Macedonia . . . while she was under your supervision."

The Bedouin paled beneath his tan. "What if I pay you . . . twenty denarii?"

Hector barked a laugh. "Twenty? I paid nine hundred."

"But my master gave me forty for the journey, and I have already spent ten."

"Thirty"—Hector smiled—"will be sufficient to offset my loss."

"But how will we travel with no coin?"

Hector shrugged. "You can hunt your food and sleep outdoors. I will accept the thirty denarii and the mare, and you may go your way in peace."

The man scuffed his shoe on the flagstones, muttering under his breath, but finally he nodded. "We are agreed. There is your horse." He pulled a leather purse from his girdle. "And here are twenty denarii."

"Thirty, and not a coin less."

Sighing, the driver gave Hector the purse, which Hector tossed toward his door. He moved to the horse and caressed the mare's strong jawbone. The animal might be lame, but she would heal. Hector would make certain she did.

"Welcome to my home," he said, feeling suddenly generous. He opened the door to his house and called for his steward, who appeared almost immediately.

"Show this man and his servant into the atrium and provide them with food and drink. Let them rest for a quarter of an hour, then see them safely away."

As the Bedouins followed the slave, Hector picked up the purse and walked the mare to the stall behind the house, his heart lifting with the comforting sound of her sure, steady hooves on the flagstone street.

Three

The sun traveled steadily toward the horizon, but it had not yet reached the tops of the merchants' tents outside the city gate. I looked up in gratitude as Ariston, my steward, arrived with the wagon while Syntyche and Lena were leaving. He helped me empty the baskets of snails into the large clay pots on the wagon, then he covered them with enough water to prevent them from drying out.

"A good day's work," he said, stacking the empty baskets. "Your helpers must be feeling quite prosperous."

"They are feeling exhausted, as am I." I smiled. "But I am sure their husbands will appreciate their wages."

Ariston climbed into the wagon and put out his hand to help me, but I shook my head.

"Won't you be coming home, Domina?"

"Not yet." I gestured to the road that led into the city. "I need to visit the market and secure our wool—we must begin dyeing tomorrow."

"Would you like me to drive you? The hour grows late."

"I would rather see the snails safely stored. I will not be long."

Ariston frowned, quietly disapproving, then flicked the reins and urged the mule toward my villa.

I quickened my stride as the shadows arose. The transient vendors' booths stood in a swath outside the city walls, and those who did not live in Philippi had already retired to their tents. The wool merchant's booth had been covered by a cloth, but a torch gleamed outside the tent behind it.

I tiptoed toward the tent and called a greeting. "*Salve!* Will you come out, sir?"

The merchant's bearded face appeared between the panels of his tent, and his eyes brightened in recognition. "The woman from Lydia! You have come late today."

"Please forgive the hour, but I have spent all day by the river." I cleared my throat, hoping I looked more like a businesswoman than a windblown wanderer. "I have been commissioned to create a purple cloak, so I shall be requiring the best wool you can provide. My client has asked that it be soft."

"An entire cloak of purple? And of soft wool." He whistled. "Would this be intended for a king?"

I gave him a coy smile. "Hush, sir, lest we be accused of treason. My client wants the cloak delivered before cold weather arrives. Since the calendar has already turned to Aprilis, I must set to work at once."

The merchant clicked his tongue against his teeth. "A cloak like that can only be intended to curry favor . . . perhaps this wealthy man intends to visit the emperor? Claudius's birthday is only four months away."

"I would not know, sir."

"And if you knew, you would not tell." Grinning, he moved closer. "You will want halo hair wool," he whispered. "It is uncommonly fine, quite soft, and outrageously expensive. No one in Philippi can afford it, so I usually sell it elsewhere."

"Price is no object," I assured him. "Have you enough of this wool on hand?"

"Not yet," he said, "but I have enough for my wife to begin the carding. We will have more when last year's spring lambs are shorn, and I will reserve the choicest bundles for you."

I did a quick mental calculation. I would need some wool this week, but if he could guarantee additional wool by early summer, I should have enough to complete the project before winter.

"Thank you," I told him. "We will dye the wool before your wife cards and spins it. If you can set aside what you have on hand, I will retrieve it later this week."

A smile curved the merchant's mouth. "Thank you, my lady. May the gods watch over you as you sleep."

"I sleep secure in HaShem," I answered, returning his smile. "And I wish the same for you."

Four

Hector filled the manger with oats and fresh hay, then rubbed his nose, which itched from the dust. Trying not to sneeze, he stepped back and admired his new mare. By all the gods, he had never seen a more beautiful beast.

As the mare snuffled and chomped the hay, he ran his hand over her, palpating her neck, spine, and the tendons in her legs. He massaged her strained foreleg and stood back to observe the results. She had not shied away from the pressure of his fingers, and from the solid way she stood, he suspected the leg would be fully healed by the morrow. In two days' time, she would be ready to travel.

He looked up as Lucius entered the barn and whistled. "She *is* a beauty," Lucius said, running his hand along the mare's flank. "Her eyes are as big as pomegranates."

"Not quite," Hector said, "but they are larger than the slitty-eyed nags we used to ride."

"We used to take pride in those slitty-eyed nags."

"Only because we had never seen animals like this."

Lucius strolled around the horse and nodded in approval. "I cannot wait to see her run. Will you take her out tomorrow?"

"Not to run." Hector shook his head. "She has a touch

of lameness in her foreleg, but nothing serious. Still, it was enough for me to persuade the Bedouin to refund thirty denarii."

"Of course it was." Lucius grunted as he ran his hand over the mare's front leg. "You applied a poultice?"

"Massage. I plan to take her out tomorrow morning, but only for a walk."

"She is worthy of an emperor." Lucius patted the horse again, then leaned against the side of the stall. "I am glad I found you. I have been meaning to speak to you about a serious matter."

Caught off guard by a tremor in Lucius's voice, Hector rested his arms on the mare's back and studied his friend. "I do not think I have ever seen you so serious . . . in peacetime, that is."

"True enough." Lucius crossed his arms. "I came because we have been together a long time."

Hector snorted. "I have never heard you complain of my company."

"But sometimes . . . sometimes a man yearns for the companionship of someone unlike himself. Like a woman."

Hector tipped his head back and laughed. "When have you ever foregone the pleasures of women? Whenever the urge struck, you found your way to the comely daughters of those who shod our horses—"

Lucius cast a look of tempered disdain in Hector's direction, then returned his attention to the mare. "I have always had your companionship, Hector, but I have never had a woman as a friend. I think they must be entertaining, even pleasant creatures unless crossed. Why would so many men marry if it were not so?"

"They marry because they are poor," Hector answered. "Their fathers force them to marry the daughters of wealthy men."

"No, wealthy men marry, too, and sometimes they wed the daughters of poor men. Like a beautiful mare, women have an allure all their own. They can be ethereal creatures—"

"I know what women have," Hector snapped. "And I know some men are addled by their charms. I have never been so easily distracted."

He turned away, hoping Lucius would change the subject, but apparently the man had not finished.

"For some time," he said, following Hector around the mare, "I have wanted to marry. If I am to take a wife, I must do it now."

Hector stopped and stared, momentarily speechless. Then he grunted. "You have forgotten the story of Lucius Iunius Brutus, who killed his own sons when they joined a conspiracy to restore a king to the Republic. Rome must always come first, even before family."

"I have not forgotten him," Lucius replied. "Indeed, my father often urged me to be proud because I bore his name. Yet though I may take a wife, I will always love Rome. Rome should therefore love me and allow me this small measure of happiness before I exit this world."

Hector allowed the silence to stretch a moment, then lifted his brow. "Have you a woman in mind or will you take the first who catches your eye? Perhaps you'd like the chief magistrate's daughter. Or the emperor's. I hear Claudia Octavia is quite beautiful."

Lucius sighed. "Jest if you like, but I have taken note of

a particular young woman in the marketplace. Her name is Celena, the daughter of a silk merchant."

"Does this girl know you exist?"

"Our eyes have met." One corner of Lucius's mouth curled upward. "She does not turn away in revulsion."

"She does not know you, then."

"How could she? She is continually chaperoned. But I believe she will make an agreeable—even a pleasant—wife."

Restless and irritable, Hector picked up a brush and briskly applied it to the mare's neck. "What if her father objects to a retired soldier? You are no longer a young man. And your wealth, while adequate, is not limitless. As to your status, you may be a newly minted Roman citizen, but you are not well known in Philippi."

Lucius straightened. "We have owned a house here for two years. I can support a family. Surely Celena could do no better."

"Her father may not appreciate your fortune because his is larger. There is plenty of coin to be made in silk."

Lucius drew a deep breath. "I am only a man, Hector; I cannot usurp the gods' will. So I will ask the silk merchant for his daughter and accept his decision. But first I wanted to speak to you."

"Why?" Hector shrugged. "Whether or not you marry makes little difference to me. Speak to the merchant. If he is willing to give you his daughter, I will not complain." He bared his teeth in an expression that was not a smile. "I might even be happy for you. If you are married, we shall no longer have to share Berdine."

He had intended to irritate his friend, but Lucius ignored the reference to the slave they co-owned. "I do not care about

Berdine. I want a son, Hector, I want a family. I want to fill my villa with children—"

"Your villa?" Hector stared as shock slapped him. "And children? Why do you think you could raise *children*?"

Lucius swallowed hard. "I was once a child. I remember what my father taught me, so I can teach children of my own."

Turning away, Hector brushed the mare and searched for memories of the man who had raised him. He recalled the soft touch of a mother, the voices of villagers, and days spent scrambling for scraps of food. In the winding length of his memories, he could not find even a trace of a father.

"Can you recall the man who raised you?" he asked. "I would wager that many more recent lessons fill your mind. Will you teach your sons how to thrust a *lancea* while charging at the enemy? Will you teach them how to destroy women and children with one strike of the *gladius*?" Hector's face heated. "When you hold your infant son, will you think of the infants you slammed against brick walls in Britannia? Will you remember the pregnant bellies you opened?"

The thin line of Lucius's mouth tightened, and his face went the color of ash. "I want to forget those things." His voice broke. "I want to raise children like any other Roman citizen. I want to be a proper father and leave a legacy for sons and daughters."

Hector closed his eyes and groaned. The softness of retirement had muddled Lucius's thoughts. In all the years of their training and toiling together, Lucius had never spoken of children and family. The only time he spoke of women was after a victory when his desire for release could not be contained . . .

Hector spat on the floor. "Did you pay no attention when

our *prefectus alae* shared reports from other retired comrades? Those who are not fortunate enough to live in Rome do not live long. Those who settle in the provinces—men like *us*, Lucius—die from old wounds, harsh weather, and pox. You have lived nearly fifty years, and you may not live another ten. How do you intend to raise a child to manhood? What kind of legacy can be obtained by leaving fatherless children behind?"

Hector waited, feeling the heat of his friend's stare.

Lucius lifted his chin. "What you say may be true, but I am in good health, I do not like Rome, and I know my own mind. A family is what I want. I want to enjoy more than a woman's body; I want her companionship. I want to claim a child and raise him for as long as the gods grant me that privilege. I want to be the *paterfamilias* of my own household, in my own house, so I beg you to name an amount. How much will you give me for my share of this house?"

Hector blinked, unaccustomed to such frankness. Until that moment, Lucius had always been easily persuaded, even when Hector suggested activities that might result in a flogging.

But something had changed. Perhaps Lucius had been moved by the sight of a man and his family at the theater, or perhaps he had wearied of Hector's friendship. Perhaps he had grown bored with retirement, and domesticity seemed an exciting new venture.

"So be it," Hector said. "Together we paid two thousand denarii for the house. But now you want out . . . and I should be compensated for the inconvenience of losing a partner."

"My portion of the estate is worth one thousand denarii." Lucius flexed his jaw. "That is what you should pay me."

Hector spread his hands. "Have I no voice in the matter? You are leaving me with a large house and slaves I will have to feed and clothe. Furthermore, you have given me no warning, no opportunity to prepare—"

"We purchased the house only two years ago," Lucius protested. "The value has not changed because we have made no improvements, and there is no shortage of housing in Philippi—"

"Then you should easily be able to find a house for your future family." Smiling, Hector extended his hand. "I will give you five hundred denarii for your investment in the house. Let us agree to the price, and I will be the first to congratulate you when you carry your bride over the threshold."

Lucius hesitated, then shook Hector's hand. "I agree, but only because I am eager to begin my new life. As to the slaves—"

"We will continue to own them together," Hector said. "If you need Titan or Berdine, send for them. I can't imagine why you would need the girl, but if you do . . ."

"To your future, comrade." Lucius gripped Hector's hand again. "May you always be as wily as you are at this moment."

Five

Ariston greeted me as I crossed the threshold, then took my cloak and handed it to Phebe, who had apparently been waiting with him in the vestibule. "I am glad you are home safe," he said, his voice a disapproving growl near my ear. "It is not good for a woman to walk alone after dark."

"I did not have to travel far."

"But, Domina, a thief could overcome you anywhere. And since—" He bit his lip, but the rest of his thought echoed, unspoken, in the entryway: *you have no husband to protect you.*

I smiled. "Do you need anything from me, Ariston?"

He cleared his throat. "The cook wants to know what you would like for dinner . . . and if you would prefer to eat in the *triclinium* or your chamber."

A sigh passed through me, a wave of weariness that ended when Phebe took my arm.

"Come," she ordered, pulling me after her. "You will eat in your room. I will tell Dione myself."

I did not argue, though I felt too tired to enjoy a meal. But I would eat because I would need strength for the morrow,

35

a day that would involve more harvesting as well as dyeing. Some of our new workers had no experience with purple, so I would have to teach them.

"I am not terribly hungry," I told Phebe. "Have Dione bring whatever she prepared for you and Ariston."

"But, Domina—"

"Thank you, Phebe." I pulled away and inhaled a deep breath of the lavender incense burning in the hallway. "I will eat, move to the atrium for prayers, and go to bed. Everyone is welcome to join me for the evening benediction."

I went immediately to my bedchamber, a spacious room that opened to the garden at the back of the villa. Everything appeared as I had left it that morning, save for Phebe's tidying the bed and draping a clean tunic over my trunk.

I sat on the edge of the mattress and rubbed the back of my neck. The day had been long, the work tedious, and the result far from satisfactory. Not only was I weary, but like an unwelcome guest, grief had shoved its way into my emotions whenever the sight of Lena reminded me of how much I had lost . . .

Thunder growled in the distance, heralding the approach of a storm. If the rain lingered until after sunrise, the women would not come to work, and we would lose a day of an already demanding schedule. Polydorus, who had come all the way from Thessalonica to deliver an order from the governor of Macedonia, had insisted that the purple cloak be finished by the time his master visited Rome in the winter.

We had seven months to finish the work, and we had scarcely begun.

I buried my face in my hands. "You have given me a new life, HaShem, and I thank you for your goodness. You have provided for my needs, and I praise you for your kindness. You have sent me faithful servants, and I can never repay your mercy. But, Abba, my heart still clings to memories that will not fade. If you will not remove them from my mind, you must dull my feelings so that I am not distracted from the work you have given me to do. Please, Abba, will you do that for me?"

I heard nothing in the stillness of my chamber, save for the expectant beating of my heart.

❖

After eating a light dinner, I went to the atrium and knelt on the tiles. As was my custom, I prayed silently for a while, allowing my servants time to join me.

When I had finished my personal prayer, I remained on my knees, drinking in the nighttime sounds of the house, the churring of insects in the garden, and the dazzling sight of thousands of blazing lights against a velvet sky.

I heard the soft sound of Dione's and Phebe's slippers, followed by Ariston's heavier tread. One by one they joined me.

I closed my eyes and begged Adonai to remind me that I was a slave, just as my servants had once been. I wanted to be nothing more than a slave to Yeshua Messiah, just as Paulos proclaimed himself to be, but it was easy to forget my status. At times I was tempted to order people about like a Roman domina; at other times I felt myself crumbling beneath the fears and failings of my past. How would I ever find balance in this new life?

"Remind me," I whispered, pitching my voice so the others could hear. "Remind all of us that though we are free from the darkness that once held us captive, we are slaves to Yeshua, who gave His life for us."

Then I recited one of the nightly prayers I had been taught at the synagogue: "Master of the universe, I hereby forgive anyone who angered or antagonized or sinned against me—whether against my body, my property, my honor, or against anything of mine, whether she did so accidentally, willfully, carelessly, or purposely, whether through speech, deed, thought, or notion—I forgive everyone. May no man or woman be punished because of me. May it be your will, HaShem, that I sin no more. Whatever sins I have done before you, may you blot out in your abundant mercies. May the expressions of my mouth and the thoughts of my heart find favor before you, my Rock and my Redeemer."

The others joined me as I continued with the benediction: "Blessed are you, HaShem, our God, King of the universe, who casts the bonds of sleep upon our eyes and slumber upon our eyelids. May it be your will, HaShem, our God, that you lay us down to sleep in peace and raise us up in peace. May our ideas, bad dreams, and bad notions not overwhelm us, may our offspring be perfect before you, and may you illuminate our eyes lest we die in sleep. For it is you who illuminates the pupil of the eye. Blessed are you, HaShem, who illuminates the entire world with Your glory."

The others fell silent as I closed our benediction: "We ask these things, HaShem, our Father, in the name of Messiah Yeshua, your only begotten Son. Amen."

My servants rose silently and left me alone. I swallowed hard, unable to rid my throat of the lump that rose when I prayed *may our offspring be perfect before you . . .*

"Domina?" Ariston's voice, low and gentle, reached my ear. "Are you all right?"

"I do not need anything." I forced a smile, though I did not turn to look at him. "You may go to bed."

When he had gone, I lifted my gaze to the night sky and searched until I spotted the North Star. "Do not leave me lonely, Abba. I have a home and a willing heart if you will send me someone else to love."

Six

Resplendent in a new tunic and robe, Lucius invited Hector to enter his new home. His *domus* was not far from the one they had shared, and though the place was a good deal larger, it was also in a state of disrepair. Hector had no sooner crossed the threshold when a stench of dampness and rot slammed his nostrils. The red paint on the interior walls had faded, several of the mosaic tiles in the vestibule had gone missing, and the plaster surrounding the niches in the study had chipped away. The empty pool in the atrium smelled of mildew, cracks spidered through the concrete basin, and weeds crowded what must have once been a beautiful garden.

After the tour, Hector turned toward his friend, broken bits of plaster grinding beneath his sandals. Lucius wanted reassurance, but Hector did not possess a gift for making light of a dire situation. "You will need to hire someone to make the necessary repairs," he said, trying not to frown. "But you will definitely have room for a wife, children, and several slaves. At least a dozen of each, I would say."

"A dozen wives?" Lucius grinned as he led the way to the

triclinium, the most serviceable room in the house. "One will do."

"Will you do all the work as well?"

Lucius shook his head. "I plan to begin by purchasing a slave with construction skills—preferably someone young. He will make the house his life's work and eventually it will reach perfection."

Hector wanted to reply that Lucius would be fortunate if the house was made acceptable in his lifetime, yet he swallowed his retort and instead studied the faded mural on the dining room wall. Though his friend had been fearless in battle and was as strong as an ox, he had never been able to look behind a man's eyes and determine his true intent. Clearly, he had not glimpsed the desperation of the man who had sold him this wreck, and he had failed to realize that this house, with its chipped moldy pillars and rotting roof timbers, would need a team of skilled tradesmen to achieve respectability.

Hector walked to the entryway and clasped his hands behind his back, pretending to study the street.

"So?" Lucius asked, an air of expectation in his voice. "What do you think? I paid only nine hundred denarii."

"You paid too much," Hector answered, not meeting his friend's eye. "But I am certain you will be happy here." He closed his eyes, choking back the torrent of words that threatened to spew from his lips. Lucius would never comprehend how deeply his desertion had hurt. For two days he had been absent from the house they shared, and Hector found the place desolate and empty without Lucius's company.

Hector still could not believe Lucius wanted to create a

family of his own, and he struggled to accept his friend's lack of loyalty. Rome required that a soldier be faithful above all else, but apparently Lucius had retired that vow when he set aside his armor.

Very well. Let Lucius take a wife and establish a family; Hector would establish a fortune.

"Tell me, have you spoken to the woman who is to be your wife?"

Lucius smiled, his scarred cheeks lifting. "Not yet, but I am making preparations. Two nights ago I attended a meeting of the city officials and introduced myself to the chief magistrate."

"Albanus Marinus? The man we tasked with confronting those Jews?"

"The same. I reminded him of our first meeting and mentioned that I hoped to raise a family in Philippi. Then, naturally, I asked about *his* family and learned he has a son and two marriageable daughters."

"Ah," said Hector, "you could not ask for a more convenient situation."

"So it seems. As soon as I get the public areas of my house renovated, I plan to invite his family to dine. I will have an opportunity to evaluate his daughters; he will have an opportunity to assess me."

"And what of the silk merchant's lovely girl?"

"Oh." Lucius flushed. "A city magistrate ranks higher than a silk merchant, no? And if you are correct, I have only a few more years to make my mark on this city. I might as well begin at the top."

Hector laughed. "I am honored, comrade, that you paid attention to my advice. I commend your plan and hope you will invite me to dine as well. I am most interested in watching you attempt this great endeavor."

The grooves beside Lucius's mouth deepened into a relieved smile. "You see? I knew you would begin to appreciate the charms of a domestic life." He gestured to the doorway and led the way to the street. "I am glad you came by for yet another reason—I was hoping you would accompany me to the marketplace. The slave seller has just received a new shipment, and I would appreciate your opinion before I buy."

"Are you sure you want only one slave?" Hector pointed to the decaying space behind him. "If you want to impress the magistrate, you will need at least a steward, a cook, a manservant, and a construction worker."

Lucius's smile faded. "I had hoped one would suffice for now. I can always borrow Berdine or Titan . . ."

"The future is not as certain as you seem to think," Hector said, clapping his friend on the shoulder. "When a powerful man declares that his daughters are of marriageable age, they are not available for long."

Seven

"This," I told the women, pointing to the border at the bottom of my stola, "is a common shade of purple. As you can see, it has a red tint because it comes from the madder root. This color is highly prized in Thyatira and beyond, but the purple we get from the murex snail is Tyrian royal purple, an unfading and balanced blend of red and blue. This is why we use snails. Our purple is of higher quality than that made from plants, and our wool more costly than that produced by the Lydian *collegia*."

I smiled at several new arrivals, who had already been grumbling about the prospect of spending several hours in the water. "That is why we search among the rocks, and that is why you earn one assárion per snail. By finding only sixteen snails, you could buy a sheep for your family and sell its wool to us. As long as purple is in demand, you will find steady work with me."

I nodded at a woman I recognized from our *ecclesia*. "HaShem once spoke of Zebulun, one of the tribes of Israel, and said, 'They shall draw out of the abundance of the seas, and of treasures hid in the sand.' These snails are the treasures HaShem planted for us. They are used to create the steadfast blue used in every Jewish prayer shawl and in the curtains at the Temple in Jerusalem. They are *true* treasures, and today we will uncover them."

"You mentioned the sea," a woman said, frowning. "This is not the sea, but a river."

"Yes, but it flows on to Neapolis and then to the sea," I said, realizing that most of these women had never ventured beyond Philippi. "When the tide comes in, seawater flows into the river, and many of the creatures find their way to us."

I pointed to the wagon, where our baskets waited. "Those of you who are new, stay close to one of the experienced workers. They will help you judge between living snails and empty shells. They will also provide you with lively conversation." I smiled. "Those of you who are harvesting, take a basket and follow the others into the river. Those who have been chosen to apply the dye, remain here with me."

The harvesters picked up their baskets and splashed into the water, squealing as the cold liquid shocked their skin. After their initial glee, they bent their heads and started searching, chattering with the freedom of women who had been silent for too long. Some of the younger girls waded farther out and dived beneath the surface, appearing a few moments later to catch a breath.

The five most experienced women remained behind, ready to learn the art of creating royal purple. As they gathered around the table, I searched the sky and saw nothing but puffy white clouds against a brilliant blue. A good day for dyeing.

Syntyche sat at the end of the wooden table, her arms crossed and her expression stony. At least she had left her daughter at home.

I gestured for the dyers to come closer, then reached into a pot of shells and extracted a handful. "Take one," I said, extending my hand. "Set the shell on the table and use a rock to break it. Once you have cracked it, slide your finger into the curve of the shell, and scrape out the snail. On the body, you will see a yellow bit, that's what we need. Do not be alarmed by the smell—the stench will not harm you. Watch how I do it."

The women scooped up small rocks and watched with uncertain expressions as I brought a rock down on the largest part of the shell. They followed my example and grimaced as they struggled to extract the gelatinous creature from the broken bits.

"This," I said, using my fingernail to separate the yellow portion from the rest of the snail. "This part must be set aside. Be careful—these tiny portions are worth twenty times their weight in gold."

My students struggled to extract the proper material, each woman crinkling her nose and holding the snail at arm's length as they extracted the element we needed.

"Good." I nodded as the last woman wiped her finger on the table, leaving the yellowed bit on the wood. "Now take another snail and do it again. Today we will extract material from the snails harvested yesterday, and tomorrow we will repeat the process."

"We will have to smell them *again*?" one woman asked.

I laughed. "You will grow accustomed to the odor. I have."

Once I was certain the women knew exactly what to do, I left them with Syntyche and picked up a basket. The waders' excited chattering had ceased, and most of the workers seemed intent upon their task.

I stepped into the water and observed the newcomers. Like the others, they wore plain wool tunics and braids that dangled over their backs. They were not women of elevated status, but they wanted to help feed their children. These were the wives of common workers: the coppersmith, the potter, the chicken farmer, and the tanner. I recognized another woman as the wife of the slave dealer, who had given me a cup of honey water the day I purchased Dione and Phebe. She had gawked in stupefaction when I asked her to be sure my new slaves had long tunics because I would free them as soon as we left the marketplace.

I caught her eye and smiled encouragement, then studied the sand beneath my bare feet. Had the slave seller's trade slowed so much that his wife had to work for me? Or had this woman grown weary of her husband's business?

I focused on my task. Last night's storm had stirred the waters and exposed more hidden treasures. I found six snails almost at once and was reaching for a seventh when I heard Syntyche shout a warning. "Stop! I saw you take snails from that other woman's basket. Come here at once, thief!"

I turned. One of the newcomers—the coppersmith's wife, I believed—stomped out of the water, her eyes narrowed into slits. Her right hand was clenched, her basket empty.

Syntyche marched toward her. "Open your hand."

The woman stiffened and lifted her chin. For a moment I feared she would either strike Syntyche or defy her, but with a look of utter disdain, the woman unlocked her fingers, revealing three snails.

Syntyche snatched them from the woman's palm and splashed into the shallows, dropping them into another woman's basket.

"As for you," Syntyche yelled, turning toward the offender, "leave us and do not return! This place is for God-fearing, hardworking women, and we have neither the time nor the patience for women like you—"

"Wait." The word slipped from my tongue before I knew I had spoken.

Syntyche halted, her gaze darting toward me.

I walked toward the thief. When I stood close enough to peer into her eyes, I spoke in the gentlest tone I could manage. "Why would you steal from someone when the sand holds more than enough snails for all?"

The flame in the woman's eyes flared. "Why? Because I have five hungry children. The youngest is a baby, so I cannot spend all day at the water."

My heart twisted, for I was acquainted with that kind of desperation.

"Here." I dumped the snails from my basket into hers. "You and I will work together for as long as you can stay. When you must go home, Syntyche will pay you for all the snails in your basket."

The woman blinked rapidly, then silently waded back into the water.

I was about to follow until I felt a tug on my sleeve. "Euodia?" Irritation flickered across Syntyche's broad face. "You asked me to assist you, so why would you undo what I have done? Why would you reward a thief?"

"I am not rewarding a thief," I answered, keeping my voice low. "I am showing kindness because Yeshua showed kindness to me."

Syntyche shook her head. "I do not think HaShem rewards theft with mercy."

"Does He not offer mercy to all who repent?" I led her back toward the table. "When we first heard about HaShem, were we not idol worshipers? In the eyes of the Almighty, is the worship of false gods not worse than stealing a few snails?"

Syntyche sputtered. "People who worship Caesar and Zeus would not forgive a thief so easily."

"But they have not been forgiven themselves, as you and I have been." I peered into her deep-set eyes. "Our place is not to judge others. Our duty is to reflect His light so others can see a new path." I hesitated, wondering how I could soften my friend's heart, and the Spirit provided an answer. "Come to dinner," I said, squeezing her shoulder. "When we are finished here, go home, wash off the sand and come to my villa. I would love to have you as my guest."

I am not sure what Syntyche was expecting, but my words clearly caught her by surprise.

"Dinner?" She lifted a brow. "You have never invited me to dinner."

"Then it is time I did." I smiled. "I will look forward to having you."

Eight

AD 49

Hector took another swig of beer, lowered his cup, and stared
moodily across the room.

"*Go to Philippi,*" they had told him. "*The women are
beautiful, the temples glorious, and the riches easily earned.*"

So he and Lucius said farewell to their comrades in arms
and left the army, each of them a freshly decreed Roman
citizen with over seven thousand denarii, riches earned from
their retirement pay and years of hoarding their wages.

Together they bought a wagon and a mule, determined
to save the rest of their coin until they reached Philippi, a
burgeoning city on a sun-drenched river near the Great Sea.
"When we arrive," Lucius had said, "we will buy the finest
house in the city, and I will marry a woman whose beauty
will put Venus to shame."

Hector ignored Lucius's predictions. A house, naturally.
After years of sleeping beneath a leather tent, it would be nice
to have a solid roof over their heads. But a wife? The army
had only one use for women, and if he wanted to indulge,

Hector had always taken his pleasure from temple prostitutes or camp followers.

On the journey to Philippi, Hector constructed a plan for their future. They would earn riches, certainly. Status, of course. And pleasure. Unbridled, limitless pleasure.

After twenty years of surviving attacks from enemies within and without Rome's army, wealth, status, and pleasure were all that mattered.

As Lucius shouldered his way to the bar, Hector sipped from his mug and studied the three slaves they had purchased at the renowned slave market in Lychnidos: Triton, a Greek scribe; Berdine, a blue-eyed female from Britannia; and a scrawny female child. The man would be used for labor and clerical work; the woman would cook when she wasn't warming one of their beds.

As for the child, she had been an extravagant waste of silver. Lucius had purchased her on an impulse, and when Hector asked why, he shrugged. "The slave seller said she had a gift. I am curious to know what it is."

"Her gift is making coin for the slave trader . . . unless she is skilled at stealing purses."

"She didn't steal mine. No, the slaver said I would discover her gift in time."

Hector sighed. When a matter pertained to women and children, Lucius could be foolishly sentimental.

Hector stared at the child, who now sat between the man and woman. She had no obvious gifts—no beauty or athleticism, and he doubted she could read or write. If she had been fortunate enough to be born into a Roman household, she might have been pampered, but this girl had the wild, unkempt look of a barbarian. Yet he could not believe she had been captured in Britannia. With no one to fend for her, he did not see how she could survive the long journey to Macedonia.

He considered the man and woman. Neither of them, fortunately, had the obstinate look of troublemakers. If they had once been defiant, a former master had beaten the resistance out of them, and for good reasons. Even the poorest slave owner knew the truth behind a common proverb: *Every slave we own is an enemy we harbor.*

For now, at least, he and Lucius should not have to worry about being murdered in their sleep. Still, he would chain them before going to bed. All slaves, even children, were skilled at covering their emotions, and few masters trusted their slaves enough to sleep without a dagger beneath their pillows.

Back from the bar, Lucius dropped a handful of coins onto the table and fell into a chair. "We will eat like kings tonight!" He sipped from his cup, then twiddled his fingers at the coins. "I won a few denarii casting lots. We will enjoy a good meal."

"Are you not forgetting something?" Hector jerked his head toward the slaves. "We must feed three others as well."

"Oh." Lucius's jovial expression faded. "Surely they do not need meat and bread."

"So we pay for three bowls of gruel. Because you insisted, we have three slaves to feed even before we reach Philippi."

Lucius grinned. "Would you do without the woman? Come the next bitter winter, you will be glad we bought her."

"I do not mind the woman, but the child? Of what use is she?"

Lucius shrugged. "She cost a mere ten assarii. She can

fetch and run errands until she grows. In a few years she will be far more useful."

"If we keep her that long."

Hector flinched when the girl's gaze met his. Then, in a high, thin voice that sliced through the noise of the tavern, she yelled, "Hector Hostilius, a man is coming to tell you about a house!"

Lucius laughed. "At least she will have no problem being heard. She could wake the dead with that voice."

"If only she truly had the gift of divination." Hector averted his eyes from the odd child. "She would be well worth the trouble if she could predict winners at the chariot races."

He looked up as a tall man in a richly embroidered cloak approached their table. "Are you Hector Hostilius and Lucius Martinus? I am Kato, and I have heard that you might be searching for a house in Philippi. I need to sell a domicile there."

Hector glanced at the girl, who was still staring at him, her eyes filled with contempt and her lips curled in a knowing smile.

Nine

Frowning, Hector squinted at a line of numbers and realized that daylight had seeped out of the room. He called for Triton, who appeared a moment later with an oil lamp. Hector swallowed his bad humor and nodded as shadows danced on the walls. "Bring another lamp as well. The room is far too dark."

He looked up when Triton did not rush to do his bidding. "Were my instructions not clear?"

"I am sorry, Dominus"—the slave lifted his head—"but I would like to ask a question."

Hector leaned back in his chair, bemused. Slaves rarely expressed their thoughts unless overtly encouraged, and he had never been the sort to encourage useless conversation. Still, he might be foolish to ignore the slave's question. Contented slaves did not make trouble.

"Ask," he barked.

Triton gestured to the parchment on the table. "I could not help but notice that you are working with figures. I was educated by a Greek tutor, so I could be of more assistance to you than I am at present. I would be happy to manage the household spending, if you wish."

Hector scratched his chin and studied the slave, wondering what had motivated this request. Was Triton bored with running errands, greeting guests, and helping Berdine in the kitchen? It might be useful to have a slave who could procure household supplies and administer a budget.

He leaned back. "The gods have blessed me with a head for numbers," he said, "or at least that's what the captain of our *turma* declared when Lucius and I enlisted. When we were not training or caring for our mounts, I was tallying figures of how much our unit spent on the beasts' feed, tack, and medicinal supplies."

"You must have been a valuable part of the army," Triton answered, bowing. "I understand why Rome's army is the greatest in the world."

Hector knew better than to pocket praise from a slave. "I mention that only to point out that I will know if your figures are incorrect. You cannot cheat me, Triton. I will discover any discrepancy, make no mistake."

"I will do my best for you, Dominus. I know you are a learned man. You know horses, property, and warfare. I cannot imagine what else you might have learned—"

"I have learned that wealthy men possess power," Hector said, leaning forward. "I saw the sons of senators and patricians enter the army as tribunes and prefects, never serving in scut jobs or lowly positions. While Lucius and I spent hours charging targets with our spears, our young *prefectus cohortis* stood on the sidelines, chewing on straw and checking his fingernails. And when our turma stood for inspection, even the prefectus cohortis stood at attention when the prefectus *equitum*, the son of a senator, rode by."

His gaze drifted to the unadorned wall. "But I have also learned much in retirement. During our time here, I have watched the city magistrate and other officials strive to please the people, desperately frightened lest some small uprising be reported to the provincial governor. The governor acts quickly so the problem does not get reported to Rome. Everyone fears someone, Triton, and the men who govern Philippi are weasels, always crinkling their noses and looking around before diving into their hidey-holes."

"I have observed the chain of command in Philippi," Triton said, "but I answer to you and master Lucius alone."

"Not Lucius, not anymore," Hector interrupted. "He has set up his own household. I alone am your master now—unless Lucius wishes to borrow you for a task." He thumped the desk. "I am glad you have spoken of this. You will keep the household accounts, and I will find another slave to assist with the work of the house. It is settled."

Triton bowed again and walked out of the room, his chin high. Hector waited until he no longer heard the slave's footsteps, then sighed and considered the numbers before him. If a man wanted to make something of himself before the gods hustled him across the River Styx, he had to make enough coin to earn an elevated position.

Though Hector had more wealth than he had ever possessed, he required far more. He would need enough to secure a position among the city leaders. He would need to be invited to their dinners and celebrations. He would need to dress the part of a man upon whom the gods smiled.

He had a house, he owned slaves, and he possessed one

of the most beautiful mares in the Empire, yet he lacked connections. Once he made the right connections, he would have the reputation necessary to secure investors. Once he accumulated the right kind of investors, he would have the thousands of talents necessary to build his racetrack, where his stallions would defeat every contender and his mares would bear foals fit for emperors.

Finally, he would use his knowledge and experience to benefit himself, not Rome. He had spent far too many hours walking colicky horses and breaking untrained stallions. Soon he would have enough coin to hire others to do the thankless work while he enjoyed the rewards.

Lucius used to say Hector had been blessed by the goddess Fortuna. Hector had believed it himself until the day his youngest slave was cursed by a wandering Jew.

Ten

Instead of dining in the triclinium, I asked Dione to serve the evening meal on trays in my bedchamber. Syntyche had not been as materially blessed as I, and I did not want to draw attention to the size of my villa.

My friend arrived just before sunset, and Ariston escorted her to my chamber. "Welcome, Syntyche." I embraced her and gestured to the upholstered bench where she could sit. "I am so pleased you agreed to dine with me."

Her uncertain expression eased into a smile. "I was surprised by the invitation."

"Should we not be friends as well as co-workers? We are sisters in the Lord, after all. We should be closer than friends."

I looked up when Ariston and Dione brought in two trays and set them on stands. A delightful aroma filled the room when the servants lifted the clay covers, and Syntyche inhaled a deep breath. "That smells wonderful."

"One of Dione's special dishes. Fish poached in white wine." I nodded at the cook. "Thank you, Dione, for your exemplary efforts. I am certain we will enjoy this."

Ariston stepped forward, his hand on his chest. "Do you require anything else, Domina?"

"Nothing, thank you. You should eat your own dinner before it gets cold."

He and Dione left us, but Syntyche's gaze followed Ariston as he strode through the doorway.

"You know what the other women say about him," she said, arching a brow.

"They talk about Ariston?"

"They say he is far too familiar with you. After all, he used to be a slave."

"And now he is free."

"Still . . . he is not your equal. And he should not take liberties."

I unfolded my napkin. "What liberties has he taken? He works hard, like my other servants. And, like them, he receives wages and is free to leave at any time."

Syntyche looked toward the doorway, as if Ariston's image still lingered there. "I would not have freed him," she said, her voice softening. "I would have kept him, if only for the pleasure of looking at him. Those broad shoulders and that hair . . . why do you think he wears it longer than most men?"

I covered my mouth to hide my displeasure. "I do not know. He is free to wear his hair however he likes."

"I am not faulting his choice, not at all. If only my husband had half as much hair on his head . . ."

I cleared my throat in an attempt to change the subject. I did not think Ariston would like to hear himself praised as an object of desire, and Syntyche was a married woman. She might admire Ariston's appearance, as did I, but as a believer, she should not allow herself to dwell on such thoughts.

"Shall we give thanks?" I asked.

She bowed her head, and I thanked HaShem for the food,

the cook, and a good day at the shore. "Abba, we come to you in the holy name of Yeshua, our Lord. Amen."

I lifted my head and tugged at the tail of my fish, pulling it free of the body. When I had exposed the meat, I pinched off a portion and smiled at Syntyche. "I have wanted to speak to you, sister, about our workers."

Syntyche froze, her hands suspended in midair. "Are they not working hard enough to suit you?"

"That is not the issue; they are good workers. But I would urge you to consider them as more than hired laborers. Though two or three of them have worshiped with our ecclesia, most of them have no knowledge of HaShem or Yeshua. They are idol worshipers, just as we once were. I hope to teach these women about HaShem while we work, and they will not listen if they dislike me. I want them to see Yeshua's gentleness in my countenance and hear HaShem's patience in my voice."

"Very prettily spoken," Syntyche countered, "but you are running a business. If you are too gentle, those women will spend the day sitting on the shore. They will say they want to learn, but while you teach, they will veil their faces and sleep. Your words about Yeshua and HaShem will fall on deaf ears—"

"I think we can work while we learn," I said, keeping my voice light. "Just as you and I can talk while we eat. One never knows what the Spirit will use to touch a listening heart. He may use something you or I say as we gather snails or the way we respond to a question."

Syntyche popped a piece of fish into her mouth and washed it down with wine. "You have already set yourself apart from others who hire women," she said, lowering her cup. "You are the only employer I know who observes a day of rest."

"HaShem commanded that we rest on the seventh day," I answered, striving to be gentle. "Surely our Creator knows what we need. And since we do not work on the Sabbath, I may invite some of the women to my home for Shabbat dinner. Would you be willing to do the same?"

Syntyche recoiled. "I could not afford to feed so many!"

"Do not worry. I will have Dione buy double the food and send half of it to your home. I am sure the women would love to share a meal with you and your family."

Syntyche scowled, her brows knitting together. "You hired me to oversee the workers, not to pamper them."

"I hired you to assist me," I reminded her. "And you have done a fine job. But if you do not want to serve them as well, I would remind you to remember the Lord's gentleness when you admonish them. Let His light shine through your eyes." I lifted my cup and smiled at her. "May the Lord bless our work so we can bless others."

Syntyche lifted her cup, too, but her face retained its scowl.

Eleven

Hector walked slowly past the wooden cages, carefully examining the men within. Ahead of Lucius, another man walked with his wife, who kept a square of linen pressed to her nose.

Hector chuckled. Yes, the place smelled of urine and filth, but he was accustomed to unsavory odors.

"I do not see why we cannot share Triton," Lucius said again. "You do not have enough work to keep him occupied."

"He is going to handle my accounting." Hector lifted his head. "When I build my racetrack, I will need a dozen or more slaves. Triton will have more work than he can manage."

Lucius shook his head. "I need only one man," he said, glancing at the line of cages. "Someone to take charge of the house and oversee the refurbishment. A man who can manage and do the work."

He stopped outside a large cage. The slaves inside had been imported from some defeated kingdom in the Empire, for their feet had been whitened with chalk. Many were white-haired and bearded, so Hector presumed they were Britons. The year before, their king, Caratacus, had been captured in battle and presented to Emperor Claudius. Most defeated kings were executed after the victory parade, but Caratacus managed to save himself and his family with a passionate, eloquent speech.

But these other Britons, who would be sold for the cost of the transport tax and a nominal fee, had to be the dregs of the captives. Most were malnourished and dirty, with scraggly beards and tangled hair. They stood or sat with their heads down, their naked flesh marked by scars and bruising. Whenever one of them looked up, Hector peered into the man's eyes and saw the dullness of defeat.

"I doubt you will find a suitable slave in this lot," he said, looking away. "Are you sure you would not rather wait for a new shipment?"

"Captives are not my only choice."

They approached another cage, this one filled with younger men. "Consider that one." Lucius pointed to a man crouching in the corner. His face was visible beneath a layer of stubble, which might indicate he had been recently enslaved.

Lucius stroked his chin. "He appears intelligent. If Greek, he may have been educated."

"You there," Hector called to the slave, who rose and slowly stepped forward. "How came you to be in this place?"

The man straightened his shoulders. "I was a free man until I could not pay my debts."

"Have you family?"

"If the gods are merciful, my parents still live."

"Where?"

"Outside Rome."

Hector shot Lucius a quick glance. A slave whose family lived far away was less likely to run.

"Are you educated?"

"I can read, do sums, and chart the stars."

"Languages?"

"Greek and Latin."

"Can you paint, chisel, and lay tile?"

The man blinked. "I believe I could."

Lucius gave Hector a victorious smile. "Not every slave is a barbarian. Does this one meet with your approval?"

"Yes, but you have not yet won the auction."

They retired to a shady spot as a horn blew. An *aedile*, a civil servant, opened the cage and ordered its occupants to walk onto the stage. Once they stood in a single line, another aedile placed scrolls around their necks. This small *titulus* not only described the slave's character but also served as a warranty for the buyer. If within six months the owner discovered defects or disease not mentioned in the titulus, the slave seller would be required to accept the returned slave and refund the purchase price and sales tax.

The first aedile shouted a command, and each slave mounted a numbered block. Hector elbowed Lucius. "If you want to examine the merchandise more closely . . ."

Lucius did not appear overeager, but under Hector's watchful eye he stalked forward and examined each man on the blocks, spending extra time on the fellow he had admired in the holding pen. Others did the same, often pinching, slapping, or manipulating the slaves, until the first aedile blew his horn.

"We will now begin the bidding," the aedile proclaimed. He pointed to the slave on the first block. "Who will give one hundred denarii for this Greek who is skilled in medicine?"

Hector leaned against a wall as the auction proceeded. He

knew these slaves had a hard life. Those sold to mines and quarries worked fourteen hours a day and slept in chains. Yet he felt no sympathy for them because he had been a slave himself, bound to Rome. In service to the Empire, he had suffered pain, injury, illness, and a constant scourge of lice. He had occasionally worked twenty-four-hour days and gone as long without food. He had forsaken the land he loved and killed men, women, and children on command. He had obeyed every order and endured every punishment assigned to his unit.

He had heard that in the early days of the Republic, every man in Rome served in the army, driven by a national sense of honor. Now nearly every man in the army served out of desperation. He and Lucius would not have enlisted if they had not faced a poverty-stricken future.

Lucius turned, caught Hector's eye, and smiled, signaling that he had won his auction. He strode toward the gate to pay for his purchase, and Hector followed.

"So?" Lucius ran his gaze over the newly acquired slave. "What do they call you?"

The slave dipped his chin in an abbreviated bow. "If you have no preference, Dominus—"

"I will call you Marcus," Lucius interrupted, the corner of his mouth lifting. He looked at Hector. "Remember our prefectus cohortis, Marcus Scaurus?"

Hector chuckled. "Indeed, I do. And now you shall have your revenge on him."

"Indeed." Lucius turned to the slave. "Go into the city, Marcus, and walk along the main street until you see the blue house. Sit on the stoop and wait. I will be along presently."

Both men watched as the man, now wearing a slave's short tunic—a last contribution from the seller—walked away.

"Now," Hector said, "let us find something to eat. I am eager to hear about the progress on your house."

"I have made no progress yet." Lucius's brow furrowed. "But since we are speaking of slaves, I meant to ask you—how is young Sabina?"

Hector drew a deep breath, knowing Lucius would not want an honest answer. "She runs errands and helps Berdine in the kitchen. She often helps Triton."

"I was afraid you might give her less pleasant tasks once I left the household."

"You are too concerned about slaves. She is my property, and I will use her as I please."

"She is a *child*, Hector."

"She is a slave, and if I wanted to rent her by the hour, what is it to you? I would have done it months ago, but there are so many temple prostitutes, no one wants a skinny girl. But with a little help from Berdine, I believe the child could be made presentable."

A tremor passed over Lucius's face. "I beg you to remember—that girl is someone's daughter."

"Then why did her parents not protect her? For all we know, they sold her into slavery. They have no right to complain about her status."

Lucius swallowed hard, then sighed and looked away. "A true shame she lost her gift. She would not have to debase herself if she could re-claim what was lost."

Hector was about to retort that a slave was already as debased as could be, but one of Lucius's words threw a spark and caught fire. *Could* the slave re-claim her gift? Philippi

67

did not have another seer, but he had heard of others with the same ability. Thessalonica was known to have astrologers and necromancers who could foretell a person's fate, so surely he could find others with similar powers . . .

He clapped Lucius on the back. "Thank you, comrade. You have given me an answer."

"I was not aware you had a question."

Hector gestured toward the butcher's booth from which emanated the delicious aroma of sizzling meat. "I will explain as we eat. If we hurry, we may find remnants of the morning sacrifices to Osiris. My stomach cries out for a slab of roasted bull."

Twelve

Trusting Syntyche to oversee the work, the next morning I left my villa and walked to the marketplace. The wool merchant's eyes lit when I approached, and after asking me to wait a moment, he returned with two bundles of the softest wool I had ever touched. "It comes from yearlings," he told me, smiling as I fingered the luxurious, long-haired wool. "The shepherds cover the lambs' bodies to keep their coats clean. After a year, the wool is shorn and sold . . . and as I mentioned, it is expensive."

I pressed my nose into the soft bundle and inhaled the aromas of animals and sunshine.

"How much?" I asked and winced when he gave me the amount. "Ten denarii per bundle? I could buy ten lambs with the same amount."

"But you would have to wait a year to shear them." He grinned. "Why should it concern you? Your clients are wealthy."

"My expenses are high," I countered. "Not only do I employ women to harvest the snails, I must also hire someone to card the wool, spin it, and weave it. I am only the manager.

The person who will benefit most from this commission is the client, who may sell it for double what he paid."

The merchant shrugged. "Still, this wool will create a cloak like none other." He squinted. "Unless it is intended to be a gift. This garment would not be meant for the emperor, would it?"

"I have already told you, I do not know who will wear it." I ran my hand over the wool again and watched the longer hairs flutter in the breeze. "All right, friend, I will buy your wool. But I will pay five denarii per bundle, not ten."

"I could not possibly take less than seven. A sheep is only a yearling once."

"Six denarii per bundle, and I will hire your wife to do the spinning and weaving. And you will reserve a dozen bundles for me after this year's shearing."

He tugged on his beard. "It is true, then—the Lydian woman is a skillful negotiator."

"I have heard the same about the Philippian wool merchant." I took the first parcel from him and smiled. "But working together, we can satisfy the most hard-to-please clients."

I paid him, tucked both parcels under my arm, and walked through the marketplace, glancing into various stalls to see if any new goods had arrived since the last market day. The sun had climbed higher, baking all of us in dry heat, so I tried to remain beneath the fabric canopies that provided a bit of shade.

I stopped at a farmer's stall and examined the pomegranates, remembering how Cassia had loved them. When a lump rose in my throat, I slammed the door on that memory and moved to the next booth, hoping it held no sorrowful associations.

I blinked at what I beheld there. A broad-chested man in a short white tunic, obviously a slave, stood behind a thin girl who could not have been more than ten or eleven. She lounged on a dining couch, her head resting languidly on one outstretched arm, one leg crossed over the other, exposing her thin limbs and frail frame. Even from where I stood, I could smell the cloying odor of overly sweet perfume.

Her pose and attire were not unusual, but her eyes . . . something about them stopped me in mid-stride. They were *old*, dark, and unfathomable. Not the eyes of a child.

Something about the girl evoked a distant memory, but I could not see her true face beneath the heavy cosmetics and the beaded wig. Only temple prostitutes wore this sort of adornment in public, and the girl's sheer garment further convinced me that she was being used for the worst sort of purpose . . .

I knew such things happened, of course. Behind every reputable slave market lurked the *lenones*, whose sole intention was to sell women for immoral uses.

I met the guard's eye and pointed to the child. "Who owns this girl?"

The man shifted as a flush crept up his throat. "Our master is Hector Hostilius."

The girl shrank back, as if the mere mention of her master's name had frightened her.

"Why has this child been put on display?"

"It is my master's wish," the man said, avoiding my gaze. "The girl needs a useful purpose, so—"

"A useful purpose?" I repeated. "You mean a *profitable* purpose. How old is this girl?"

"I do not know."

"Surely you have some idea."

"She is a slave," the man answered. "She must do as commanded without argument. Please, mistress, move along before you make matters worse for us."

I stepped back, horrified by the implication. Did they have a quota to fulfill? What sort of man asked this of a mere girl?

Overcome by disgust, I covered my mouth and turned away. I was not naïve; I knew such evil existed in every corner of the world. The temples of Diana and Bacchus and Osiris and even Caesar offered prostitutes, children and adults, who would do anything to satisfy the worshipers' carnal desires. This girl's owner was offering the same services as the temples . . . but for a different reason.

The owner of these slaves was not seeking to appease a god, but to earn filthy lucre. Apparently, he did not care how he obtained his wealth.

I hurried away from that horrible booth, clinging to my parcels and trying to focus on the work that needed my attention. But something about the girl had struck me, and I could not forget the sad aspect of her countenance. That heavily painted face . . . had I seen it before, or was I transposing Cassia's image onto the girl's? Cassia had not been that thin, but she also had olive skin and long fingers . . .

I shook my head in a vain attempt to dislodge the awful memory, though I could think of little else as I walked to the river. By the time I reached the women, I knew what the Lord wanted me to do.

❖

I was still pondering my plan when I woke the next morning. When Phebe finished arranging my hair, I sent for Ariston.

"How may I help?" he said, hesitating in the doorway.

I turned from the looking brass and hurried toward him. "There were two slaves at the marketplace yesterday, and I do not think their owner deserved to be given a booth. He was prostituting a slave, a mere child. I would like you to find this man, Hector Hostilius, and inquire if he is willing to sell the girl."

Ariston frowned. "Sell the slave . . . to you?"

"Of course." I smiled as his eyes widened. "Do not worry. I do not intend to add a slave to our household. But no one, especially not a child, should be used in that way. I will free this girl and care for her until she is old enough to make her own decisions."

Ariston cleared his throat. "I am happy to serve, Domina. But if he agrees to sell, what price are you willing to pay?"

I closed my eyes, trying to remember how much I had paid for my other servants. This would be a private sale, so the cost might be higher than usual . . . or lower, considering the girl's age.

"What is the standard rate for a child at the slave market?"

Ariston's expression darkened. "A captive child would never bring more than a nominal price. Male slaves in good condition might sell for a thousand denarii, a woman for a few hundred."

"And a child? I do not believe this girl is more than ten or eleven—she does not appear to have reached marriageable age."

Ariston crossed his arms. "Is she especially beautiful?"

"I could not see her true face beneath the cosmetics."

"If she is handsome and accomplished, she might fetch a high price, even as much as a grown woman."

"Let us hope she is not accomplished, then." I opened my strongbox and pulled out a pouch of denarii—three hundred at last count—a gold *aureus*, and a handful of brass *sesterces*. I thought it was enough to buy two or three slaves, but I wanted Ariston to have different coins available in case he had to negotiate. "I hope the seller will accept two hundred denarii. If he accepts your offer, bring the girl to me at the river, and we will let her spend her first day of freedom in the sun. We will also make sure she is comforted and well fed."

Ariston nodded—a bit reluctantly, it seemed—then departed.

I went to the kitchen, picked up a basket of honey cakes for my workers, and set out for the shore.

❖

I had just finished distributing the honey cakes when Syntyche spotted Ariston on the road. "Euodia," she called, her voice slicing through the women's chatter. "Your servant approaches."

I put the basket beneath the table and hurried to meet Ariston. I stared, speechless, when I realized he was alone. Had Hector Hostilius refused my offer?

"What happened?" I asked when I reached him. "Are we to summon her, or will he deliver the girl to the villa?"

Ariston's face flamed. "Domina, you do not want that girl."

Astonishment stole my breath. "And why not?"

"Do you not remember? She is the slave who used to stand in the town center and tell the fortunes of those who passed, whether they wanted to hear them or not! She muttered and chirped in strange voices, but her masters grew rich when the wealthy paid to meet with her."

For an instant I thought Ariston had lost his mind, then the memory broke through—no wonder she looked familiar! She used to scream at Paulos whenever he preached in the town center. I noticed her several times during those weeks, but a year ago she looked more like a wild animal than a child. Her owners—two men, as I recalled—had clothed her in rags and tattered furs to emphasize her feral nature.

Of course I did not recognize her! The girl in the market stall had been calm, wide-eyed, and dressed like a seductress. Her eyes had not blazed with demonic fire, but neither had they brimmed with life. And her masters were still using her for profit.

I clenched my hands and looked toward the water, not wanting Ariston to see the storm that had to be manifesting on my face. This could *not* be endured. I did not have the power to stop the practice of slavery, but if HaShem was willing, I could help one girl find freedom.

I turned back to Ariston. "I *do* want that girl," I insisted. "And I will have her. Go back to the marketplace—"

"It is closed, mistress."

"Then find out where her masters live. When you find them, relay my offer, increase it as needed, and bring the girl to me. I will not rest until she is safely under my roof."

A shadow flitted over Ariston's face. Then he broadened his shoulders and adjusted his cloak. "I should carry a weapon," he said, his jaw tightening. "It is not safe to venture into the area where I am likely to find her masters tonight."

He was not asking for permission; he was telling me because he knew I would not approve of carrying a weapon to a negotiation. I drew a breath, about to insist that he leave his blade behind, but a man with a purse tucked into his tunic made an obvious target.

"I understand," I said, swallowing my reservations. "Do whatever you have to do."

Thirteen

AD 50

The cloudless sky had shimmered with heat haze when the troublesome men first came to Philippi. Most people remained indoors, avoiding the sun, but four strangers strode into the city and went immediately to the town center. Two were bearded and wore the fringed prayer shawls favored by Jews. One even wore small black boxes on his forehead and arm, the unmistakable mark of a Pharisee.

Hector leaned against the frame of his front door and watched them, his curiosity aroused. During his time with the army, he had observed many Jews. They were a strange people, keeping to themselves and subjecting everyone in their community to a "holy Law." They refused to eat pork and a host of other foods, their women covered their hair, and they were unusually devoted to their children and the worship of an invisible God. But what marked them as decidedly obnoxious was their stubborn refusal to mingle with their neighbors. No devout Jew would join a Gentile neighbor for a meal, buy anything from a non-Jewish merchant, or worship at a Roman temple.

They had been an infuriating people from the beginning. Two hundred years before, one of the Jews' leaders had asked Rome for help, and Rome had generously helped expel the Seleucid king Antiochus IV from their territory. The Jews had been content to rule their own land under a series of Hasmonean kings, but when one of those kings waged war against his brother, Rome was again asked to extend aid. As a result, the Hasmonean dynasty ended, and Rome installed Herod as king over Judea. Early in Hector's childhood, Herod died and then Rome declared Judea a province.

But Judea did not behave like the other provinces. Syria, Cyprus, Macedonia, Aegyptus, and even Britannia were grateful for the protection, opportunities, and freedoms the Empire granted to its people, but the Jews refused to adopt or adjust to Roman culture. Rome had always allowed assimilated peoples to worship their old gods in addition to the gods of Rome, but not even the gifts of religious freedom, paved highways, and a rich culture could convince the Jews to look upon the beneficent Empire with loyalty or affection. While steadfastly refusing to obey any law that would force them to bend their rigid traditions, some of them immigrated to Rome and settled on the banks of the Tiber. Instead of buying from Roman merchants, however, they created their own neighborhoods and did business only with one another.

Ten years ago, when the Jews refused to erect a statue of the emperor in their Temple, Caligula prepared to march on Jerusalem, intending to utterly destroy it. Hector and Lucius were certain they would be dispatched to fight in what was certain to be a bloody and one-sided battle, but one of the gods intervened, Caligula died, and the Jews were spared . . . though perhaps temporarily.

Hector chewed a dried bit of beef as he studied the four approaching strangers. Behind them, a group of women followed, their hair modestly veiled. The group made their way to the paved space in the center of town, then the women and three men sat as the rabbi began to speak. Within a few moments, he drew a crowd.

Hector turned to his slave girl, who crouched near his feet.

"Go," he told her. She rose, her eyes fixed on the Jews, and strode toward the gathering.

Hector crossed his arms and smiled. Philippi welcomed newcomers, but it had no need of Jews. Especially a rabbi who stood in the town center and disturbed the peace.

Hector walked toward the gathering and strained to hear the rabbi's words. The man declared that he and his friends were proclaiming good news about HaShem, the invisible God, who had sent His Son to earth . . .

Hector spat and leaned against the wall of a small shrine, grateful for a sliver of shade. The Jews' invisible God could not be as powerful as Osiris, an important god in Rome and Egypt. Osiris reigned over the earth's fertility, as well as the living and the dead. Unlike the invisible God of the Jews, Osiris's body had green skin, the color of growing things, and was never depicted without his crook and flail.

Confident that the rabbi would say nothing worthy of his attention, Hector returned to his office, where a stack of coins waited to be counted. Berdine bowed at his appearance and resumed waving her fan while Triton whitewashed the walls.

A few moments later, Lucius entered and coughed for Hector's attention. "The girl is yelling at strangers in the city square."

Hector looked up and grinned. "I am not surprised."

"Should we not stop her?"

"What is the harm? Let her speak. And if perchance some of the listeners recognize her gift, we will be richer for it."

"You should go," Lucius insisted. "We do not know who these men are."

"They are Jews."

"But which Jews? They may be powerful."

Sighing, Hector stood and followed Lucius. The man would not let go of an idea once it entered his head, so he might as well take another look at the rabbi and his minions.

They walked to the town center and halted.

Lucius was correct—the girl was yelling, but in a voice unlike any Hector had ever heard.

"These men are servants of the Most High God!" she yelled in a sharp, shrieking tone.

The rabbi glanced at the girl and stepped away, but she followed, as persistent as a flea on a dog. "These men," the girl repeated, "are not from this place. They are the servants of the Most High God!"

Hector shifted his attention to those who had stopped to watch the entertainment. Some of the observers laughed at the sight of strangers being discomfited by a mere child. Others drew their children closer to them, as if the girl's madness could be contagious.

Hector smiled. "Do you see?" he asked Lucius. "Someone here may wish to know the future. This is not a problem, it is promotion. Many of these people know about her gift, but others do not. What more could she do to spread the word?"

The girl's gift had manifested itself the day they bought her, and it had proved beneficial when they arrived in

Philippi. They made an offer on a house not far from the town center, then retreated to wait for the owner's answer. But before the man could respond, the girl looked at Hector and, in a guttural voice that raised the hair on his arms, declared, "The house can be yours for another one hundred denarii."

Hector did not know what to think of the girl's declaration, but before five minutes passed, a servant appeared with an answer to their offer of nineteen hundred denarii. They could have the house if they increased their offer by one hundred.

The girl had been bringing customers to their house since. A widow came to hear the voice of her dead husband. A young woman wanted to know if she should marry the baker or the butcher. A young man came in search of wisdom— should he follow his father's wishes or his mother's? One by one, the people of Philippi visited the house Hector and Lucius shared, and the men welcomed them with enthusiasm.

Now, watching the girl flit around the rabbi like a gnat, Hector resisted the urge to kiss Lucius on both cheeks. "Ah, Lucius. How grateful I am that you purchased that slave. Her gift will make us wealthy." He pulled his purse from his tunic and jangled it before Lucius's wide eyes.

Lucius stared at the purse. "Has she really earned so much?"

"And her fame is only beginning to spread." Hector shoved the purse back into place. "We may be wealthy even sooner than we hoped."

Lucius crossed his arms. "So, you will stop complaining when I buy extra food and clothing for the slaves?"

"Buy whatever you must for the girl, but be prudent with

the man and woman. No slave should eat more than coarse food and fallen olives if they can be found."

"As soldiers, we received nothing but grain from the emperor, yet we were allowed to eat meat we could kill. Should we forbid our slaves the same opportunity?"

Hector shrugged. "I suppose you are correct. If they catch a dormouse, they may eat it."

"That is not what I meant!" Lucius flushed. "A little salted fish would be beneficial to them and only a slight expense for us."

"Would you clothe them in silk, too?" Hector shook his head. "We will conform to the usual practice. A new tunic every year, a cloak and shoes every two. Except for our young fortune teller. If a better tunic would draw more customers, a better tunic she shall have. But for now, I think the feral look is more intriguing."

A muscle clenched along Lucius's jaw. "We do not have to treat our slaves as the army treated us."

"We do not," Hector replied. "We do not have to do *anything* for them, but we shall do our best to keep them alive." A smile tugged at his lips. "You should enjoy your liberty, Lucius. After everything we endured for Rome, we deserve to live as we please."

Lucius sighed. "I suppose you are right."

Hector glanced out the doorway. The girl was still flitting around the Jew, screeching her refrain and drowning out the rabbi's words. "Of course I am right. I always am."

❖

For three weeks the Jews and their companions continued their routine, every day save the seventh of the week, when they remained cloistered at the Lydian woman's villa. Hector had heard that Jews reserved the seventh day for their God, so he was content to use the slave girl for other work on that day.

During those weeks, Hector and Lucius shared many laughs as they watched their slave bedevil the Jewish teacher. Each morning when the Jews and their followers walked past his house, Hector would release the girl, who immediately ran after them, shouting in that unearthly voice: "These men are servants of *El Elyon*, and they are proclaiming to you the way of salvation!"

Hector often followed the parade, which always ended at the town center. The rabbi, a Jew called Paulos, consistently spoke of the Jewish God and His Son. While he spoke, Hector watched the crowd, ready to note the slightest sign of unrest. The audience, which varied in size from day to day, listened politely, yet few appeared genuinely interested in learning about an unknown God. The talk of gods and their sons was nothing new, since Greeks, Romans, and Egyptians had been worshiping such deities for hundreds of years.

When Paulos's voice began to rasp, the other Jew, Silas, would speak while Paulos attempted to engage individuals at the fringes of the crowd. These people usually wandered away, but every day several of them stopped to marvel at the slave girl. Whenever this happened, Hector strode forward and advertised his slave's services. "She can divine the future," he declared. "And she will answer any question for a single denarius."

Every afternoon dozens of denarii fell into his hands, and with each clink, he heard the sound of pounding hoofbeats. Every coin brought him closer to his racetrack.

Hector was happy to thank his gods for the visiting Jews until the day Paulos lost his patience.

That day began like all the others. Paulos, his companions, and the women paraded down the street, so Hector released the girl. She took off like a hunting dog, but instead of ignoring the slave, Paulos stopped and stared at her, exasperation visible in every line of his face.

Hector blinked in curious, tingling shock. Why would Paulos acknowledge the slave today? He had ignored her for three weeks.

Then Paulos spoke, and in the rabbi's voice Hector heard the strain of exhaustion. "I command you," the rabbi said, raising his voice above the girl's eerie screeching, "in the name of Messiah Yeshua, come out of her!"

The slave stopped in mid-breath and snapped her mouth shut. The fiery expression left her eyes, and her hunched posture straightened. Then she bent at the knees and sank to the ground like a child whose life has deserted its body.

The group around Paulos retreated as Hector ran forward to examine his slave. He held his hand above her nose and relaxed only when he felt the gentle brush of breath against his palm.

"Girl." He shook her shoulders. "Slave, wake. At once."

Her eyelids lifted. "Dominus?"

"Rise, slave, and continue. These people are waiting to hear from you."

The girl clambered to her feet and stared at the crowd, her eyes wide with bewilderment.

Hector folded his arms. "Speak."

He became aware of hot eyes upon him, and in the rabbi's eyes, the sharp sting of contempt. Then, without a word,

Paulos continued walking toward the town center, leaving Hector with a suddenly mute slave.

"He has bewitched her," Lucius announced, stepping out of the house. "He has cursed her."

"Jews." Hector spat the word. "No wonder they insist on remaining apart from society. They practice the black arts."

"How is she?" Lucius peered at the girl's blank face. "Child, are you well? You have appointments this afternoon."

A flicker of shock widened the girl's eyes. "Why?"

Lucius glanced at Hector, then replied in a calm voice, "To answer their questions, of course. To divine their futures."

The girl's face rippled with despair. "How . . . how can I do that?"

Hector gripped the slave's arm. "These Jews must not be allowed to disrupt our lives. We are reporting them to the authorities."

They stormed forward, passing through the town center, turning heads as they rushed toward the city's administration building. Hector left the slave with Lucius while he marched into the chief magistrate's office. "Albanus Marinus," he barked, "you must come out and deal with this matter. This Paulos, this *Jew*, has destroyed our business."

Albanus, who had scowled when Hector entered, smoothed his features. "You have a legitimate complaint against the outsiders?"

"You are aware of what this man has been doing?"

"Of course."

"You are aware that my young slave has the gift of divination?"

"I have heard of it."

"She has the gift no longer. Paulos cursed her this morning."

Albanus left his desk and followed Hector outside. "Where is this man?"

"There." Hector pointed toward the town center.

"I will call the guards."

"No need." Albanus had turned, but Hector nodded to Lucius. Together they strode into the town center, grabbed the rabbi's arms, and held him securely as they dragged him to the magistrate.

"This man and his companions," Hector began, not loosening his grip on the Jew, "are throwing our city into an uproar! Being Jewish, they advocate customs that are not permitted for us Romans to accept or practice."

Hector spoke in as reasonable a voice as he could manage, but his fervor expanded the sound, drawing those who had been listening in the forum as well as sellers in the marketplace. Men and women spilled from their booths, declaring that their businesses had also been affected by the Jews, who discouraged their listeners from purchasing idols, sacrificial animals, and incense. The merchants joined Hector's protest, their fists beating the air as Albanus Marinus eyed Silas, who had walked over to see about his companion.

Finally, the magistrate had heard enough. Albanus ordered the chief jailer to beat the Jews, so the jailer's guards ripped the tunics from Paul and Silas, then chained them to flogging posts. When the men were securely confined, the guards took stiff rods and beat their prisoners.

Hector crossed his arms and watched with a great deal of satisfaction. Several of the women wept while other onlookers flinched with every blow. But Hector, who had been flogged himself, basked in the knowledge of his growing power. The magistrate had listened without questioning his report, so his status in Philippi had already risen considerably.

When the jailers had finished administering the required number of stripes, the Jews were unable to stand. They dangled from the flogging posts, their backs bruised and bleeding. Albanus Marinus stepped forward to make certain the men still breathed, then commanded that they be thrown into the city prison.

"Clement Gavia," Albanus called to the jailer, "I entrust these men into your care. We will question them on the morrow."

❖

That evening, Hector smiled when the chief magistrate sent a written message. Both men had been stretched and secured in the stocks, where they would remain until morning.

"Good." Lucius nodded. "Perhaps they will learn not to curse those who have been gifted by the gods. Perhaps Sabina will now recover her gift."

But when the men called for the girl at dinner, they found the slave as bewildered as ever. She retained not even a trace of her gift, and instead of replying to their questions with impudence, as had been her habit, she cowered before their threats.

Hector propped his chin in his hand. "I fear," he admitted, "those Jews have sent powerful magic against us. Despite their suffering and imprisonment, the slave remains useless. Have they blinded her? Made her insensible?"

Lucius shook his head.

Defeat left Hector numb. "Unless we can find another slave with a similar gift . . . or torture the Jew until he reverses his curse . . ."

He sighed, knowing such a task might well be impossible.

Fourteen

APRIL AD 51

As the sun hovered over the western horizon, we tidied our work area and loaded the wagon. I filled the tall jars of snails with water and tucked fistfuls of dyed purple wool into woven baskets.

I glanced toward the road several times but did not see Ariston. Finally, I climbed onto the wagon, picked up the reins, and urged the mule homeward. Once I reached the villa, I left the mule outside the barn, then went into the house and sat in the vestibule to wait. What was taking Ariston so long to bring the girl?

"Dione wants to know if you will eat," Phebe said. "Your dinner is waiting."

With a sigh, I said, "You may set my tray here."

When dinner arrived, I ate quickly. "Have Dione prepare trays for Ariston and the girl," I told Phebe when she came to take my tray away. "They will be hungry when they arrive."

One hour passed, then two, and my concern intensified with each drop of the water clock. Had I sent Ariston on a fool's errand? Had he been beset by thieves? Though he did not dress like a wealthy man, he carried himself like a king. I had heard stories about men killed for the cloaks on their backs, and I would not want any harm to befall my devoted manservant.

My prayers had become frantic pleadings by the time I heard the crunching of gravel. I hurried to open the door and saw Ariston at the threshold, the girl in his arms. Her eyes were closed, her face marked with bruises.

My hand flew to my throat. "What—?"

Without being directed, Ariston carried the girl to one of the spare bedchambers and gently placed her on the bed.

I caught his sleeve. "You found her owners, yes? You bought her?"

Ariston held a finger to his lips and motioned that we leave the room. I led the way to the atrium, where we sat on a bench. "Tell me everything," I said, turning to face him. "Do not spare any details."

Ariston propped one hand on his knee. I saw that a bruise marked his cheek as well, and his knuckles were swollen. "The girl was owned by Hector Hostilius and Lucius Martinus, two retired army veterans," he began. "The girl worked in Hector's house because Lucius has established a household of his own."

I nodded. "Go on."

"When I inquired at the tavern, I heard that Hector was away on business. When I finally found Lucius Martinus, he refused to let me see the girl. He said she had been rented for the night. We argued loudly outside his house and exchanged a few blows. I did not think he could be persuaded, even by force, but when he saw the gleam of silver in my hand, he led me to a tent outside the city. The man who paid for her had already taken his pleasure and knocked the slave about, so I threw the purse to Lucius and carried the girl away."

"The bill of sale?" I asked, my mind racing. "Lucius signed it?"

Ariston lifted his hands. "I had no scribe, and I was carrying the girl. I sensed that I needed to take her away before Lucius had second thoughts."

I closed my eyes, remembering that a deathly pallor lay beneath the girl's bruises. "Do you think she will live?"

"She does not appear to have any severe wounds." He lowered his head onto his hand. "I am sorry I was not able to find her sooner. And I should have negotiated a better price for you."

I snatched a breath. "You gave him the entire purse."

"I did not want to delay. I feared he would demand to wait until Hector returned, and that fellow would not have been easily persuaded. As I said, Lucius seemed determined to keep the slave until he saw the girl's bruises. Then he relented and let me take her."

I closed my eyes, horrified by what the child had endured and terrified that she might die. "I must check on her." I hurried to the bedchamber and studied the small figure on the mattress. She had not moved.

"Has she a name?" I asked Ariston, who had followed.

"Lucius did not mention it. Now that she is yours, you may name her anything you like."

I bent and pushed strands of hair away from the child's wide forehead. Her face bore the flush of fever, a bruise marked the skin of her left cheek, one eye appeared swollen shut, and a blood trail ran from her nose to her lips. As I surveyed her body, I saw angry handprints on her upper arms and a bite mark on her tender skin.

I groaned. "HaShem help us. Who has ravaged this child?"

"She has been rented to animals," Ariston growled, "who dare to call themselves men."

"She was better cared for when she had an unclean spirit." As I smoothed her hair, my chin trembled, and a tear ran down my cheek. "Clearly, her owners have little regard for her." I opened my mouth to speak again, but an unexpected and agonizing wave of emotion paralyzed my tongue. I looked down and saw my daughter on that bed, my precious Cassia . . .

I swallowed the sob that had risen in my throat and kept my head down, not wanting Ariston to see how I suffered.

He handed me a damp cloth and I took it, grateful to have something to do. I wiped the smeared blood from her nose and lips as gently as I could. "What of the other owner?" I whispered. "Was Hector Hostilius part of this business?"

"According to Lucius, renting the girl was his idea," Ariston said. "But if Hector questions the sale, I am sure I can find witnesses who saw us fighting in the street. They must have seen us leave together."

Confident that my emotions were under control, I met his gaze and smiled, grateful that the Lord had sent him to me. "Ariston, you have done the right thing, as always." Feeling awkward, I reached up and lightly touched his bruised cheek. "Get a cool cloth for your face and take your rest, and be sure to eat dinner. Phebe and I will tend this child. You have done your part."

"Yes, Domina."

Ariston bowed and left the room. A few moments later,

Phebe entered with towels, a basin of water, and a clean cotton tunic.

"Thank you," I said, realizing that she must have been listening in the hallway. "This girl is still breathing, but we must do what we can to be sure she does not stop."

❖

The next morning, I tiptoed into the girl's bedchamber and found her asleep. I pressed my hand to her forehead, which felt cool and dry, then bent to listen for the sound of breath.

"How is she?" Phebe asked, slipping into the room.

"Asleep. But in better condition than she was last night." I pulled the thin blanket over the girl's chest and lightly stroked her bruised cheek. "Have Dione prepare a tray for her. Bread, of course, fruit . . . and diced meats, in case her teeth are in poor condition. And honey water; bring the pitcher. This child needs more flesh on her bones."

While Phebe hurried away, I picked up the blood-smeared towels we had used last night. I was about to leave when a trembling whisper broke the silence: "Domina? Who are you?"

I turned. The girl had risen on her elbows, and her peaceful face had shifted into the desperate lines of a trapped animal.

"I am Euodia, a dyer of purple," I said, speaking in the gentlest voice I could manage. "Some call me Lydia because I came from that region not so long ago." Not wanting to frighten her, I sat on the bench facing the bed. "What is your name?"

The girl moistened her dry lips. "I am called Sabina . . .

and my master will be angry when he hears you have stolen me."

I laughed, overjoyed and relieved to know her spirit had not been broken. "Why," I asked, struggling to temper my smile, "do you think you were stolen?"

Like a cat scenting the wind, she glanced from one side of the room to the other. "Why else would I wake in a chamber like this? You should fear my master, lady—he used to be a soldier. He knows forty different ways to kill a slave."

My smile faded as a chill scrambled up the bones of my spine. "And how do you know that?"

"He reminds me. Nearly every day."

I inhaled a slow breath and searched for words. How was I, a woman who could not break free of the past, going to teach this child to do the same thing?

"Whatever *used to be* no longer matters," I told her. "You belong with me now. I paid a high price for you last night, and you are worth every coin." Moving slowly so as not to startle her, I shifted from the bench to the bed, then pushed a stubborn curl away from her eyes. "No one in this house will hurt you, Sabina. You need not fear anyone."

The wariness in her expression disappeared, replaced by a disbelieving stare.

"How are you feeling?" I asked, determined to win her trust. "You were not well when my servant brought you home."

"What do you mean, I belong *with* you? Do I belong *to* you?"

"Yes," I said, "and when you are feeling strong, I will take you to the magistrate. I will sign your manumission papers, and he will give you a cap of freedom. You will take my family name and can stay with me for as long as you like. I keep no slaves in this household."

"But . . . you have servants."

"They are paid for their labor. Everyone in this household works, including me." Hoping to set her mind at ease, I smiled and tapped her knee. "You are welcome to work with me as well. When you are stronger, you can decide whether you want to work in the house or at the river. I employ more than a dozen women, and I daresay they enjoy their work . . . and their wages."

She stared, eyes wide, mouth slightly open. Her confusion was so obvious, I wondered if she had trouble hearing.

"You may stay here until you are strong," I repeated, raising my voice. "Then I will grant you freedom."

She blinked. "I will be *free*."

"Yes. You can go anywhere you want to go. But know this—a woman who does not work at *something* usually does not eat. But for now, your only job is to get well." I stood and stepped toward the door. "Dione will soon bring you a tray, and you should eat your fill. I will summon a physician to examine you as well. All I want you to do is rest and regain your strength."

Sabina nodded almost imperceptibly, then curled into a ball beneath the blanket. I gave her a smile and turned away, my eyes stinging with tears that had sprung from some deep and ever-aching place.

❖

My heart brimmed with dreams and prayers as I returned to my chamber and sat before my looking brass. Phebe was waiting to arrange my hair, but my thoughts wandered as she braided the long strands. What would become of Sabina? I had hopes for her, of course. When she was well, I hoped she would enjoy working with us at the river. What youngster did not enjoy a beach? Cassia had loved the water, and perhaps Sabina would, too.

I hoped she would have a happy life with me. I would hire a tutor so she would not remain ignorant, and I would demonstrate how a young woman should behave before God. I would allow her to join meetings of our ecclesia and I would teach her about the only true God, the One who worked miracles for Israel and sent His only Son to live and die as a man. I would tell her about Paulos and Silas, even young Timothy and Luke, the scribbling physician.

One day, when she had fully recovered from the trauma her masters had forced upon her, I would find her a suitable husband, a believer who would love her as Yeshua loved the ecclesia. Someone who would cherish her as I had cherished Cassia . . .

My daughter's face ruffled through my memories like wind on water. Cassia had been about Sabina's age when I lost her. Like Sabina, she possessed a wide forehead, silky brown hair, and a pointed chin. Her laughter filled a room like the sound of tinkling bells and never failed to lift my spirits. My husband adored her as much as I did, and for ten years we had been a happy and prosperous family. Our neighbors said we were blessed by the gods.

"Are you well, Domina?" Phebe asked.

A glance at the looking brass revealed Phebe's look of concern. "Yes." I forced a smile. "I am well."

"You are so quiet. I thought you must be worried about the girl."

"I am concerned, yes. Deeply. But I am sure the Lord will guide us as we care for her."

Phebe bound off one plait and began another. "What will you do with her? She is not much hurt, I think—nothing that food and rest cannot make better."

"You may be right. As far as my plans are concerned, they are simple. When she is well, I will let her choose where she wants to work. And I will love her."

Phebe's jaw flexed. The house servants tended to be a bit jealous of newcomers, and I understood why—they did not want to be replaced.

I caught my maid's hand and squeezed it. "Do not worry. I already have a handmaid and a cook. If Sabina wants to work at the house, I will find something else for her to do."

The corner of Phebe's mouth rose in a half smile. "She could work with the chickens. We need someone to feed them and bring in the eggs. Someone to teach the rooster how to behave."

"Yes, we do. But if she is to be free, she must decide what she wants to do."

I released Phebe's hand and wondered how I would feel if I were in Sabina's place. I could not imagine what the girl was feeling, as I was no longer a child and had never been a slave.

Yes, you have.

The voice, coming from someplace within me, rattled my composure. Paulos had spoken of hearing such a voice, beginning on the day he met Yeshua. I had heard the voice before, always when I faced a decision and sought guidance from the Spirit . . .

"Is that *you*?" I whispered.

Phebe cast me a quizzical look. "Domina?"

"Nothing." I smiled and waited until she had finished with my hair. "Thank you. You may go."

When she had gone, I closed my eyes. "I am listening, Lord."

When I drew you, you were a slave to false gods. But when you believed in me, you surrendered your life. My yoke is easy, and my shackles are light.

My heart warmed as I realized the truth. I had been a slave to Roman traditions, pagan rituals, and society's expectations, but the Spirit of the Lord helped me to see even when I lived in Thyatira. My friends and neighbors, even my husband, thought I had gone mad when I began to visit the local synagogue.

But within those stone walls I discovered the God who listened to Hagar and Rachel and Sarah. I found people who valued *all* their children, even those who were sick or crippled, because God decreed them a blessing. I saw men who respected their wives, and women who loved and exalted their husbands. Within those walls I found people the Romans called "peculiar," but their God seemed more consistent, just, and loving than the gods in Roman temples.

I had not loved my husband when we married, nor did he love me, even when I gave him a daughter. And when we lost Cassia, everything we had built seemed to blow away like dust . . .

I shook my head, unwilling to dwell on the past. I needed to concern myself with the present, with the girl in the west bedchamber. Though she was young, she was still enslaved to the forces that had held me in darkness. Paulos had freed her from an unclean spirit, but she had not yet discovered the Light of the world.

Sabina had no one to guide her to Truth. Her owners had whisked her away as soon as Paulos cast out the spirit, so no one had shared the news about Yeshua. As far as I knew, she was not even familiar with HaShem, whom I now called *Abba*, father.

"I will teach her." I lifted my eyes to the sky above my garden. "I will lead her in the path of righteousness, just as I would have led Cassia."

Perhaps Sabina was my second chance. My daughter was with God, but this lost, wounded, and frightened girl would be my responsibility.

"I will love her," I promised. "I will love her as if she were my own flesh and blood."

My words floated toward the heavens, unheard by any human ear save my own, but noted by the One who mattered.

❖

On Shabbat morning, I knocked on Sabina's door and entered. She was lying on her bed, her hands fastened across her stomach, her eyes fixed on the ceiling. Despite a day of good food and many cups of honey water, she remained pale and thin.

I found it hard to believe such a frail body could still house a soul.

"A blessed Sabbath to you," I said, pulling the bench closer to her bed. "Today is a day to rest and honor God."

Her eyes swiveled toward me. "Which god?"

"The God above all gods, and the only One who can provide salvation. The Jews call Him HaShem, or The Name, because His name is too holy to be spoken." I smiled. "Since

I will not be working today, I thought we could talk. I would like to hear your story."

She blinked. "I do not know what you mean."

"Surely you have some memories of a time before you were a slave. Do you remember living with your parents? A mama and papa?"

"No."

I closed my eyes, my heart aching. I could not imagine being without memories of my parents because they had taught me about love.

"What is your earliest memory?" I smiled again, hoping to erase the worry from her eyes. "Surely you can recall something."

Her mouth twisted in a pained expression, then she returned her gaze to the ceiling. "I remember water. I remember splashing in silver water."

"Silver?" I could be mistaken, but I did not think she was remembering the sea. The waters of the Great Sea were blue, and the waves crested with white foam. Of course, the color might depend on the time of day and the angle of the sun. On our riverbank, a fiery sunset often tinted the waters orange and pink.

"I remember trees," she said. "I remember being in a cart and watching trees beyond the bars."

She had to be thinking of a slave wagon. They frequently traveled Roman roads, picking up slaves at one city and disgorging them at another. If this was her earliest memory, how did she come to be enslaved at such a young age?

Gently, I pressed for more details. "Were you alone?"

She shook her head. "There were others, and at night we

slept chained together. I slept next to Doreen, who kept me warm."

Doreen was a Gaulish name. Caesar had conquered Gaul more than a hundred years before, but Gauls had been sold as slaves throughout the Empire ever since. This child *might* have come from Gaul, but *Sabina* was a Roman name.

"Were Hector and Lucius your first masters?"

Sabina sat up. "I do not know."

"How long were you with them?"

Her brow wrinkled, and something moved in her eyes. "From the market . . . until your servant took me away."

I sighed. Would I ever know the story of this girl's past? I did not know much about the two army veterans, but I knew enough to be grateful Ariston had removed the girl from their custody.

I had one more question. "Do you remember Paulos? About a year ago, you met him in the town center. Your masters had him arrested after he spoke to you."

Sabina lowered her head. "I remember seeing him look at me," she said, speaking slowly, "but I do not remember much before that day. But when he looked at me, I remember feeling . . . as though I had been given wings."

I leaned back and closed my eyes, my heart singing with joy. Sabina might not remember being tormented by a demon, but she certainly remembered her moment of release.

"That man, Paulos, is my friend," I told her. "And through him I was freed, too. Not in the same way as you, but I am free because Paulos told me about Yeshua."

Sabina's brow crinkled. "Who?"

I opened my mouth, eager to tell her the good news of Yeshua, but her eyelids were half closed, her shoulders slumped. The strain of captivity and abuse had drained her, and she needed rest.

I clasped her hand. "I will tell you all about Him when you are stronger. And know this—with His help, I am determined to make sure that from this day forward, your life will be better than before."

On the first day of the week, I rose early, dressed, and asked Phebe to look in on Sabina. "Find her a suitable garment," I said. "Nothing that looks like a slave's tunic. Braid her hair and have her ready to leave at the usual time."

Phebe frowned. "Where are you taking her?"

"I want her to meet the others in our ecclesia."

Phebe's eyes widened, but she left to do what I asked.

Half an hour later, Phebe led Sabina out of her bedchamber. Dione, Ariston, and I stared as the girl came toward us, her eyes downcast, her hair neatly arranged, and her face clean, with only the shadow of a bruise on her cheek.

"How nice you look!" I stepped forward to embrace her. She stiffened in my arms, but at least she met my gaze.

"Sabina," I said, gesturing to the others, "I know you have seen these people, but I would like to formally introduce you to Ariston, our steward, and Dione, our cook. You have already met Phebe."

Her dark eyes flitted from face to face, but she said nothing. Why would she? The child had never been in a position to learn about social graces.

"Come," I said, stepping into the cloak Ariston held for me. "This morning we are going to worship HaShem."

We left the house, with Sabina following close behind

Phebe. Ariston and I led the way, and occasionally I glanced back to see Sabina walking behind Dione and Phebe, her head low, like a slave walking behind her owners.

She would need time, perhaps months, to break those ingrained habits.

Because the group of believers had outgrown my villa, we walked to the river, where some of the men had situated rocks in the design of an amphitheater. These were our seats, the open sky our ceiling, the wind our choir.

Clement, keeper of the Philippian prison, opened our meeting with prayer. Then he led us in a psalm. After he recited the first line, we recited the second, lifting our voices to the Lord.

"Sing to Adonai a new song," Clement said.

"For He has done marvelous things," we answered.

"His right hand and His holy arm have won victory for Him."

We responded, knowing that Yeshua was HaShem's right hand: "Adonai has made His salvation known. He has revealed His righteousness before the eyes of the nations."

"He has remembered His lovingkindness," Clement said, glancing at the parchment in his hand. "His faithfulness to the house of Israel."

The last line was special to us, for though we had not sprung from Israel, we had nonetheless received God's saving grace: "All the ends of the earth have seen the salvation of our God."

"Amen!" Ariston shouted, lifting his hands.

I glanced at Sabina to gauge her reaction to our worship. Though her wide eyes appeared to take everything in, they revealed nothing of her thoughts.

Clement gave us a message of exhortation, then spoke of man's sin and God's salvation. I looked at Sabina again. Did she understand his meaning, or had she lived so long with Romans that she had no concept of holiness? She was only a child, but even children could understand right from wrong. Paulos had taught us that God's eternal power and His nature were evident through creation, so anyone who turned against the Creator was suppressing the truth.

What did this child believe about the Creator? From what she had already told me, I surmised that she had been sold into slavery at an early age . . . and somewhere, somehow, she had opened her mind to an unholy spirit. Paulos had freed her from the demon, but what was the condition of her heart?

At the end of the service, Clement offered a blessing, and afterward we sang a hymn and then moved toward the wooden table that usually held baskets and snails. Today, however, our people had brought wine and bread, which we ate and drank in obedience to the Lord's command. Sabina did not come forward to partake of the commemorative meal but remained seated on a bench, her hands folded in her lap.

"Do not worry," Ariston said, coming to my side. He nodded at Sabina. "She is mired in her old life, but she is listening . . . and watching."

"May it be so," I whispered, blinking tears away. "I pray you are right."

Fifteen

Hector had gone to the port of Neapolis to examine several horses, and when he returned, he did not expect to find himself short one slave.

When he could not find Sabina at his house or the marketplace, he went to Lucius's home and entered without knocking. He found his friend in the triclinium, eating grapes and cheese while he watched his slave paint the wall.

Hector frowned at the irritating odors of sweat and sawdust, then came straight to the point. "Where is the girl?" he asked, startling Lucius into nearly dropping the grapes.

"Hector." Lucius swallowed and extended his hand. "Would you like some fruit?"

"I want the girl. Has someone killed her?"

Lucius glanced at his slave. "That will do for today, Darby. Take your tools and go."

Hector swallowed hard, trying to tamp down his anger as the slave gathered his brushes and hurried from the room.

"Would you like wine?" Lucius asked.

"What do you think? The day is warm, and my throat is parched."

Lucius picked up a brass pitcher from a tray, filled a cup, and gave it to Hector. "How was your trip?"

"Uneventful. An entire boatload of sorry horseflesh. A waste of time."

"Nothing at all interesting?"

"Nothing over fifteen hands, just more Roman ponies." Irritated by his friend's inflated sense of hospitality, Hector gave Lucius a black look. "Enough useless conversation. Where is the girl?"

"And that brings me to my surprise." Lucius pulled a leather pouch from his tunic. "You will be pleased to hear we made a profit on a nonprofitable slave. I sold her to the Lydian woman's steward."

Hector weighed the pouch on his palm. "For how much?"

"More than double her value, I'd wager."

Somehow Hector resisted the urge to fling the purse in Lucius's face. "I do not care how much we profited. You sold her without my permission."

Lucius's face went idiotic with surprise. "I thought you would be pleased. You complained that she was barely earning her keep."

"But I have a plan! When it is complete, we will earn more than your so-called profit in a single day."

Lucius stared, red-faced, and slumped against his couch. "What sort of plan?"

Grinning, Hector perched on a nearby stool. "I have worked it out. If the gods gave the gift to the girl, they could bestow it a second time, no?"

Lucius frowned. "I cannot speak for the gods."

"All we must do is take her to a priest, another fortune-teller, or a necromancer. Surely one of them can restore her power."

Lucius's mouth pursed in a rosette, then unpuckered enough to ask, "Do you know of a necromancer with a similar gift?"

Hector batted the question away. "We live in the Roman Empire, home to millions of citizens and thousands of temples. We will find someone."

"But what if you cannot find someone to do what you want? Then Sabina is only a skinny girl of little use. You should be glad she has been sold."

Hector gritted his teeth. "I will *not* fail."

Lucius shrugged and poured more wine. "I applaud your idea, Hector, but the deal is done. The Lydian woman's steward took the girl, and I accepted payment. Half of it is yours, so count out your portion and think about your horses. Two days ago, I heard about a promising stallion in Thyatira."

He picked up another stem of grapes and tossed one in his mouth, so casually, so foolishly that Hector's irritation erupted into rage. Lucius had never possessed the ability to look beyond the present, and he had blindly, stupidly given away the girl who held the key to their future success.

Hector pulled his dagger from his belt and lunged. He should have known his quarry would respond instinctively, and Lucius did, scattering food as he used the tray for a shield.

"What's this?" he asked, his brow rising. "Would you allow so trivial a matter to come between us?"

"This matter is *not* trivial!" Hector shouted, breathing hard. He lowered his arm as tension crackled between them. "We were partners, and you sold the slave without consulting me."

"I bought the slave without consulting you, too, yet you

ceased to complain about that when she brought us profit."
Though he still held the tray, he gestured toward the brass
pitcher. "You need more wine. You are weary, and all sense
has fled—"

Sputtering with rage, Hector reached for the pitcher and
then swung it toward his comrade. The pitcher struck Lucius
on the side of the head, a surprisingly solid blow that sloshed
red wine over his tunic.

Lucius toppled sideways and fell onto the tile floor. Hector swallowed a surge of righteous satisfaction, then bent
over his friend. "Lucius." He nudged the inert body with
his foot, then drew a deep breath and felt a dozen emotions
collide.

No stranger to violence, he knew the signs—the empty
eyes, the slack facial muscles, the fading color of the lips.
Lucius was dead.

Hector sank onto the couch, his fury dissipating in a mist
of fatigue. "Your dreams were never big enough," he said,
his voice trembling in the chamber. "Why should you settle
for a house and a family? You should have kept up. You were
never able to keep up."

He picked up the Lydian woman's purse. "And you should
have driven a harder bargain."

He cast a last glance at his friend's body, then called for
the slave.

❖

After leaving Lucius's villa, Hector went at once to the
city authorities to lodge a complaint. Albanus Marinus,
the chief magistrate, listened to his story about the missing
slave, then cleared his throat. "I must speak to the slave's

co-owner before I can render a decision. If you say the slave is gone—"

"She *is* gone, but not missing. You will find her at the home of that Lydian woman."

"But I must speak to the co-owner before—"

"Lucius Martius is dead. We fought and I hit him."

Shock flickered over the magistrate's face. He then narrowed his eyes and asked, "Did you *intend* to kill the man?"

"Of course not." Hector stiffened at the challenge in the magistrate's words. "We were friends and comrades."

A cloud seemed to settle over the magistrate's face. He drew a trembling breath and stepped out from behind his desk. "We must go to the home of Lucius Martius. Lead the way."

Hector led the magistrate and two guards to Lucius's home. The front door stood open just as he had left it. They crossed the vestibule and entered the triclinium, which smelled of paint, sawdust, and spilled blood. Lucius's body still lay on the floor. The slave, Darby, was kneeling by the corpse.

"Slave!" Albanus snapped. "What are you doing?"

Darby leapt up and held out his bloodstained hands. "I did not kill him. I found my master exactly as you see him."

The magistrate gestured to the guards. "Bind the slave."

"But I did not do this!" Darby looked at Hector. "Tell them I did not!"

Hector folded his arms. "I have already said this is my doing. We argued, I struck him, and he fell."

The slave blinked in bewilderment. "If that is so, why must I be bound?"

"You are property," Albanus said, surveying the room. "The bonds are to ensure you do not escape." He glanced

at Hector. "The law imposes no penalty for accidental man-
slaughter. Did Lucius Martinus have an heir?"

"He did not."

"Brothers?"

"None living."

"Wife?"

"No."

The magistrate's lips flattened in a tight smile. "Then I
suppose you are the man's heir. The choice is yours—you
may sell this slave or keep him. The house is now yours as
well, as is the responsibility for burying this man and paying
off his debts."

Hector struggled to repress a smile. "I would be honored
to do so," he said, bowing to the magistrate, "but let us not
forget the other matter. My slave girl is still missing."

"Oh yes." Albanus quirked a brow. "Why do you care so
much about that wisp of a girl?"

"She is beloved. A pet."

The magistrate shrugged and walked toward the door.
"I will send someone to adjudicate the situation," he called
over his shoulder. "Be patient, Hector Hostilius. I will see
that your property is returned."

❖

Hector pushed past the hanging beads adorned with dead
insects, rats, and bones, and stepped into the dark interior
of the magician's shop. The walls were crowded with shelves
of charms and small bags, doubtless filled with potions and
medicinal remedies. The air was thick with the tang of herbs,
old earth, musk, and various creatures long dead.

The gaunt little man who appeared from the darkness

stepped forward and bowed before Hector. "May I be of service, Dominus?"

Hector glanced around. "I wish to purchase a curse tablet."

The corner of the man's mouth quirked in a half smile. "We have several available and many prewritten. You have only to supply the name of the person you wish to curse."

"I will not have one so common." Hector scowled at the collection of scrawled lead sheets lying on a table. "I want a curse that will be unique and effective."

"Certainly." The man reached into a trunk and pulled out a fresh sheet and a sharpened stylus. "Is it a man or woman you wish to curse?"

"A woman."

The man licked his thumb, then picked up the stylus and drew a simple image: head, trunk, arms, and legs. "Would you like to write the curse or dictate it?"

Hector frowned, reminded once again that he had never learned to read or write. "How much?"

"One sesterce for the *defixio*, two for the table and the writing."

"You write it," Hector said, crossing his arms. "I will pay."

The man held out his palm. "Payment in advance is required."

Hector placed the coins in the magician's hand. The old man sat at a desk, licked his thumb again, and nodded. "The name of the cursed? Any other identifying details would be useful. We do not want the gods to bring their fury upon the wrong person."

"I wish to curse the seller of purple who lives near the river," Hector said. "They call her 'the woman from Lydia.'"

The man scratched furiously, filling the top of the sheet. "Which gods would you like to act against her?"

"All of them," Hector said, rancor sharpening his voice.

"I find," the magician said, "that curses work best if you address the gods as individuals. No one likes to be lumped with a group."

"Jupiter, then. Mars, Minerva, and Apollo."

The man nodded in approval. "Good choices. Now, what would you like the gods to do?"

Hector's temper flared as he considered the matter. "I want the gods to destroy, crush, kill, and strangle the Lydian woman and her entire household. May she languish and rot. May her womb shrivel so she never has children. May her heart burst, and may her hands and feet burn with the heat of a thousand fires. May every piece of flesh on her body be covered with suppurating sores. May her hair fall out and blow away. May everyone within the sound of her voice suffer. May her servants vomit on her, curse and desert her. May her business fail so she lands in abject poverty. When she dies, may dogs lick her blood and her memory die when she does."

He halted, fury almost choking him. The magician held up a finger as he scribbled furiously, then used the stylus to scratch the picture at every area Hector had mentioned: womb, heart, hair, hands, and feet. He looked up. "It is a most thorough curse. Anything else?"

Hector considered a moment, then shook his head.

The magician picked up a long nail, wrapped the lead sheet around it, pulled the nail free and drove it through the center of the cylinder. He handed the curse tablet to Hector. "You must bury it someplace deep where it is not likely to be disturbed, such as in a lake, the soil, or in a grave. Place it as close to the cursed one as possible."

"And this will work?"

The magician smiled. "I have had no complaints."

Clutching the defixio, Hector left the shop.

Sixteen

After we returned from worship, Sabina crept back to her chamber and did not venture out again. I thought she might be sleeping, but then I wondered if she felt uncomfortable mingling with us. When I mentioned Sabina's withdrawal to Ariston, he shook his head.

"A slave does not venture forth when the master is in the house," he said. "Unless you summon her, a slave is to remain hidden until needed."

I accepted this news with surprise, wondering why I had never noticed. My parents owned slaves and so did my husband. I had always assumed the slaves were busy elsewhere, but apparently they were hiding from us.

Well, if the slave would not come to the mistress, the mistress would go to the slave.

I followed the aroma of fresh-baked honey cakes and found Dione in the girl's bedchamber. "I thought I'd join you for dinner," I said, pulling the bench toward the bed. I nodded when Dione placed the tray on a stand between us. I smiled at Sabina. "We should get to know each other, should we not?"

Sabina did not meet my gaze but looked at the tray. "May I eat, Domina?"

"Of course."

Shyly, she lifted her head. "Will you eat, too?"

Ah, another detail I had missed. The mistress had the right to eat first. I lifted one of the honey cakes and took a big bite. Thus assured, Sabina picked up a piece of salted fish and nibbled at the edge. She reminded me of a mouse, glancing furtively about while taking small bites, ready to rush back into hiding at the slightest provocation.

I set the cake down and clasped my hands. "I am going to give thanks," I said and bowed my head. I prayed, "HaShem, my Father in heaven, I thank you for this food and for Dione, who prepared it. Bless her and use this food to strengthen us to do your will. I ask this in the name of Yeshua, your precious Son and my Lord. Amen."

When I lifted my head, Sabina was chewing slowly, her eyes averted. I wondered if she would speak at all, but it seemed her curiosity overcame her reticence. "You pray to the Jewish God?"

"I do. What do you know of Him?"

She lifted one shoulder in a shrug. "Nothing. The voice spoke of Him once . . . until the rabbi sent him away."

I stared at her, puzzled, then the pieces fell into place. The voice must be the demon that had tormented her. The rabbi had to be Paulos.

"I remember that day well," I said. "I was with Paulos the day he freed you of the unclean spirit."

Her eyes glittered briefly before she took another piece of dried fish from the tray and looked away. Her hand froze in midair. "May I eat this piece as well?"

"You may eat anything you see before you."

A smile flitted over her lips as she devoured the fish. "My masters were not pleased with what the rabbi did," she said, dipping the fish into a bowl of sauce. "They wanted to destroy him."

"I remember. They accused Paulos and Silas of throwing the city into an uproar, but everything had been perfectly quiet until your masters stirred up trouble." I struggled to repress a shudder. "I will never forget watching as the jailer scourged my friends. I thought the chief magistrate would surely release them after that, but to throw them in prison?" I shook my head. "While the experience was terrible, I learned something that night. I learned that when all hope seems lost, God has an alternate plan."

Confusion filled Sabina's eyes. "What plan?"

"That was the night HaShem sent an earthquake to open the prison doors and loosen the chains of every prisoner, even those that held Paulos and Silas in the stocks. Yet they remained in their cell."

"Why did they not run?"

"They knew better." I smiled. "That, too, was HaShem's work because when Clement the jailer saw that they had chosen to remain, he brought them out of the jail and asked them how he could be saved."

"HaShem did that?" The girl's voice sharpened. "Does He control earthquakes as well as spirits?"

"HaShem created the world, so why should He not control everything in it? He is the God above all gods."

Sabina remained silent for a moment, then snorted softly. "The Romans say Jupiter is father of the gods. How can you doubt it when we can *see* Jupiter hurling lightning bolts while his thunder rattles the heavens?"

I tilted my head. "I used to worship Jupiter. And when I joined the fullers' collegia in Thyatira, I had to sacrifice to Jupiter before every meeting. But after he failed me—"

"Jupiter failed you? How?" The girl's eyes had gone wide.

I hesitated. Because she was a child, she might not understand the depth of my grief. Yet she, too, had experienced loss. "I lost my family," I answered. "My husband and daughter died from illness. I begged Jupiter to save them, but he did nothing. Then I heard a woman at the collegia speak of the Jewish God. I attended synagogue with her and listened as men read from the Torah, the Jews' holy book. I learned about the unseen God who formed the world with His words, who created the first man and woman, and who called the Jews to be His special people. Adonai—that is another of His titles—opened my mind to thoughts I had never considered and led me to places I had never been. I met Paulos soon after that."

Interest flickered in Sabina's eyes. "The rabbi?"

I nodded. "Paulos and his companions came to the water's edge, where my workers and I were meeting for prayer on Shabbat. Paulos asked if I had heard of HaShem, and I told him I had. He asked if I had heard about Yeshua. I listened because I had never heard that name or His story."

Sabina's dark brows came together as she frowned, but she did not interrupt.

"Paulos told me that the rituals of sacrifice to atone for sin or win favor no longer meant anything because HaShem had sent His own son to be a blood sacrifice for us. By believing in Yeshua, we can turn away from our wrongdoing and turn to God, trusting Him to guide us through life and welcome us into the afterlife."

Sabina looked away again. "I do not know who I am, but I am not a Jew. Why would I worship their God?"

"Because HaShem created you. Because He extends mercy to all who call on His name, whether Jew, Macedonian, Gaul, or Roman."

She gave me a tight-lipped smile. "Thank you for talking to me. If you will allow it, I would . . ."

Poor child. Her head was bobbing, her eyelids drooping. She was still exhausted.

I leaned back, disappointed that my words had not made an impression. Regardless, I would let her sleep. "Yes, you need to rest, Sabina. But before I go, tell me one thing—what has Jupiter done for you?"

She chewed her bottom lip. "Jupiter has given me nothing. But Athena has saved me from death many times, even the night your servant took me away. My master bade me go with a man who wanted to kill me. He might have done so if I had not fainted. Athena brought me to this place. So even though I do not understand why I am here, at least I am not dead."

"Athena did not save you, Sabina. The Spirit of HaShem urged me to send for you, and Ariston carried you here." I gripped her hand. "I do not want you dead, sweet girl. I want you to heal and grow as a free woman." I wanted to say more, but I did not think the girl had ever dreamed of life beyond her chains.

I released her. "I was hoping you would come with me to the river, perhaps later this afternoon. Phebe and I will be leaving soon. The work is not difficult, and the fresh air would be good for you."

Sabina stiffened. "Leave the house? I could not. I will remain here."

"Are you certain? The sun is known to have healing properties, and the water feels wonderful on one's feet . . ."

Sabina turned and curled on the bed. My heart squeezed in anguish as I realized that my words about Yeshua had had no effect. When Paulos shared the Gospel of Yeshua with me, I accepted it immediately, but the Spirit had prepared me to receive that glorious news. Sabina was not ready, yet I would continue to pray while the Spirit worked on her heart. Until that work was complete, I would keep Sabina safe and love her as if she were flesh of my flesh and bone of my bone.

Because until Sabina wanted a new life, she would remain ignorant, frightened, and a captive.

A girl had to yearn for freedom before she could accept it.

We were dining from trays in the atrium—Ariston, Dione, Phebe, and me—when Phebe suddenly straightened and lifted her head.

"What?" I asked, wondering what had caught her attention.

"I heard something," she whispered. "Outside."

I shrugged and went back to eating the roast chicken Dione had prepared. I was just about to compliment her on the vegetable stuffing when Ariston stood.

"You too?" I asked, puzzled by the look on his face. "I heard nothing."

"I did," Phebe insisted, looking at Ariston.

"You heard the wind," I said, "or a stray dog. You know they often prowl the riverbank at night."

"It did not sound like a dog," Ariston said. Before I could stop him, he had left the atrium and was heading for the door.

"Ariston!" I called, but he did not answer. I sank back onto my chair, reminding myself that freed slaves had the right to do as they pleased and could no longer be punished for disobedience. I was happy to be surrounded by freed slaves, but allowing them such independence was often inconvenient.

Phebe, Dione, and I continued eating, though I was no longer as relaxed as I had been. A flicker of apprehension coursed through me, and Phebe had gone as tense as a harp string. Only Dione appeared calm, probably because she was busy analyzing the flavors of our meal.

"Where do you think Ariston has gone?" I asked. "He has been away long enough to walk to the river and back."

"I fear for him," Phebe said, no longer eating. Her hands gripped the edge of her dining tray, her knuckles shining in the lamplight. "He should have returned by now."

I stopped eating and concentrated on the sounds floating through the open roof—the shrill cries of crickets, the windblown leaves, but little else. I flinched when the front door opened with a complaining screech. "Ariston!" Though my voice rang with a note of rebuke, I felt nothing but relief that he had returned. My relief disappeared, however, when he stepped into the atrium with something in his hand.

"Mind your shoes!" Phebe cried, pointing to his footprints on the tile.

"Domina." Ariston extended his hand, showing me the object. "I saw a man digging outside the house. I did not recognize him because he wore a cowled cloak, and I could not see his face in the dark. Since I could not determine his intentions, I let him finish, then walked over and uncovered what he had buried."

I stared at the mud-covered object in his hand. "Is that—?"

Ariston dipped his chin in a sober nod. "A curse tablet. Probably intended for you."

Phebe stood so abruptly that she nearly knocked over her dinner tray. "Remove it at once! It is cursed!"

I lifted my hand, silently telling Ariston to wait. I had heard of such things but had never seen one. "You think this was meant for me?"

Ariston flushed. "It saddens me to say so, but yes. And I am equally sure this came from one of the girl's owners." Apparently aware that Sabina could be listening, he lowered his voice. "Lucius is a reasonable man, but that other one—he is hard, Domina, and could make trouble. I would not be surprised if this came from him."

I waved the object away. "Thank you for your efforts, Ariston, but you may dispose of it now."

"What should I do with it?"

"Bury it, burn it, whatever you like. It has no power over me."

Phebe gasped, and even Ariston flinched.

"You should curse the soldier," Dione said, lifting her head. "My mother always said a curse held no power as long as you cursed the curser before he cursed you."

I sighed. "I will not curse anyone. I am surprised by the lot of you—are we not protected by the Spirit of God? Is the power in us not greater than the power in the world?" I looked at each of them, allowing my words to resonate. "My dear friends, if Paulos were here, he would laugh at your fears and remind us that our Lord is always with us. And if He is with us, who can harm us?"

"A Roman soldier," Phebe said. "Or two of them."

I smiled and picked up another piece of chicken. "They may kill the body, but they cannot touch the soul. Never forget that, friends." I looked at Ariston. "Please remove that silly thing and return to your dinner. Dione has outdone herself tonight."

He walked away, his face red, and I resumed eating. But though I was unafraid of the curse tablet, I was a bit shaken to realize I had made an enemy . . . and a powerful enemy at that.

On the first day of the week, Ariston and I were preparing to leave for the river when a pair of mounted officials approached the villa. I remained in the house, watching from the doorway, as Ariston strode forward to address our visitors.

Partially concealing myself behind the door, I searched the men's faces for some clue about their reasons for coming to my home. One of them seemed vaguely familiar, and when I spotted the reddish color of his hair, I recalled where I had seen him. The man was a city official, and I had noticed him when he helped arrest Paulos and Silas. What had brought him to my villa?

The men dismounted and met Ariston in the road. They said something and gestured as if they would push past him, but he widened his stance and blocked their path, his voice rising as they argued. The second man produced a document and waved it about, then strode around Ariston and came directly to my door.

I stepped out to meet him. "Is there some problem, sir?"

"Are you the woman from Lydia, the *univira* who dwells in this villa?"

I startled, having not heard myself described as a univira—a complimentary term meaning the widow of only one man—since my first days in Philippi.

"I find it odd, sir, that you describe me as an honorable widow and yet come to my house waving papers and upsetting my steward."

The man lifted his chin. "I am acting under the authority of Albanus Marinus, chief magistrate of Philippi, and I have come with a warrant for the retrieval of a slave girl rightfully belonging to Hector Hostilius, a retired soldier of the imperial army."

I glanced at Ariston, who stood behind the man, his face a study in frustration. "I *told* you," he said, clipping his words, "the girl was properly sold to my lady Euodia. I gave Lucius Martius a purse of silver, which he accepted in exchange for the girl."

"Where is the bill of sale?" The official looked from Ariston to me. "Have you the bill of sale, my lady?"

My throat tightened. "I-I do not. The girl was nearly dead when Ariston brought her home, and we were so concerned with caring for her—"

"There were witnesses," Ariston interrupted. "In the street outside Lucius's villa, several men heard me make Lucius an offer and saw the purse in my hand."

"Yet Hector is co-owner of the slave, and he does not recall seeing you at all."

Ariston heaved an exasperated sigh. "I declare to you, I gave Lucius a purse filled with coin, and a sale was concluded. When I took the girl, Lucius made no move to stop me. I could go to his villa now and find at least four men, including Lucius, who would agree that we were negotiating the purchase price of that slave."

"If there was no bill of sale," the official persisted, his voice flat, "there was no transfer of ownership."

The second official placed one hand on his belt. "Bring the girl out"—he glanced at Ariston's broad form—"or we shall send men to arrest your mistress for theft and retrieve the slave by force."

Ariston's nostrils flared. "By my life, you will do no such thing!"

I closed my eyes, dreading what appeared to be an inevitable confrontation. I had not been thinking about receipts the night Sabina arrived. I had been far more concerned for her life, her well-being, and her soul.

"I can assure you, magistrate, my servant does not lie, nor do I." I met the official's gaze and did not flinch. "If you will speak to Lucius, I am certain you will learn that a proper sale was concluded. In any case, I can sign a bill of sale in his presence, and all will be well."

The official's mouth twisted. "I am afraid that is impossible."

"Has the fool run off?" Ariston clenched his fists. "He's probably hiding, waiting for his partner to retrieve the girl. They want both, the silver *and* the slave. But if you search, I am certain you will find this cowardly Lucius—"

"I would never call a Roman soldier cowardly," the official retorted. "And as to your suggestion, Lucius is not hiding. Lucius Martius is dead."

❖

I stood by the gate, biting back tears of loss and frustration as Ariston went into the house and returned a moment later with Sabina. The girl, who must have intuited the situation the moment she saw Ariston's face, took one look at the officials and meekly put out her hands, ready to be bound and returned to her master.

"Stop!" The cry slipped from my lips before I could think. "You cannot take her. Can you not see how she has been abused?"

"A man has a right to use his property however he wishes," the official said, wrapping rope around Sabina's wrists. "The owner has pressed his claim, and you have no bill of sale. That is the end of the matter. You should count yourself fortunate that Hector Hostilius considers this a simple misunderstanding."

Ariston scowled, doubtless thinking of the curse tablet. "I am surprised he has not called for us to be arrested."

"You are not a party to this action," the official said to Ariston. "Hector Hostilius understands that your lady is responsible for instigating this matter."

My face burned at his reply. Yes, I was the driving force behind it, but by discounting Ariston's role, the official had quietly and thoroughly reminded Ariston of his low standing. A freedman, a mere worker, was not a citizen and therefore of little importance.

The second official led Sabina away. My heart tightened when she turned, and in her young face I saw sadness, resignation, and a ripple of fear. An instant later, her expression became as smooth and blank as the riverbank after a wave had wiped it clean.

As the officials mounted their mules, I stared at the back of Sabina's head and felt my heart break.

I had promised to protect and guide her, yet I stood weak and helpless, unable to prevent her from being taken from me. We had not stolen her! We had procured her legally and truthfully, so why was the Lord allowing this injustice?

"Please." I strode forward and respectfully placed my hand on the official's shoe. "I beg you—the girl has no one to speak for her, and I do not want to see her harmed. She was abused in that man's custody, so if your heart holds even a shred of mercy, you will leave her with me."

"I have honor," the official replied, his voice rough. "And I know the law, and it is firm. If you have no bill of sale, you cannot have the slave."

He kicked his mount's flanks, and the men rode away, pulling Sabina behind them.

I watched her go, my heart in my throat, and waited to see if she would turn to look back at me.

She did not.

Seventeen

Hector smiled with satisfaction when he saw Albanus Marinus outside his house with the slave. The girl appeared a little dusty, but otherwise unharmed.

"My property has been returned." Hector pulled a silver mina from his purse and presented it to the chief magistrate. "Thank you for enforcing the law of Rome."

"You are too generous," Albanus protested, but he did not return the valuable coin.

"I will not forget your efforts on my behalf," Hector finished. "If I may ever be of service to you—"

"I will call on you, Hector Hostilius. Farewell."

Hector waited until the magistrate had gone before pulling the slave into the house. "I am glad to have you back. This is your place, nowhere else."

The girl did not speak but stood before him with her head bowed.

"What stories you must have to tell," he said, taking his dagger from his belt. He pulled the girl closer and cut the rope around her wrists. "I have plans for you, and I believe you may enjoy our next outing."

She lifted her head. "What will you have me do, Dominus?"

"Nothing taxing, I promise you. We are going on a journey. Along the way we may visit cities even larger than Philippi. Your world is about to expand, slave, and I hope you appreciate my efforts on your behalf. If all goes well, we shall both prosper in the future. Now go."

The girl blinked in confusion, then turned and walked away.

Hector went to his desk, currently covered in a map. He sat and ran his finger along the line representing the Via Egnatia, the major Roman road that ran from east to west.

On the morrow he would command Triton, Darby, and Berdine to mind the house while he left Philippi with the girl. They would take the mare, and as they traveled west, he would inquire about seers and necromancers at every opportunity. If the gods did not lead him to someone who could restore the girl's gift by the time they reached the port at Dyrrachium, he would book passage on a ship bound for Rome. In such a large city, home to Caesar and the Senate, surely someone would be able to restore the spirit that had turned his young slave into a profitable investment.

Once her gift was as powerful as before—or even more so—he would return and use his profits from the girl's gift to build the greatest racing arena Rome had ever seen. He would become wealthy, not only because he had an eye for choosing great horses but also because he had a slave who could peer into the future and predict the winner of every race.

The next morning, Hector rose early and charged Berdine with waking Sabina, setting Darby to work in the garden and telling Titan to feed, groom, and saddle the Kohl-ani mare. He had considered taking a wagon and another slave, yet he could travel more swiftly on horseback. The sooner they left Philippi, the sooner he would be on his way to wealth and status.

After eating his fill of dates, cheese, and bread, he walked to the temple of Caesar, bowed before the statues of Augustus and Claudius, and gave the priest a denarius for the *immolatio*. The priest left him for a moment, then returned with a ram that had already been washed and adorned with ribbons and strips of scarlet wool. The priest consecrated the beast, sprinkling it with *mola salsa*, a salted, roasted wheat flour, and then splashed wine on its forehead.

Hector folded his hands and watched as the priest passed the sacrificial knife along the animal's spine, completing the consecration. Then, with great gravitas, he presented the blade to Hector.

Hector accepted the knife and studied the ram with a narrowed eye. The success or failure of his journey hinged upon the next few moments. If all went as it should, the gods would bless his efforts and reward him for his faithfulness and generosity. But if the animal had an internal flaw—a disfigured organ, a blemished liver, or any other sign of disease—his plans would be doomed to failure.

Hector met the ram's gaze. The ideal sacrifice should show no sign of fear, lest it pollute the offering. Ideally, the animal should also demonstrate its consent to slaughter by lowering its head. When this ram did not voluntarily do so, Hector gripped the ram's horn and applied downward pressure, deftly forcing it to a lower position. While he held the horn, the ram bleated in protest until the priest slammed the beast's forehead with a poleax, stunning the creature. An instant later, Hector cut the animal's throat.

The ram staggered and fell back, splashing warm blood onto the tiles. As the life flowed out of the beast, the priest helped Hector turn the dying animal onto its back. When the ram lay belly-up, Hector opened the soft abdomen. Inhaling the coppery stench of fresh blood, he thrust his hands into the steaming organs, examining the liver, lungs, biliary blister, peritoneum, and heart. Hector found no deformities, which meant the gods had accepted his sacrifice.

He glanced at the priest to make certain he had not spotted any ill omens. The priest nodded and gestured to his assistants, who pulled out the entrails and put them in a golden bowl reserved for the gods. Then, with Hector's assistance, they divided the ram for the midday banquet. The coals were already heating, the skewers freshly oiled.

"The divine Caesar blesses you," the priest intoned, bowing toward the statue of Claudius. "And so do his priests."

"I will bless you as well," Hector replied, "when I return for the banquet. I am about to undertake a journey and will require the goodwill of the gods."

"Then you shall have it," the priest said, bowing. "For your generosity, the divine Caesar will ensure your journey is safe, swift, and prosperous."

❖

Sol, god of the sun, had ridden his blazing chariot halfway across the sky by the time Hector returned to the temple with the slave girl. They climbed the marble steps, bowed before each of the statues, and entered the triclinium, where priests were serving roasted meat from the morning sacrifice. At least twenty men reclined on the dining couches, many of them retired legionaries. Hector called greetings to the men he knew, then reclined on a flower-bedecked couch as Sabina sat cross-legged on the floor near his feet. One of the priest's slaves brought a heavily laden tray and set it before Hector, an appropriate gift for the man who had furnished the sacrifice.

"A delicious meal," he told the girl, pulling tender cuts from the skewers on his tray. "Fortification for the journey ahead."

He was surprised when the girl responded. "The Lydian woman fed me," she murmured, her voice so low he wondered if he had imagined it.

"Did you say something?"

She lowered her head. "I am sorry, Dominus."

He laughed. "You may have enjoyed your day or two in that woman's house, but you have no place there. You are my slave, and I did not agree—I would *never* agree—to the sale."

"Master Lucius—"

"Master Lucius is dead. I am now your only master."

She raised her head as if she would speak again, but Hector lifted a warning finger, having no interest in her words.

Many a slave owner, even high-ranking generals, slept uneasily on account of their slaves, but Hector did not believe the girl capable of harming anyone. She was too small, too weak, and, since losing her power, too *empty* to be dangerous.

"When I retired"—he lowered his voice to reach her ears alone—"at first I found it difficult to adjust to life as my own master. I was accustomed to being told what to do and when to do it. But one has only to look at the stars to know that some were created without much light, others have a middling glow, others blaze with glory. You are a slave, a dim star. Created with only a little light, you can never be anything else."

She lifted her head slightly. "After the army, you learned to live free."

"I was born into freedom, but you have always been a slave, no? But you are not alone. Triton, Darby, and Berdine are your family, and I am your master. This is how the gods arranged your life, so this is how you are destined to live. Take what you are given and do not desire more."

He pulled a bit of meat from a skewer and tossed it to the girl. She nibbled at the edge, then devoured the rest.

"Here." Since she had decided to cooperate, Hector threw her a larger piece. "I do not know when we will eat again."

❖

After finishing his meal and receiving a benediction from the priests, Hector mounted the mare and pulled the girl up to ride behind the saddle. Most slaves walked or ran along-side their masters, but the girl would never be able to keep up with the mare.

A sense of nostalgia overtook him as he rode out of the city. More than two years before, he and Lucius had traveled the Via Egnatia on their way to Philippi and little had changed since that time. The road was still nineteen paces wide, and though it had been heavily traveled for more than two hundred years, very few of the paving stones had cracked.

Numerous other wayfarers crowded the highway. Most people traveled in groups for companionship and security, forcing Hector to maneuver around them. In addition to numerous people, carts, and flocks, he spotted two riders for the *cursus publicus*, a system that carried important documents from one civil authority to another. The riders exchanged their horses for fresh mounts at eight-mile intervals, and he had heard that a message could travel from Rome to the farthest outpost in only two days.

If only he could fulfill his goal in so short a time.

He settled into his saddle and steeled himself for a long journey. Unless he found a quick solution to the problem of a now-useless slave, this road would take them through scenic mountain passes, grassy highlands, and along a rushing river. But would it provide an answer?

He looked over his shoulder and glimpsed the girl, who clung to the lip of his saddle. Was she relieved to be back in his household or did she not care where she lived? She could not have enjoyed life in the Lydian woman's villa. He had seen that woman and others working along the river, and rumor had it that she worked as hard as her employees. A well-bred woman should not work alongside servants; the very notion contradicted the laws of man and nature. He had also heard that the Lydian woman was a faithful follower of Paulos, which only fortified her reputation as a renegade.

He shook his head at the thought of the troublesome Jew. No one could deny the importance of religion in a man's life, but any man who spent his life as an emissary for only one god was far too shortsighted.

As the crowds thinned, the mare responded to the nudge

of his heels and quickened her pace. Hector sighed in satisfaction—at last, they were making progress.

Aware that he might be away indefinitely, Hector had left his slaves to mind his home, but he also arranged for someone from the magistrate's office to check the house every day. If any of the slaves disappeared, the magistrate would conduct a search and recover them. If any items from his house went missing, he would beat the slaves until the absent item was returned. After all, a man's wealth was measured by his possessions—the sum of his slaves, houses, treasures, and coins.

He had taken precious little with him. In his backpack, Hector carried a blanket, a dagger, and a bag of dried fish, enough to provide for his comfort if he could not find a *mansio*, an inn for government officials. A bag of wheat kernels would suffice for the slave.

His sword, as always, hung from his saddle.

In his former life, the army never ventured into battle without sacrificing a bull and searching for omens in the entrails. He had done the same at the temple, but still he felt uncomfortable setting out alone. He had the girl, of course, but slaves were not proper company.

Perhaps he would feel less discomfited if he focused on his purpose. Barring an unforeseen accident, he would reach Amphipolis on the morrow, where he could easily find safe shelter. He did not expect to find a seer in that city, but considering the vast number of people who traveled the Via Egnatia, he might learn of a reputable necromancer in a dining room or around a campfire.

Memories of army campfires brought thoughts of Lucius, for whom Hector had conducted a proper but hasty ritual of cremation. Lucius had been a fine companion when they served Rome—courageous, strong, and the best rider Hector had ever seen. He once commented that Lucius's thighs must be cast iron because no one else sat a horse with such tenacity, but Lucius had batted away the compliment by claiming he stayed in the saddle only because he had coated it with honey.

Lucius had been a faithful comrade-in-arms, yet he proved to be nothing but a hindrance after their retirement. His perspective was clouded by domestic dreams, and his eyes watered when he spoke of floors of mosaic tiles and walls with painted murals. Retirement had made him soft, even maudlin, and if Lucius had been thinking clearly, he would have been grateful that Hector had compassion enough to kill him.

When they reached a stretch of open road, Hector urged the mare into a trot. He thought he heard the clatter of the girl's teeth as she bounced on the mare's hips.

They made good time until the road curved to skirt Mount Pangaeos, where Hector allowed the horse to walk so he could drink in the sight of the snow-covered mountain. Through the sparse trees he glimpsed the remnants of gold and silver mines, and higher up, evidence of workers who had extracted slabs of marble. No wonder the people of this area had fractious relationships with their neighbors. The mountain contained wealth for anyone with the strength to extract it, but too many men wanted to claim the entire mountain for themselves.

"I heard a story once," he said, unable to bear the heavy silence. "They say the gods distributed soil through a sieve throughout the world, then dumped the remaining stones in

Macedonia." He waited for a snort, a breath, or a comment, but the girl remained silent.

"Slave?"

"Dominus?"

"Never mind."

He was a man on the rise, and he would not resort to conversation with a slave.

He flicked the reins and urged the horse to trot.

Eighteen

After the shock of losing Sabina, I fasted, prayed, and wept for a full day. Unable to face the women at the shore, I charged Syntyche with overseeing the work and asked Ariston to convey a message to the wool merchant and his wife. We would pay for the halo hair wool when it became available. We would pay for the wife's spinning and weaving when the cloak had been completed. Until I returned, Syntyche and her workers would be carrying on, trusting that all would be well.

I would do the same, even though the coin I had set aside for the wool and weaving had gone to Hector Hostilius.

"I do not understand," Syntyche said when she stopped by the house the next morning. "When you gave Ariston the purse to buy the slave, you knew you would need it to pay our expenses. So why did you buy her?"

"I was certain the Lord would provide," I said, biting back fresh tears. "I thought I was acting in accordance with His will. But when we lost the girl, I had to wonder—was I obeying the Spirit or my own impulse? Now I have lost a great deal of coin and have nothing to show for it. If I acted out of my own will, I cannot ask the Lord to bless my foolishness."

Syntyche examined my face with considerable concentration, then shook her head. Clearly, she did not understand my reasoning.

"You should know," she said, watching me with a wary expression, "they say Hector has taken the girl and left Philippi."

"Left the city?" My throat tightened. "Where has he gone?"

Syntyche shook her head. "No one knows."

The information rattled me, but after earnestly seeking the Lord, I still felt as though He wanted me to pursue Sabina and free her.

An hour later, I knew what I had to do.

"We cannot stop our efforts to reach Sabina," I told Ariston. "The Spirit has shown me that no kindness done in Christ's name is ever wasted. I want you to visit the people who live in the tents near the city gate. Find out where Hector has gone."

Ariston gave me a dubious look. "And how would this information be helpful?"

"I intend to find her, redeem her, and bring her home. I promised her freedom, and I will not break my promise."

Ariston might not have understood my reasoning either, but he bowed and did not argue.

❖

When I called for Ariston that afternoon, Phebe said he had not yet returned. I spent the next hour writing instructions for Dione and Syntyche.

Ariston returned with a worry line between his brows. "I have made inquiries, Domina—and yes, Hector has left the city. Yesterday he sacrificed a ram at the temple of Caesar and departed on horseback, taking the girl with him." He lowered his voice. "I also heard rumors about events before his departure. Many believe he killed Lucius, his closest companion, before departing."

I stared in disbelief. "Why?"

"Apparently, they fought." Ariston folded his arms. "I know a slave who is owned by the magistrate. Hector told Albanus they argued and fought, but because he did not intend to kill Lucius Martius, Albanus did not charge him with murder."

"So he took Sabina . . . and our purse."

Ariston dipped his chin in a reluctant nod. "Now the Roman has everything. I do not know what he is planning, but he has not sold his house or his other slaves. I spoke to Triton, his steward, who told me Hector plans to return. Apparently, he believes there is coin to be made elsewhere."

"By selling Sabina?"

"I cannot say. Triton did not know his master's intentions."

I considered this new information. If I had focused on my work and not been distracted by the sight of that pitiful child, she would still be in Philippi. She would still be subject to the whims of an uncaring master, but would that not have been better than being taken away and sold . . . or used for some other purpose?

"Adonai, have I made the situation worse?" I begged the Lord for guidance, then lifted my head. I might not have coin to spare, but I had obligations to my workers, my client, and a helpless young slave. I had promised the Lord I would care for Sabina, but first I would have to find and free her.

Aware that I would need help to fulfill my plan, I placed my hand on Ariston's arm. "Go back into town, visit the tavern and the baths, and see if you can learn where Hector has gone. I will make arrangements to continue the work here, and on the morrow I will set out to follow him."

"Alone?" He lifted a brow. "Domina, you cannot travel alone."

I searched his dark eyes, hoping I could rely on the inherent strength I saw there. "I will take Phebe, if she is willing," I said, "and I would like you to accompany us. But only if it pleases you to do so."

I waited, my heart in my throat, knowing he was right—I could not travel without him.

"My lady," he answered, "I would sooner die than let you chase that malicious man unprotected."

❖

While Ariston went back into the city to see if he could learn more about Hector's plans, I walked to the beach to make certain all was going well with our latest commission.

Syntyche was overseeing both groups of workers—the women who searched for snails in the water, and the women who worked at the table, dipping handfuls of halo hair wool into the malodorous dye. She seemed content with her workload, and I did not think she would mind if I took a few days to search for Sabina.

The wind snapped my headscarf as I hugged Syntyche and complimented her on the women's progress. "I see you have everything well in hand," I said, "so I will not worry while I am away."

Her eyes widened. "You are leaving? How long will you be gone?"

"I cannot say. As long as it takes for me to find Sabina and bring her home."

"You speak as if she is your daughter, but—" She bit her lip.

"Please, speak your mind."

Syntyche drew a deep breath. "That slave is not your daughter. Your girl's ashes are scattered in Thyatira, not Philippi. You have a new life now, a new purpose, and these women are depending on you."

Her words stung, yet I forced a smile. "Perhaps that is why the Lord sent you to me. I know I can trust you to make sure the work proceeds as it should. You understand how important it is that we finish this cloak by autumn."

"What if I run out of coin to pay these women? The purse you gave me is already light."

I sighed, acknowledging her predicament. "If you run out of coin, sell some of the raw wool in storage—it should fetch a good price. Not the lambs' wool; we will need that for the cloak. And sell small amounts, only enough to replenish our purse."

"And if the wool merchant demands a deposit for the additional halo hair? We do not have nearly enough for a full cloak."

"Tell him he must be patient. We will pay him when he delivers the wool."

Syntyche frowned. "I do not understand why you are having difficulty with the budget. You have never run short before."

"I have never spent most of the advance payment on something else . . . but it could not be helped." I gripped her hand, resigned to suffering some degree of loss. "If you run short of funds, go to my house and ask Dione to help you select whatever furnishings you can sell on market day."

Syntyche gave me a twisted smile. "I could never sell your beautiful things."

"They are only things," I said, readjusting my head covering. "I am leaving to find something far more precious."

I was turning to leave when Syntyche grabbed my hand. "If you are traveling west—"

"Yes?"

She hesitated, but then her words came out as if they'd been glued together. "I have a favor I need to ask of you."

❖

Ariston was waiting when I returned to the villa. As I came through the doorway, he removed my traveling cloak and brushed a few grains of sand from my shoulder. "Is all well at the river, Domina?"

I nodded. "Syntyche has the work well in hand. I will not worry about her while we are away." I turned to face him. "Did you learn anything else about Hector's plans?"

Ariston's face darkened. "I am sorry to say that I did. I found an old woman who brought food to Lucius after he left Hector's house. She was in the kitchen when Hector last visited there."

"The day Lucius died?"

He nodded. "She said Hector was angry because Lucius sold the girl. Hector said he had come up with a plan to restore the girl's gift."

I stepped back, astonished. Dozens of questions bubbled in my head, so I chose the uppermost: "How could he do that?"

Ariston's eyes narrowed with disapproval. "He intends to take the girl to a witch. Hector is convinced a necromancer will be able to order the spirit of divination to return."

My hands trembled as I sank to a couch. "Can this cook be trusted? We have only her word on this matter."

"The woman said she used to stand outside the triclinium and listen to Lucius's conversations. She holds no love for Hector and swears by her gods that he killed Lucius intentionally. Out of fear for her life, she fled the house when she heard Lucius fall."

"Do *you* believe her?"

"I do. She has nothing to gain by lying."

I covered my mouth for a moment, horrified by Ariston's news. Sabina had been in the grip of an unclean spirit, but through the power of Yeshua, Paulos had freed her. She was so close to salvation, but if Hector had his way, she would be thrust back into darkness. She could find herself in a worse state than before . . .

Paulos had shared a story with us, a tale Yeshua told about unclean spirits who left a man and wandered about restlessly. Then it said, "I'll go back home where I came from," and when it returned, it found the house vacant, swept clean, and put in order. So it went and brought along seven other spirits more evil than itself, and they went and lived there. That man's last condition was worse than the first.

I did not know if such a thing was possible in Sabina's case, but I could not let this happen to her. I turned to Ariston. "Where would Hector go to find a necromancer?"

"He could go anywhere. But he would be most familiar with cities to the west since he retired from the legion in Britannia."

The west . . . the Via Egnatia led west, winding through several cities until it reached the port of Dyrrachium. From there, if he had enough coin, Hector could board a ship and cross the Ionian Sea. Within several days he could be in Rome, where he would be one of nine hundred thousand people.

I had never been to the imperial city, but I had heard enough about Rome to dread even the possibility of visiting that place. "Let us hope," I said, "we do not have to chase him all the way to Caesar's villa."

"Agreed."

I drew a deep breath and stood. "Tomorrow we will rent a conveyance and travel west, making inquiries along the way. We will ask the Lord to help us find Sabina, wherever she might be, and free her from Hector's evil plans." I lifted a brow. "Have you ever been west of Amphipolis?"

He grinned. "I was born in that city. I did not leave until I was fourteen."

My heart contracted at this unexpected news. I did not know much about Ariston's past, and I had never thought to ask about his roots. He was a slave when I met him, but he was rapidly becoming a friend. I should have been more considerate and less aloof.

I met his gaze. "When we reach Amphipolis, will you know where to search for a man like Hector?"

"I might. Every city, no matter how large or small, has dark corners where men meet to drink, carouse, and enjoy forbidden pleasures. I can find those places. And we can always search the temples."

I frowned, suddenly aware of what our search would entail. We were believers in the true God; we must not allow ourselves to be drawn back into our former practices. I could not ask Ariston or Phebe to venture into situations where they might be tempted.

"Ariston, I would not want you to revisit your old life. But if you can make inquiries in good conscience—"

"For the sake of a lost soul, I can do almost anything. The Lord will strengthen my spirit and my resolve."

I clasped his hand. "Then I will depend upon your direction once we begin our search."

He smiled, his warm fingers wrapping around mine. "I would be honored, Domina, to be your guide."

Nineteen

After spending the night in the woods, Hector rose at day-break, saddled the mare, and woke his slave. The girl had remained quiet throughout the evening; she slid off the mare without complaint and fashioned a bed of wet leaves when Hector spread out his blanket. He had considered command-ing the girl to sleep with him solely for the sake of warmth, but a girl that small could barely warm herself, let alone another.

He rode in silence for a while, surveying the road, and startled when he heard rapid hoofbeats in the distance. He directed the mare to the right, certain he was hearing the approach of a rider for the cursus publicus, and gaped in surprise when the rider called his name. "Hector Hostilius! Halt!"

Hector wheeled the mare around. The approaching stranger rode a mule, so this was no imperial messenger. The man also looked vaguely familiar, but why?

Hector pulled his dagger from his belt and concealed it in his sleeve in case the magistrate had sent this man to arrest him for Lucius's death. "Who goes there?"

The man slowed the mule, whose sides heaved as it trudged forward.

"Hector Hostilius," the man called. "I was not certain I would find you."

"We have established my name," Hector replied. "Now let us establish who *you* are."

The man's brows rose like startled birds. "You do not recognize me? I am Marcus Tullius. My house is but a short distance from yours."

"You have come all this way because we are neighbors?"

The man grinned. "I have come with information that should interest you. I have ridden hard, slept on the ground, worn out two mules—"

"This must be serious, then."

"It is." The man studied Hector's face. "It is the sort of knowledge for which a man might pay a great deal."

"How would a man know the correct price," Hector answered, "unless he is familiar with what the information is?"

The man's smile flattened. "I am brother to a Philippian merchant called Omri, a man whose wife works for the Lydian woman."

Hector shifted uneasily in the saddle. "And?"

"My brother mentioned that the Lydian woman is preparing to leave Philippi. Indeed, I saw her servants making preparations as I passed her villa. She will be traveling with her steward, a maid, and my brother's garrulous mother-in-law. They have rented a *carpentum*."

Hector forced a polite smile. "I am delighted for her."

"It is her *reason* for leaving Philippi that should concern you. Omri said she is determined to re-claim the slave you took from her."

Behind him, the slave girl caught her breath. Resisting the urge to turn, Hector remained focused on the messenger. "Why should I be concerned about a mere woman? The city magistrate has affirmed that the slave belongs to me."

"The Lydian woman believes otherwise. And like many other Philippians, she follows the God of the Jews. She was hostess to Paulos and his company when they created havoc in our city. She may be asking her God to create havoc for you."

The wisp of unease that had seeped into Hector's mood billowed into a cloud. While Paulos and his friends were only men, they had exhibited inexplicable power. If not for Paulos, Hector would not have been forced to take this journey.

But what could the woman do to him? A traveling party of four would never overtake a man on horseback. If, by chance, they did, three women and a steward were no match for a trained soldier of Rome.

He pulled a denarius from his purse and tossed it to Marcus Tullius. "I hope this proves sufficient for this news. I thank your brother for the report."

Tullius frowned at the coin. "I had hoped the news would be worth more to a neighbor."

Sighing, Hector took out a second denarius from the purse. "She travels with only a few servants?"

"That is what I heard, though the man is a big fellow. Nevertheless, he is only a steward, more accustomed to dealing with merchants than men of arms."

Hector tossed the coin to the man, then flicked the reins. "Travel safely, friend. I will consider what you have said."

"Wait." Tullius edged forward. "I hope you will recall that I have done this for you."

"I am not so old that I am losing my memory."

"Still, I may need a favor from you someday."

Hector smothered a guffaw. He would never have need of a plebian like Marcus Tullius, but he might as well keep the man on his side. "You have only to ask," he said. He waited until his visitor turned his mule before nudging the mare.

As he pressed the horse forward, he could not help admiring the Lydian woman's resolve. She would re-claim the girl? How?

Few women would have the courage or the means to undertake such a journey, especially when failure was guaranteed. What had given this woman the confidence to proceed with her foolhardy plan? And why was she so concerned for his slip of a slave? She might be off her head, but at least she had courage.

"Did you hear that, girl?" he asked, not turning. "The Lydian woman seeks to take you from your lawful master."

The girl did not answer, nor did he expect her to. But as the mare whickered and bounced her head, Hector thought he heard a low, quiet sob.

❖

The road finally turned southward, heading toward the sea and Amphipolis. Within a mile Hector encountered other travelers—families on foot, merchants with their carts and clattering iron-shod wheels, the occasional wealthy family in a closed carriage. He slowed the mare to a walk and let the nimble beast pick her way through the crowd.

Years as a soldier had taught him to eye outsiders with suspicion, so his gaze darted automatically to every traveler's hands and then to his clothing, where the hilt of a sword or the outline of an axe-head might be straining against the fabric.

Rome was currently at peace with its neighbors, but the *pax Romana* did not extend to all men. Thieves and miscreants traveled among family groups, along with escaped slaves, foreign spies, and insurrectionists.

Rome despised insurrection, in part because men of all stations could be caught up in a wave of discontent. Roman soldiers still talked about Spartacus, a former captive-turned-gladiator who led a slave uprising during the time of the Republic. Thousands died in what turned into all-out war, and afterward the Romans became acutely aware of potential insurrectionists.

Only twenty years before, Rome had crucified a Judean who claimed to be king of the Jews, successfully eliminating what could have become a bloody war in the East. Like Spartacus, whose body was never found, the Judean's followers claimed he had escaped death and traveled about the countryside for days thereafter. But he had not been sighted in years, and most of his followers were Jews, a people who were unnaturally disposed to quarreling among themselves.

Yes, enemies of Rome walked every highway, including the Via Egnatia, and nothing in their appearance would give them away. Hector would have to engage them in conversation to learn of any disloyalty to the Empire, but he would be well rewarded if he discovered such traitors—

He clipped the thought. He was no longer a soldier, so he should stop thinking like one. His only duty now was to care for himself and take pleasure in his remaining years.

They were only a short distance from Amphipolis when the wind picked up and swirled dead leaves over the paving stones. A dark cloud rolled in from the other side of the mountain, blocking the sun and compelling travelers to shelter in the forest.

Glancing around, Hector saw no structures of any kind. Tall trees lined both sides of the road, yet experience had taught him that sheltering beneath a tree was risky. In a high wind, the tree could fall and trap those beneath it, or lightning could strike the treetop, injuring or killing anyone in the vicinity.

He spurred the mare into a gallop. Spits of rain struck his cheek, and the girl clung to his waist, her bony fingers needling his ribs as the heavy cloud sagged toward the earth. The trees thrashed about, thunder rumbled, and Jupiter's lightning bolts zigzagged in the heavens, causing the mare to rear up. Hector barely managed to remain in the saddle. Somehow the girl still clung to him.

With the next crack of thunder, rain began to fall in sheets, drenching rider, horse, and slave. Hector searched for shelter but saw none. Then a burst of lightning illuminated the area, and he spotted a structure. He yanked on the reins, trying to direct the mare, but she reared again, unseating him and the girl. Hector landed hard on the paving stones while the mare galloped into a nearby forest.

"By Jupiter's left eye, come back here!" He tried to move his leg, but it had twisted in the fall. He could see a bruise forming around his knee. Now he had lost the mare and the slave, too.

But he hadn't. He felt a tap on his shoulder and looked up to see the girl shivering beside him. She must have realized his predicament because she extended a hand to help him up. Surprised that she had not run away, he took her hand

and pulled himself upward, nearly bringing her down in the process. After he regained his balance, she stood beneath his arm and helped him hobble into the woods, where someone had built a three-walled structure with a roof.

Once inside, Hector dropped to the ground, realizing they had found shelter in a goat shed. Two goats stood near the opposite wall, suspicion radiating from their golden eyes.

Hector propped his arms on his bent knees and stared out at the road. Wordlessly, the girl sat cross-legged beside him, hugging herself as she shivered in the cold rain.

By all that was holy, what was he to do now? He would have to make his way to Amphipolis on a wounded leg and with only a skinny girl to assist him. His costly mare could be anywhere, along with the supplies he had packed for the journey. His purse remained safely tucked inside his tunic, but his blanket, sword, and food were with the mare.

He pushed a curious goat out of his way and straightened his injured leg. Though the ankle was still swelling, the knee felt solid, despite the bruise. He had incurred far worse injuries in battle.

He glanced at the girl. She had curled herself into a wet ball of flesh and linen and was staring blankly into the rain. She was his property, she had lived with him for over two years, and he knew nothing about her. He did not particularly *want* to learn anything about her, but without Lucius to provide conversation, he could think of no other way to pass the time.

He cleared his throat. "Why did you stay?" he asked, not looking at her. "You could have run."

"Where would I go?"

He shrugged. "People live in these woods. Some of them would welcome a child to work on their farm."

The corner of her mouth drooped. "They would know I am a slave."

"So? They might allow you to stay."

"Escaped slaves are hunted down, returned to their owners, and branded. Everyone knows this." She spoke slowly as if measuring the risk of each word before forming it on her tongue. But at least she was talking.

"Is living in my house so bad?"

"You are a soldier. A soldier knows nothing but killing."

"True enough. But I am a soldier no longer."

"You talk of killing every day. And you killed Lucius."

He threw her a sharp look. How could she have known? Had she heard the story from Darby, or did she still retain a vestige of the power that allowed her to see the future?

"I regret Lucius," he said, returning his gaze to the rain. "I struck him in the heat of anger. He sold you without my permission."

"Does Rome allow its citizens to kill each other without consequence?"

He whistled, amazed that so many words had come out of her mouth in one string. "Listen to you! I had no idea you carried such weighty thoughts."

"All slaves have thoughts, though not many masters realize it."

He nodded. "You may be right. And to answer your question, if I had visited Lucius with murder on my mind, I would be guilty of a crime, but that was not the case. We fought and I won. I regret his death."

She looked at him, her eyes sharper than a child's ought to be. "Lucius did me a kindness in selling me. That woman was going to grant my freedom."

He scoffed. "And what would you do with freedom? Where would you go? How would you find food and shelter?" He closed his eyes and let his head fall to the wall at his back. "Trust me, girl—one day you will be glad you belong to me. I have great plans for you, and when they are complete, you will never want for anything again."

❖

When the storm stopped, Hector hobbled out of the goat shed. Even with the slave's help, the act of moving from the shed to the road convinced him that he would not be able to proceed without help. He looked around for a stick that would bear his weight, but though fallen branches littered the ground, most were rotted or too small to be of use.

He leaned against a tree trunk and sighed. "We will wait," he said, "until a wagon comes along."

An hour passed, an interval in which he saw dozens of travelers walk by. He watched for the Lydian woman's rented *carpentum*, a four-wheeled wagon with an arched roof of cloth or wood, but he saw no conveyances of any kind. Finally, as the sun was about to disappear behind the horizon, he heard the distinctive grind of iron-shod wheels.

"Help is coming." He leaned on Sabina's shoulder and walked carefully toward the road. "We will ride with these people."

His hope expanded to buoyant confidence when the vehicle came into view. This was no farm wagon, but a Roman *plaustrum*, a supply vehicle. As it approached, he straightened and saluted the driver.

"*Salve*," he called. "I am Hector Hostilius, formerly of the

157

Second Augusta legion, and I need transport to Amphipolis. My horse spooked and fled in the storm."

The soldier pulled on the reins, his eyes darting from left to right as he stopped the team of mules. "An honored legion," he said, lifting a brow. "Did you see much action in Syria?"

Hector chuckled. "We served in Britannia, as you well know. I was with an *alae* and rode in a regiment five hundred strong."

The driver grinned with no trace of his former suspicion. "Climb aboard."

Hector gestured to the girl, who ran to the back as the driver extended his hand and helped Hector onto the seat.

"How is life in retirement?" the driver asked, glancing at Hector as he flicked the reins. "Is it worth twenty years of a man's life?"

"Depends on where you settle," Hector answered. "I have great hopes for a future in Philippi."

"Then may Jupiter preserve you. I hope you have many years to enjoy the fruits of your labor."

They had gone no more than a short distance when Hector heard a whinny. Looking ahead, he saw the Kolh-ani mare halfway up a hill, her reins caught in tree branches. "She's still here," he said, marveling. "I wonder that no one stole her."

The driver laughed. "Who would steal a horse with a Roman sword dangling from the saddle?"

Hector joined in the man's laughter. "Any thief would probably believe it a setup." He clapped the driver on the shoulder. "If you would remain a moment, I could use help mounting the horse. After that, I will be on my way."

As he worked to free the agitated mare, a thought occurred—
one that had been lost during the events of the last hour. A
foolish woman was following him, and he did not want her
to interfere with his plan. Yet here was a legionary, a fellow
soldier. For a coin or two, he might be persuaded to handle
Hector's problem.

Leading the mare by the reins, he limped over to the supply
wagon. "Before I go," he said, looking at his new comrade,
"I wonder if you could be persuaded to take care of a matter for me."

The man smiled. "Name it."

"Three women and a man are following me in a carpentum. I need someone to discourage them from proceeding."

The driver lifted a brow. "How discouraged should they
be?"

Hector shrugged. "An injury, perhaps, or even a severe
fright." He grinned. "They are civilians; it will not take much
to dissuade them."

"How will I recognize them?"

Hector thought a moment. "The woman always wears
purple on her garment, though she is no one of importance."

"I am surprised she has not been arrested for violating the
sumptuary laws. Perhaps the law is different in the East, but
I thought only senators and the emperor were allowed to—"

"Such laws are only useful in Rome, friend. No one in
Philippi cares if the woman wears purple. She wears it not
to signify her rank, but to advertise."

Hector climbed onto the wagon, then swung his leg over
the horse and settled into the saddle. He snapped his fingers
at the girl, gesturing that she should climb up and sit behind
him.

"I am happy to serve a brother," the driver said, picking up his reins. "Consider it done."

"*Vale.*" Hector extended his arm in a quick salute. "May the gods go with you." He urged the mare into a trot and left the legionary behind.

With little daylight to spare, he finally spotted the city of Amphipolis, perched on the top of a mountain. "There it is," he announced. "We will go into the city and find something to eat. Then we will make camp in the woods."

The girl did not respond, and for a moment he wondered if she had fallen asleep. But as the mare began the steep climb toward the city, she clung to his saddle to keep from sliding off the horse's rump.

He smiled. Given a choice, she would choose to stay with him. But slaves, being slaves, had no right to make choices.

❖

The markets of Amphipolis were famous for wood, fine wine, and olive oil, but Hector had no interest in purchasing any item that couldn't be stuffed into his saddle pack. Instead, he bought a bag of cracked wheat from a woman near the city gate, then turned the mare toward the forest, guiding her through shaded trees and gray rocks until they came upon an abandoned mine. Hector dismounted, taking pains to spare his injured leg, took his pack from the horse and moved into the mouth of the cave.

The girl hesitated, then slid from the horse and landed in a heap on the ground. As rain began to drizzle from the dark skies, she scrambled to a spot beneath a budding tree. When Hector glanced over a moment later, the girl was curled into a ball and shivering.

He spread his blanket on dry ground and munched the cracked wheat. He had taken solid steps to stop the Lydian woman, so what else could he do to ensure the success of this mission? He had buried the curse tablet, which might take effect as the woman traveled. He had offered a sacrifice to Caesar, though thus far the divine emperor had done nothing to answer his prayers. But Amphipolis was the first city he would reach, and if the gods willed, he would find what he sought within its walls. "May it be so," he whispered. "May I find the necromancer soon, because every step I travel west only increases the length of my journey home."

He closed his eyes and willed his leg not to ache. Perhaps . . . perhaps he felt uneasy because he missed Lucius. He needed the assurance of an honest friend, someone who would speak plain truth. Or perhaps he was discouraged because he was in a fair amount of pain, exhausted, and sorely in need of sleep.

He stretched out on the blanket and set his sword by his side. As always, he ran his hand along its length and thanked Jupiter that it had become part of his right hand. The short-bladed *gladius* was every soldier's primary weapon, and Hector could not imagine being without it.

Before finally drifting into unconsciousness, Hector had one cold, lucid thought. On the morrow he should visit a temple and beseech another god for help. Jupiter, known as Zeus in Greek Macedonia, was father to the other gods. Since the divine Caesar had not yet helped him, why not petition the mightiest god of all?

Twenty

We had covered about half the distance between Philippi and Amphipolis, or so Ariston assured me, when the wind cooled and the clouds moved to block the sun. I shivered and wrapped my *palla* more closely around me, then turned to see if Phebe had remembered to bring my cloak. The woman was sleeping, her head resting on my trunk, and I did not want to wake her. Tabitha, Syntyche's mother, also slept.

We had been fortunate to find an available carpentum in Philippi. Wealthy Romans usually used a carpentum to travel safely over long distances, but Omri, Syntyche's husband, had one he used to visit customers in Neapolis. His conveyance was covered by stretched leather, not wood, but it would still provide shelter from the weather and a bit of privacy. Best of all, considering the dire state of our finances, we would not have to pay a single assárion. All we had to do was take Syntyche's mother back to her home in Amphipolis.

"Apparently, the woman has worn Omri out," Ariston had explained. "And he is so delighted to be rid of her that he offered his mule, as well."

I was grateful for this development because I did not want

to leave Syntyche without my wagon and mule. And truth be told, I could not help but admire Ariston's resourcefulness. From the first, I suspected he would make an excellent steward, and he had proven himself a hundred times over.

Behind me, lulled by the creak of the carpentum and the grind of iron-shod wheels, Phebe and Tabitha slept soundly, thank the Lord. Tabitha had spent the first hour of our journey complaining about Philippi, and by the fifth hour she had narrowed her complaints to Syntyche's housekeeping. Phebe and I had listened, nodding occasionally, but we could not break into the conversation because the woman's words flowed in an unending stream.

Sitting behind Ariston, I shivered and wearily regarded the road, bordered by thick forest as far as I could see. The trees whispered to themselves as our creaking vehicle passed. Ariston sat at the front edge of the wagon bed, his legs dangling behind the mule's tail, his hands firmly grasping the reins. He had no support for his back and no padding for his hips, however, and I knew he would be weary at day's end.

For the first time, we found ourselves alone on the road. The pedestrians had fallen behind, and those who traveled on horseback and in chariots had raced ahead.

I was about to remark on the unexpected solitude when I sensed a change in Ariston's posture. I glanced at him—his back had gone ramrod straight, the cords in his neck had tightened, and his eyes were narrowed as they scanned the trees to our left.

"Euodia," he said, his voice as cool as a winter wind, "move to the back of the wagon."

"But—"

"Now," he added, and his tone left no room for argument.

I stared at the thick brush and saw nothing alarming, but only a fool would have argued in that moment. Careful not to disturb the sleeping women, I moved to the back of the conveyance and crouched between two trunks. I considered waking Phebe, but if Ariston sensed danger, I did not want to complicate the situation.

Ariston pulled back on the reins and clicked his tongue. The mule stopped, flicked his ears, and brayed, the sound echoing in the narrow vale between the forests to the north and south.

"I may be imagining things," Ariston said, his voice low, "but would you please hand me a weapon?"

A what? I glanced around and saw nothing fitting that description, then remembered the knife Phebe had packed in case we needed to catch rabbits for dinner. I opened her trunk, found the blade, and placed it in Ariston's out-stretched hand.

Ariston urged the mule forward. The beast took three slow steps, then shied to the right as two men burst from the brush, swords flashing and faces disguised with carved masks. I shrieked despite my intention to remain hidden, and Ariston leapt from the wagon bed, armed with a blade that appeared utterly unsuitable when compared to the swords wielded by our attackers.

Both men pointed their swords at Ariston and gestured to the ground. "Down!" one of them commanded. "Or you and the women die today."

I blinked. How did they know our conveyance contained women? Tabitha and Phebe lay with their heads down and could not have been visible from the road . . .

Fear blew down the back of my neck as Ariston obeyed

and dropped his knife. One man ordered him to lie on the ground while the other lifted the leather flap at my right. By some miracle, Phebe and Tabitha had not yet opened their eyes.

"I'll take whatever coin you have," the man said, his dark eyes flashing through slits in his mask. "Offer it quickly, lady, or I will drag you out and search for it."

Though it pained me to do it, I pulled my purse from my girdle. The man took it, jingled the contents near his ear, and nodded. "That will do," he said. "Many thanks to you, mistress."

Phebe, who had finally awakened, squeaked and clung to me as the man walked toward his companion. The man guarding Ariston nodded, and for an instant I thought we might escape without harm. But before parting, the second man cut Ariston—once on the upper thigh and again on the right arm. Then both men disappeared into the forest.

I crawled over Tabitha, then jumped out of the carpentum and crouched beside Ariston. Both wounds were bleeding profusely.

"It is nothing," Ariston said, lifting his head. "Just a scratch."

I pushed his head back down. "Phebe"—I steeled my voice—"find some sort of linen in my trunk. Use one of my stolas or undergarments. We must bind these wounds."

Phebe scrambled to obey, and after a few harrowing minutes—and a half dozen protestations from Ariston—we managed to stanch the flow of blood.

"Good thing I was lying on my back," Ariston muttered as I bandaged his arm. "If he had cut the backs of my legs, the miscreant might have hobbled me."

"The Lord was with us," I managed to whisper. The rush of courage I felt when the men attacked had disappeared, and without it I felt drained. "They could have killed you. They could have killed all of us."

"Caesar does not want his roads strewn with corpses."

I gave the bandage on his arm a final tug. "What does Caesar have to do with this?"

Ariston snorted. "Those men were legionaries."

"They were ruffians. They wore no uniforms."

"They carried Roman swords, and the one who cut me knew what he was doing. There are places in the thigh and upper arm . . ." He bit his lip. "You are right—the Lord was with us. We are alive." He struggled to stand, so I extended my hand and helped him up. "How much did they take?"

"I gave them my purse. But they did not know that I always sew my largest coins into the hem of my cloak, a trick I learned when traveling throughout Lydia. We will not have coin to spare, but we will have enough to continue our journey."

"Continue?" Phebe's voice quavered. "How can we continue? Ariston is badly hurt, we have been robbed, and we do not even know if we are traveling in the right direction—"

"We will continue," Ariston interrupted. "And I will see a physician when we reach Amphipolis. Euodia has extra coin, and the fact that we have been attacked means we are on the right path."

I blinked, amazed by his deduction. "How can you be sure?"

He gave me the smile one gives a confused child. "Any soldier who would destroy the peace of Rome risks his life. Who do we know with ties to the army?"

The realization struck like a physical blow. "You think Hector arranged this?"

"I would not be surprised."

Phebe, whose face had compressed into a frustrated knot, retreated to the back of the wagon and held Tabitha's hand. The old woman had slept until I shouted for linen, then she woke and began to call down curses on her son-in-law.

I ignored her and helped Ariston climb back into the carpentum. He sat at the front edge, but I told him to slide over. "I will drive to Amphipolis."

"It is my duty—"

"You are wounded." Gently but firmly, I took the reins from his hands. "You must rest your arm. This mule and I shall get along very well. You will see."

While Ariston sputtered in annoyance, I flicked the reins. The mule twitched her ears as if confused, then hurried forward, as eager to leave the area as we were.

Twenty-One

Hector woke the next morning with an inexplicable sensation of being watched. He reached for his sword, then sat up and discovered the slave girl sitting beneath a tree, staring at him with those eyes that seemed older than the hills. Why?

Perhaps she was hungry.

He glanced at the ground and saw the empty burlap bag. Last night he had eaten all the cracked wheat, but he had reserved a hard loaf from his dinner at the temple. He attempted to break it, but the loaf had solidified, so he threw it to the girl. She pounced like a wolf attacking a lamb.

He shifted his gaze to the hobbled mare, who was browsing vegetation beneath the trees. "Hear me, Jupiter." He set a sliver of crust on the ground in case the god was hungry. "Hear my prayer and bless this day's venture. Lead me to your servants and aid me in my cause. Dull the pain in my injured leg, for I have much to accomplish."

The girl looked at him, probably expecting him to continue, yet he had no talent for ornate language.

"Give to the wicked what the wicked deserve," he finished, "and to the just give what is proper. Do not let me become like those who are greedy for undeserved wealth and have no righteous motivations. Bless me in my quest, for I seek only what I deserve."

Hector stood and limped toward the horse, then released the hobbles and attached his bedroll to the saddle. He mounted, grimacing when he shifted his weight to his bruised leg, and extended his hand for the girl. She came straightaway and settled on the mare's bony hips.

They set out for Amphipolis.

As he suspected, the temple of Jupiter had been built at the highest point of the city. He left the mare in a stable and paid a groom to be sure the horse ate well. Then he took the girl by the arm and led her up the mountain. Six resplendent columns stood at the temple entrance, topped by an ornate pediment adorned with sculptures of Jupiter's immortal offspring.

Hector tipped his head back and squinted at the statuary. "Jupiter is at the center," he said, hoping to enlighten the ignorant slave. "The other gods flank his sides, as he is the father of all."

The girl looked up but did not speak.

Grimacing with every step, Hector climbed the stairs and limped over floors of bleached limestone. Inside, dozens of skillfully worked statues towered over the morning worshipers, a mute testament to the gods' power and immortality. The bald priests, wearing white tunics, mingled among the people, accepting offerings or coins for sacrifices. An altar stood in the center of the room, where several priests were engaged in the ritual slaughter of a bull.

Hector dragged the girl toward the altar and thrust a handful of coins toward a priest. "I have an urgent request of

Jupiter," he said, pushing the girl forward. "This slave used to have the spirit of divination, but after a Jew called upon his God, the spirit left her."

A muscle quirked above the priest's eyes. If he'd had eyebrows, they would have risen to an impressive height. "And you want the spirit to return?"

"Of course." Hector stepped back. "Do with her as you will."

The priest took a long look at the slave, his eyes burning with curiosity, then led her to the lifeless head of the fallen bull. Chanting in Greek, he dipped a flail in the streaming blood and flicked it at the girl. The other attendants followed the priest's cue, chanting as they dipped their flails in blood and spattered the girl. She stood still and wide-eyed, flinching with every snap of the priests' flails.

The chanting grew to a crescendo as the priests circled the bull, sprinkling the girl each time they passed. Hector backed away—he had come to pay homage to the god, but he had no desire to be bathed in blood. He had experienced that state far too many times on the battlefield.

At last the priests dropped and pressed their faces to the bloody floor. The air seemed to shiver with anticipation. The girl, Hector noticed, had been thoroughly drenched, but was it enough to earn an answer to his prayer?

The chief priest lifted his head, caught Hector's eye, and dipped his chin in affirmation. "Jupiter has heard your prayer," he said. "He will honor your request."

Hector glanced toward the girl, wondering when her renewed gift would manifest itself. "It may take time," the priest added. "Be patient and you will behold our father's glorious work."

Hector bowed in deference, then took the girl's arm and led her outside. Drawn by the scent of blood, flies swarmed the slave, so he led her to the public bathhouse. The facility in Amphipolis had a section reserved for women. He directed the slave to the women's entrance and told her to meet him after she had bathed. "Do not rush," he warned. "If you stink, you will walk the rest of the journey."

Realizing that he also stank of blood and death, he limped toward the men's baths, his soul stirring with hope. Perhaps Jupiter would set things right by the time he returned.

❖

Hector entered the bathhouse at the *apodyterium*, where he stripped and put his belongings in a niche carved into the stone wall. A muscular slave stood nearby, so Hector tossed him a denarius to guard his possessions. "If even a single lepton is missing from my purse," he warned, "I will see you crucified."

The slave answered with a terrified nod, and Hector nodded back, certain his belongings would survive the pickpockets who loitered at the public baths.

He entered the vestibule and surveyed the layout of the complex. Even at this early hour, the *tepidarium* was moderately crowded and the *frigidarium* overflowing. Only in the steamy waters of the *caldarium* would a man have room to move about. He was fortunate—hot water, he had learned, eased the ache of bruises and strained muscles.

He slid into the steaming pool and breathed deeply of the scented air. The Greeks tended to begin their bathing with cold water and move to warm, but Romans, ever practical, preferred the opposite. Hector cared more for comfort than custom and knew warm water would not only ease his aching limbs but do a better job of cleansing his body.

He sat on the ledge that ran around the edge of the pool and nodded at the other bathers who looked his way. A strigil lay within reach, so he grabbed it and began scraping his flesh, whisking dirt and dust away from his tired muscles and battle scars. When his body was a rosy pink, he tossed the strigil over his shoulder and dropped beneath the surface, content to simmer in the warmth of the bath.

When a muffled voice cut through the water, Hector came up sputtering. Through blurry eyes, he saw another man watching him.

"Apologies," Hector said, shaking water from what remained of his hair, "but I could not understand your words."

The stranger, who appeared several years older than Hector, smiled. "I said you have the look of a soldier, but I do not recognize you."

Hector squinted, but because the man wore no clothes, Hector could not tell if he was being addressed by a merchant, an official, or the emperor himself.

"I *was* a soldier," he said, sitting on the marble ledge. "Part of the cavalry. I am now retired and living in Philippi."

"Ah." The man stepped into the water, sat on the ledge, and propped his elbow on the rim of the pool. "A prosperous city, Philippi. What brings you to Amphipolis?"

Hector leaned forward, realizing that the man might be the answer to his morning prayer. "I have a slave," he whispered, "who once had the gift of divination, but no more."

The man's brow furrowed. "The gifts of the gods do not usually disappear."

Hector snorted. "A Jew"—he spat the word—"cursed her."

"Must have been a powerful curse."

"You know the Jews. They are odd."

The man lifted his chin in silent agreement. "We have many Jews in Amphipolis. They tend to keep to themselves."

"I wish they had done so with regard to my slave. She used to bring in a tidy profit; now she is useless."

"There are other ways to profit from a female, my friend."

"I have tried. She is too young and not at all desirable. So I am looking for a necromancer or priest who can restore her gift and make the girl useful again."

The man scratched at his temple. "I have heard about an enchantress living in Lychnidos. She is called Magaere, and she lives beside the lake. They say her performances are quite entertaining."

Hector frowned. "She *performs*?"

"Indeed. Because people come from all over Macedonia to see her, the city officials have built an amphitheater for her use." The man arched his brow. "They say she works signs and wonders like the gods."

The hair on Hector's arms rose. "Have you seen her?"

"No, not I." The man smiled as if embarrassed. "I hear she can raise the dead and heal the lame. She also speaks with other voices and in languages of men from long ago."

A tremor of anticipation touched Hector's spine. Was *this* the work of Jupiter or mere coincidence?

"I visited the temple of Jupiter this morning," Hector said, "and asked the father of all gods to restore my slave's gift."

"And?"

"I have seen no evidence of her restoration, but you may

have acted as Jupiter's emissary. If I do not find a necromancer here, I will take my slave to Lychnidos."

"You may find such a person in Thessalonica, which is closer. With so many people entering its gates, it should not be difficult to find someone who can win favors of the gods."

"True." Hector nodded. "I will consider your suggestion."

"A pleasant journey to you, then. Gods protect you."

"And you, friend."

Hector climbed out of the pool, bowed in an overflow of goodwill, and hurried to claim his possessions.

Twenty-Two

The great city of Amphipolis, I noticed when we were yet some distance away, had been built atop a terraced hill. Ariston—who sat behind me and fretted because I would not let him drive—said the city was naturally fortified by a river that snaked around three of its borders. The ancient city's founders constructed a wall on the vulnerable eastern side, and at the conclusion of our first day of travel we drove through its wide gates.

I nearly wept with relief. Not only had we been attacked and robbed, but the journey had been far from pleasant. Though the Via Egnatia had been paved with smooth flagstones, my bones felt every jostle and jounce as our carpentum rolled over the road. Walking travelers jeered at us when yielding space for us to proceed, and I couldn't blame them for feeling irritated. I felt the same annoyance every time a Roman official on horseback or driving a chariot forced us to pull over so he could leave us in the dust.

By the time we entered the city, my arms felt as heavy as lead, and blisters had risen on my thumbs and index fingers. My back ached, and my ears had gone numb from Tabitha's whining. I completely understood why Syntyche's husband was so eager to be rid of his mother-in-law. Fortunately, the woman slept through the attack, but after she woke, she complained about everything from the weather to the thieves that frequented the road we had chosen to travel. Ariston looked at me, about to point out that the Via Egnatia was the *only* road we could travel, but I shook my head. No sense in inviting more argument.

Even Phebe, as patient a person as I had ever met, bore the look of a woman who had spent far too much time with demanding children.

When Amphipolis first came into view, I had asked Ariston to tell me what he remembered of his birthplace.

"The people here are proud," he said, propping his injured leg on a trunk. "Proud to be Greek and Macedonian, and proud to be living in the city where Alexander the Great planned his conquests. Amphipolis is home to many powerful and wealthy citizens, as well as the poor and lowly."

I saw what he meant as I drove slowly over flagstone streets crowded with vendors and their carts, women carrying laundry, and wealthy women peering through the silk curtains of their slave-carried litters. A mix of the impossibly rich and the utterly poor.

What had Paulos and Silas thought of this place? They and their traveling companions would have come through Amphipolis after leaving Philippi. Had Paulos stopped to preach here? If so, did anyone accept his message? If we lingered, we might be able to find fellow believers, perhaps even attend a meeting of an ecclesia . . .

But we did not have the luxury of time. Hector was ahead

of us and eager to accomplish his dark purpose. Was this his ultimate destination? We would be fortunate if that were so.

"Domina," Ariston asked, uneasiness creeping into his voice, "I hope you do not mind, but I must ask a question."

"What is it?"

He slid forward and sat beside me. "I admire your determination to find the girl and right the wrong that has been visited upon her. But once we find Hector and Sabina, how do you plan to convince him to release her?"

I sighed. The same question had occurred to me more than a dozen times in the passing hours, and I had not formulated an answer. I knew I did not have the power to convince Hector to surrender Sabina, and though Ariston was strong and courageous, I had already seen that he was not capable of overcoming a trained soldier. But while I lacked definite answers, I possessed infinite faith.

"I do not know," I admitted, keeping my gaze on the road. "I only know that God has set this task before me, so I must find Sabina and set her free. My resolve may seem foolhardy, but once we find her, I will trust the Lord to show us how His will should be accomplished."

"You believe God will tell you what to do? I have followed the Way for many months but have not yet experienced a direct revelation. I do not hear God's voice aloud."

"Nor do I, but I have heard His voice in the quiet of my soul, and I know He wants me to save that girl. I have already paid to redeem her, so claiming her will be a righteous act."

Ariston's jaw flexed. "I will do whatever you ask me to do. You gave me freedom, so my life is yours."

"Your life—and mine—belong to the Lord," I reminded him. "We are slaves to Him."

After a few minutes, Ariston pointed to a mansio. As always, other inns had been built near the government-run establishment, including several *cauponae*, cheap inns usually inhabited by prostitutes and thieves. Fortunately, several nicer guesthouses were nearby, one advertising itself as a *taberna* with an attached stable. We would stay there.

After hopping down from the carpentum, I waited for Ariston, Phebe, and Tabitha, and together we walked into the taberna.

"Come," Ariston said, apparently realizing I was too weary to take charge. "I will see you and Phebe safely to a room, then I will escort Tabitha to her home. Once she is settled, I will search for Hector Hostilius."

"But your injury," I protested. "You promised to see a doctor."

"I will," he said. "As soon as you are safe."

"And when will you sleep? You have been awake all day; you cannot search all night."

"I will rest," Ariston insisted, but he refused to meet my gaze. I wondered at his hesitation, then decided to leave matters in his hands. He had never given me reason to mistrust him.

Perhaps he did not want me to know what transpired after dark in Amphipolis.

◆

After rising early the next morning, Phebe and I broke our fast in the taberna's common room. Though I looked for Ariston with an inappropriate and somewhat brash curiosity, I saw no sign of my steward.

"I hope he is safe," Phebe said, shyly averting her eyes as

a grand lady and her retinue of slaves passed our table. "It is not like him to disappear."

"He is faithful," I reminded her. "And Amphipolis was once his home. I am sure he is following every report of Hector Hostilius."

"What if Tabitha decided to keep him?" Phebe said, her eyes twinkling. "She might have knocked him over the head just to keep him around."

I smiled, though I found the idea far from humorous. "Keeping Ariston would be easy," I said, "but *feeding* him would probably cost more than Tabitha can afford."

Midday arrived and we had not yet heard from Ariston. "Should we send someone to look for him?" Phebe asked, her face shadowed by concern. "Perhaps someone took advantage of his weakened condition. Or what if his wounds started bleeding again? What if he was robbed and beaten and is lying in some alley?"

I forced a smile. "He promised he would see a doctor to have his wounds properly tended. And do not forget—he might still have connections in this city. Perhaps he is visiting friends."

Phebe ignored my attempt at optimism. "If people here know him, they remember him as a slave," she whispered. "I would hate to think someone mistook him for a runaway and had him arrested."

"He has manumission papers," I replied, "but perhaps I will ask the innkeeper if he has heard anything."

With Phebe trailing behind me, I left our small chamber and approached the owner at his desk. "Ladies," he said, smiling. "Will you be staying another night?"

"I cannot yet say," I said, "but I wonder if you have seen

the man who arrived with us? Last night he went out and has not returned. Is this the sort of place where a traveler might be . . . accosted?"

The man pressed his hand to his chest. "By Jupiter, I should hope not! Still, though most areas are safe in daylight hours, after dark . . ." He shrugged.

"Danger prowls the streets?"

The owner grimaced. "I would not use those words, but who can say what might happen? Some people might take advantage of a stranger who drinks too much at the temple, attempts to steal from a merchant, or meddles with another man's wife."

"Ariston is not likely to have done any of those things." I drew a deep breath and forbade myself to worry. "He is an honorable man."

"Then I would not be concerned." The owner clasped his hands together. "I am certain he will return when he is ready. Now, may I offer you ladies dinner?"

"Ariston did say he would try to sleep," Phebe whispered. "Perhaps he is sleeping longer than he intended."

"But where?" I turned, hoping to spot Ariston stretched out on a bench or a dining couch, but he was not in the common room.

I thanked the owner for his time, and we returned to our chamber, where I fell onto my knees. "Father," I prayed, "you sent us on this journey, and I am already lost. Guide us as you guided Paulos and Silas. Keep us safe, bring Ariston back to us, and help us find Sabina. Most of all, Abba, give me the words to say and the strength to act when we find her. I am trusting you, *only* you, to tell me what to do in that moment."

"Amen," Phebe said, and when I lifted my head, I saw her

swipe a tear from her lower lashes. Had my prayer moved her so much, or did her feelings for Ariston run deeper than I suspected?

❖

Phebe and I had just finished praying when we heard a knock. I froze, my heart thumping as Phebe opened the door and announced what my eyes had already discerned.

"Ariston is back," she said, dimpling.

My gaze met his. "Are you well? We were worried about you."

"You need not worry about me, at least not here." He closed the door behind him. "And I am grateful to be back."

"We missed you," Phebe said. Ariston threw her a quick smile, then his attention shifted to a platter of fruit. Realizing that he might be starving, I gestured for him to eat.

"What business have you been about?" I asked, trying to keep my voice light. "We were beginning to think you had been robbed or assaulted."

"I saw a doctor," he said, settling onto the bench with a bowl of figs, "and he stitched up both wounds. He said I have the constitution of an ox."

I smiled at his exaggeration. "I am glad to hear it. What news did you hear of Hector?"

"I looked for him," he said, rubbing a fig against his tunic. "I did hear reports of a man and a slave girl riding through the gate, but the man made no attempt to prostitute the girl. Apparently, Sabina was with him when he made a sacrifice at the temple of Jupiter."

"He did not take her to a witch?"

"If he did, I have heard nothing of it. He visited the baths after a temple sacrifice. I do not know where he went afterward."

Frustrated, I pressed my lips together. We could not plant a spy at every street corner, so how could we know where Hector was going next?

"Fortunately," Ariston continued, his mouth curling upward, "I have a friend who works at the women's baths."

I blinked. "Surely you jest."

"It is a long story, but I did not think you would mind if I took an hour to inquire about the woman who raised me. My mother died giving me life, but the slave who raised me still serves the same master. I went to his house last night and asked for her."

"Wait." I lifted my hand, overwhelmed by the realization that I knew so little about the man who lived in my villa. "You were raised *here* by a woman still living."

He nodded. "Her name is Demetria, and she was overjoyed to see me. She gave me dinner and rejoiced when I told her I was a freedman." A smile flickered across his strong face. "I told her why we had come to Amphipolis, and that is when she told me about seeing a young girl at the baths." He glanced at the couch, where Phebe was doing needlework, and lowered his voice. "Demetria is not a believer, and sometimes she dabbles in fortune-telling. When the girl entered the baths, Demetria went over to help her. She said the girl seemed lost and . . . empty."

My mind flitted back to the days Sabina spent in my house. Yes, *empty* was a good description of her demeanor. As if she were waiting for something to fill her. I nodded. "Go on."

"The girl cleaned herself, and Demetria helped her scrub

her tunic. Not until then did Demetria realize she was helping another slave."

Of course. Slaves wore simple, unadorned tunics of inexpensive fabric, purposely designed to reveal their place in society. If Sabina's tunic was covered in blood, I could understand why Demetria would not have known whom she was helping. "Please, continue."

"Demetria was going to ask if she could read the girl's palm, but she said it was forbidden."

"By whom?"

Ariston shrugged. "She did not know. She only knew she was not allowed to do it, so she bade the girl farewell and sent her out of the baths."

I closed my eyes to sort through this new information. I did not want to know anything about divination or witchcraft, but a surge of hope rose within me nonetheless. Was the Spirit of God protecting Sabina? I did not understand how such a thing could be true, but if it were, God be praised.

"Help me understand." I leaned forward. "Are Sabina and Hector still in Amphipolis?"

"I do not believe so. They are traveling on horseback, so if they departed after the sacrifice, they could be nearing Thessalonica."

I sighed. "That is good news. That is a large city, so if they linger there, perhaps we can catch up with them next week. But Shabbat begins tonight, which means we cannot travel tomorrow."

"And if we do not find them in Thessalonica?"

"We will keep going," I assured him. "Even if we have to follow Hector all the way to Rome."

Ariston's lips pursed in a thoughtful expression. "Going

to Rome will take time. You may not finish your commission for the governor."

The possibility haunted me. "I know. But I believe—I hope—Syntyche can finish the job."

"The journey will not be an easy one. The Via Egnatia is a difficult and steep road, especially for a woman who is hated by a soldier of Rome."

"That curse has no power over me. And I am not worried, so long as I have you and Phebe with me." I glanced at my maid and saw that she had fallen asleep, needlework in hand.

Ariston's chest rose as he inhaled a deep breath. "Servants barely count as people, Domina. Yesterday's attack convinced me you are not safe, and I do not want to see you subjected to further danger. But know this—if, as I suspect, Hector had a hand in yesterday's attack, he will not stop until you are dissuaded."

"Would you have me break my vow? I promised Sabina freedom, and I am determined to see that she gets it."

"I would have you survive. I would have you *live*."

I was about to wave away his concern, but the memory of yesterday's ambush had quickened my pulse and dampened my palms . . .

Ariston had a point. I was a widow traveling with servants, and if a thief murdered me in the woods, little fuss would be made over my death. I was not famous or of noble blood, and though I made a comfortable living, no wealthy father or husband or brother would seek justice for my death or take up Sabina's cause. Though I cared little about justice for *my* life, I cared passionately about justice for Sabina.

I swallowed and met Ariston's gaze. "I will heed your

warnings, but what else can I do? I must pray for the strength to stay on this course."

"There is something you can do." Ariston lifted his head. "You can marry me."

I blinked, certain I had misheard, then I laughed. "I am sorry, but I thought you said—"

"Marry me, Domina." He leaned toward me, his eyes and voice brimming with intensity. "It can be a marriage in name only if you wish, but allow me to be your husband. A man traveling with his wife will be accorded greater respect than a woman alone. If we were married, we would not be given a room on the ground floor"—he gestured to the open window with its flimsy blind—"but an inner chamber with greater security. Make me your husband and I will continue to serve you as I do now. But I will be able to remain by your side where I can better protect you."

My laughter died in my throat. Take Ariston as my husband? Impossible. While I had given him his freedom, he had been a *slave* . . .

"I can see my proposal has astounded you," he said, looking away, "and anyone would understand why. You are a woman of quality and education; I came from poverty and chains. You are also a woman of strength and courage, and I value your life above my own. As your husband, I would live to serve you."

I pressed my hand to my forehead as questions ricocheted through my brain. Was he *serious*? Though my first thought had to do with the difference in our social status, perhaps I could set that aside. But did he not understand that I had already failed at being a wife and mother? I had lost both my daughter and my husband. After much suffering, I had become resigned to live like Paulos, unattached and free to serve the Lord.

I drew a deep breath. "Ariston—"

"I know I am not worthy of you," he interrupted, "but I urge you to consider my offer nonetheless."

I turned away, unable to look him in the eye. Did he think my hesitation sprang solely from the differences in our social status? Aside from a certain respect in the small Christian community, in Philippi I was still an outsider. Neither did my hesitation come from a selfish desire to hoard my wealth. Nearly everything I earned was either invested into my business or given to support Paulos and his mission. So why did the idea of marrying Ariston strike me as profoundly ridiculous?

"I do not consider you unworthy," I began, struggling to find words. "But I must know why you would suggest such a thing. Apart from wanting to keep me safe, is there another reason? A marriage would last far longer than this one journey. You may not wish to be joined to me once we return to Philippi."

His gentle gaze rose to meet mine. "If I have learned anything from the teachings of Yeshua, it is this: the greatest love offers the greatest service. That is what I offer you, Domina. I will serve you whether or not you marry me, but I may be able to serve you better as a husband than as a steward. I will do so willingly for the rest of my life."

His eyes shone with sincerity, and in that moment I came close to accepting his extraordinary proposition. But I could not agree without prayer, so I thanked him for his kind consideration and told him I would give him an answer at the close of Shabbat.

"In that case," he said, his voice grave, "I should give you time to think without distraction."

An unexpected dart of apprehension shot through me. "Are you leaving again? Where will you go?"

"It is not proper for an unmarried freedman to stay with you in a chamber as small as this one," he said, standing. "But I will remain close at hand."

Without another word, he turned and left.

❖

After Ariston had gone, I went to bed, though my thoughts were too frenzied for rest. Marry my steward, a former slave? I knew my attitude was wrong, for all believers stood on level ground before HaShem, but I could not easily shake off the conventions I had been taught since childhood. How could a freeborn woman marry a noncitizen? More important, how could I marry a man with whom I had little in common?

Hoping to find something that might disqualify him from this proposed union, I sorted through memories of Ariston, beginning with the day I first spotted him in the slave market. Even then, he had stood apart from the sullen captives who clearly resented their fate. Though he wore a dirty tunic like the others, he had taken care to wash and shave, revealing the resolute strength in his jawline and chin. His deep brown eyes gleamed with intelligence, and he stood proud and erect. Broad-shouldered and tall, he had the look of an Olympian.

When he ascended the slave block, I could not help but think of Joseph, son of Jacob, who had himself been a slave before HaShem lifted him to a place of authority in Egypt. Did I signal the auctioneer because I imagined him as a nobleman in disguise? Surely not, and yet I could not deny the two men had much in common. Joseph was handsome, too, righteous and a believer in HaShem.

I bid more than I had planned, but at the conclusion of the auction, Ariston belonged to me. My new slave was surprised and grateful when I showed him to the chamber that would become his.

"A room?" His brows shot up. "For me?"

"I know the custom is for slaves to sleep anywhere they can lie down," I answered, "but my household keeps no slaves; my servants are all free. So yes, you will have a room, as do Phebe and Dione."

He stared at me, apparently bereft of words. "I am to be—"

"Free," I whispered, smiling at the astonishment in his eyes. "I will draw up your manumission papers on the morrow, and we will visit the magistrate. You will be wearing the cap of a freedman before sunset."

He fell to the floor, prostrating himself before me. In that humble position, I glimpsed scars on his limbs and suspected that the flesh on his back looked even worse. His previous owner must have been a hard taskmaster, which made his spirit and determination even more remarkable. Yet I did not ask for details, and when I gave him a long tunic, the garment of a freedman, I backed away, afraid he would kiss my feet in gratitude.

Though from that day he was free to leave my household, Ariston remained, filling whatever role he thought appropriate. He was my butler when guests arrived, my escort when I needed to go into the city, my gardener when plants crowded my atrium, and my guard when strangers knocked at my door. Yesterday he had been my defender, willingly surrendering to renegades because he knew he could not defeat two armed men without putting me and the other women in danger.

He did not love me, I was certain of that—at least not in the way of those who wrote romantic poetry about eros and pathos and intertwined limbs. I thought he respected me, though, and respect was a rare thing between men and women. He had never given me a reason to doubt his loyalty, and if he wanted the marriage to be an arrangement of convenience, it would be.

So why did I hesitate? My dyers, none of whom were highborn or wealthy, would be astounded to hear I had married a former slave. But I had no family in Macedonia, so no one would protest the union. In my newfound faith, I found only one consideration that might negate the idea of marriage: Paulos's encouragement to remain unattached for the sake of the Gospel. A year ago, I assumed his words applied to me, but had that belief come from the Lord or my broken heart?

Paulos would not care about Ariston's past. Had he not said that in Christ, we believers were neither Jew nor Greek, slave nor free, male nor female? We were all one in Messiah Yeshua.

The man who wanted to marry me was no longer a slave. His protective feelings for me had undoubtedly been born of gratitude, but was gratitude enough to sustain a lifelong union?

I rolled over, exhausted from my unsettling thoughts. When I was ten or eleven—Sabina's age—some of my friends were married to men they barely knew. Though I pretended to celebrate with my parents and the other wedding guests, inwardly I was terrified at what lay ahead for my friends.

I was equally terrified on the day I married Lysander Cassius. The physical act of marriage, while not exactly what I expected, was not frightening. What truly alarmed me was the realization that I would forever be under my husband's authority. He could kill me if I displeased him, he could deny me food, dignity, and control over my own life. The law recognized the complete authority of a husband and father, and I would remain under his firm control until death.

Was I reluctant to accept Ariston's proposal for that reason? I had been independent for years. I ran my own business; I had women working for me. If we married, everything I owned and did, every word I spoke, would be under Ariston's control.

The very idea sent a spasm of panic through my body.

But, another voice persisted, you grew up under the authority of your father, who had the same degree of control. Yet you did not fear him, and he was never cruel or spiteful toward you. Rather, you flourished under his care because . . .

Papa loved me.

My father had given me remarkable freedom, allowing me to be educated, to grow. He even postponed my marriage until I had reached my seventeenth year. His position did not chafe, nor was it cruel because he chose to love, not dominate.

But Ariston—did he, *could* he, ever love me? Or would his gratitude fade into indifference and his respect shift to disdain? This time I had no loving father to arrange a marriage; I would have to make this decision alone and then live with the consequences.

Perhaps Ariston had already provided the answer. A marriage in name only would not change our current relationship, but it would give me the security of a husband's protection. I knew Ariston and believed him a good man. We did not have to change.

For now, Ariston and I shared a common goal: we were both set on finding and freeing Sabina. Once we accomplished our mission, the Lord would continue to direct our united path . . . if this marriage was indeed His will.

I closed my eyes, asking HaShem to make my way clear. "I know I asked you not to leave me lonely, Abba. I asked you to send me someone to love, and you sent Sabina. But then you took her away, and I do not understand why you would now send Ariston, whom I do not love more than I love any believing brother . . ."

A dark memory crept out of the shadows and took my thoughts hostage.

Lysander and I had enjoyed an auspicious beginning and held our wedding on a festival day. After a sacrifice to Jupiter amid a gathering of wealthy friends, we came together to honor the provisions of the wedding contract. I wore the traditional woven tunic belted with the knot of Hercules. My handmaid carefully arranged my hair and covered it with the traditional orange veil, dyed to match my shoes. It was the perfect Roman wedding.

Lysander appeared completely calm when he took my hand, but he was twenty years my senior and ready to establish a family. My voice trembled when I recited my vows, but no one blamed me for being nervous. Years later, however, they blamed me for a marriage that ended in tears, shame, and death.

If I married Ariston, our wedding would be neither Roman nor perfect. But tomorrow night, and for many nights afterward, at least I would not be alone.

Was it right to marry for such a selfish reason?

Twenty-Three

When Hector finally caught a whiff of sea air, he knew they were nearing Thessalonica.

"We will sleep in the city tonight," he announced. "I look forward to a good meal and sleeping in a warm room. What a pleasure it will be to spend the night without gnats in my eyes."

The girl did not respond, though the news should have pleased her. He kicked the mare into a canter.

The ancient settlement of Thessalonica, the largest city Hector had ever seen, had been built on a slope that began at the Horiates Mountains and ended at the sea. A shimmering marble temple crowned its peak, while the base boasted of a bustling port, where merchant ships crowded the docks and white sails dotted the horizon.

After entering the city, Hector made a few inquiries and then headed toward the barracks for auxiliaries from the Legio IV Macedonia, the legion responsible for keeping order in the province. If they were fortunate enough to have an empty bed, he would rest beneath their roof. He stabled the mare and told the girl to follow, then carried his bedroll to the tribune's office and saluted the man in charge. After reciting his name and former rank, he explained his situation. Moments later, a centurion escorted him and the girl to the barracks.

Hector stepped into the building and inhaled the familiar odor of sweat and urine. "Smells like home," he said, grinning.

"Latrine ditches are outside," the centurion said, pointing to a rear door. "The empty bunk is here. You are in luck—last week we lost a man in a drunken brawl, so you are welcome to his bed."

After stashing his sword and bedroll beneath the bunk, Hector joined a group of men around a fire in the courtyard. They were sharing a roasted goat, so Hector joined them, ordering the girl to sit behind him. As he ate, he occasionally tossed pieces of fat and gristle over his shoulder. When a supply officer sent a loaf of bread around the circle, Hector broke off a piece and gave the crust to his slave.

Once he had finished eating, he went to the barracks, stretched out on the bunk and covered himself with his blanket. The slave would sleep on the floor. He soon drifted into a doze, but then woke abruptly when he felt a hand on his shoulder. "Soldier?"

Hector's eyes flew open. "Who speaks?"

"Me." The man, dressed only in his loincloth, gestured to the floor. Hector peered over the edge of his mattress and saw the girl's foot protruding from beneath the bed.

The soldier pointed again. "Who have you brought to us, brother?"

"My slave." Hector let his head fall back to the mattress. "She will not trouble you."

"And you served with the cavalry?"

"Aye." Annoyed, Hector lifted his head again. "What of it?"

"So you will not mind if I take her to warm my bed for a while."

Hector sat up so quickly, he nearly hit his head on the bunk above. He did not want this man using the girl, but how could he deny a fellow soldier? The girl was a mere possession, and if he did not share, the others would consider him disloyal. He was a guest in this barracks, and a guest should show proper gratitude.

But why should he share what he had worked twenty years to acquire?

The answer came to him as he squinted at the soldier. "You want her?" He forced a laugh. "I would not have her in *my* bed."

The man cocked a brow. "Why not?"

Hector sat up and lowered his voice. "Until a few months ago, she possessed a spirit of divination. Yesterday I asked Jupiter to give her even greater powers, and I am sure he has." He shrugged. "What if you were enjoying her and she decided to curse you? She could command the gods of the underworld to shrivel your manhood."

The man took a quick step back. "By Jupiter's toes, surely you jest."

"A wise man would ignore her," Hector said, settling back on his bunk. "That is what I try to do."

The soldier cast a worried glance at the bed, then walked away, mumbling an incantation against evil.

Sighing, Hector pulled his blanket to his chin, ready for sleep.

❖

The sound of snoring had wrapped around Hector like a blanket, and when he opened his eyes, for a moment he thought himself back in Britannia with the men of his turma. The hand dangling off the upper bed surely belonged to Lucius, and the snuffling from the far side of the room came from Decimus, who always sneezed throughout the months of spring.

Then he heard movement beneath his bed. When he looked beneath the bed frame, he saw the sleeping girl.

He dropped back to his mattress, recalling the events that had brought him to Thessalonica. Before meeting the man at the Amphipolis baths, he had been blindly searching, yet now he had direction. Today he would leave the provincial capital and travel as swiftly as possible, avoiding anything that might delay his arrival in Lychnidos. He would remain open to learning about other necromancers, but why waste time searching when he knew of a woman who could solve his problem in a moment?

As the gray light of dawn crept through the high windows, he turned and studied the slave beneath his bed. Why had this girl fascinated the Lydian woman, and why was the woman so determined to have this child? He had cursed the woman and set a trap on the road to Amphipolis, but he could not be certain his hireling had completed the work to his satisfaction. Thus he would set another trap in Thessalonica in case the woman made it this far. Something simple, something that did not involve bloodshed. Something that could not fail.

He went outside and searched for the latrine. His injured leg had stiffened during the night, causing him to stumble over a boulder near the ditch. He sat on the rock, wincing, until the pain subsided. Though the warm bath in Amphipolis had helped with the ache, he would not take time to visit the baths today. Better to press forward and take care of business.

When he returned to the barracks, the room had emptied. The other men had departed, as had his slave. Where had the onion-eyed minnow gone this time?

He would find her, but first he wanted to handle the Lydian woman. He rolled up his blanket, strapped on his sword, and limped out to the courtyard, where the legionaries stood in formation as the centurion assigned their daily duties. Hector glanced around the perimeter of the courtyard but did not see the girl.

He hefted his bedroll onto his shoulder, left the fortress and walked to the city gate, where several of the elders sat in the shade of a sprawling olive tree. A few merchants had set up booths outside the gates, and a group of men lounged nearby, probably hoping to procure work for the day.

He had a job available.

He spotted a young man, clean-shaven with a spark in his eye and a smirk on his lips. He wore the simple tunic of a plebeian and appeared to be the sort who would not mind earning a few coins for a small task.

Hector approached the man, whispered the nature of his task, and received a nod in return. Then he whispered further instructions and pressed two drachmas into the youth's palm. "If you fail," he said, gripping the hilt of his sword, "I will find you as easily as I found you today, and you will not see another sunrise."

The young man's face twisted as he nodded.

Hector, satisfied that the task would be completed, lumbered toward the stable, favoring his injured leg as he searched for the girl behind stones, between buildings, and near fountains.

Finally, he spotted his slave, sitting on the edge of a fountain. A group of women was washing clothes in the bubbling waters. They sang a rhythmic tune as they pounded their garments, though he did not recognize the song. Someone had set words to an unfamiliar melody. Then he caught a phrase he had heard before. Paulos had uttered the same name when he looked at Sabina and told the spirit to come out of her . . . in the name of *Messiah Yeshua*.

Sabina sat with her head tilted to one side, her eyes wide and burning with what appeared to be curiosity. One of the women seemed to be singing especially to her as if a bond existed between them. What would drive a grown woman to befriend a slave?

"Slave!" he shouted. The girl turned at the sound of his voice, and the singers' smiles faded as they fell silent. He limped over and grasped the girl's arm. Glaring at the women, he dragged his slave away.

"That name robbed us of your gift," he muttered, gripping her firmly as he walked toward the stable. "I will not let it destroy your chance to become whole again."

He looked at her, hoping for any sign of spirit in the child, but she kept her head down. When he forcibly lifted her face, he saw only the inscrutable face of a slave who had learned to disguise all genuine feeling.

Hector left the girl outside the stable and went in search of the mare, moving as quickly as he dared in case the girl decided to run back to the women at the fountain. But she was still waiting when he returned, so he hoisted her onto the mare's back, then used a stool to mount the beast.

He would waste no more time searching for a necromancer. He would press westward, find the enchantress of Lychnidos, and pay her to restore the girl's power. If for some reason the witch could not help, he would sell the child straightaway.

Lychnidos was also famous for its bustling slave market.

Twenty-Four

Phebe's hands trembled as she sewed the curls above my forehead into place. "Well?" she asked, bending to peer at me. "Have you made a decision?"

Because I had not yet made my choice, I feigned ignorance. "About what?"

She snorted. "I did not sleep much last night, either. I lay awake long after Ariston left, wondering what you would do."

"So you were only pretending to sleep, and you heard everything."

"I believe I did."

I sighed. "Which would be more foolish—marrying him or not marrying him?"

"He is a good man," Phebe said, her tone clipped. "Tall, pleasant, and righteous. The mere sight of Ariston would send set most thieves to flight."

"But he is my *steward*," I pointed out. "That is like a rabbit marrying a lion."

Phebe's mouth dipped into a frown. "You are too hard on yourself, Domina. Unless you see him as the lion."

I shook my head. "A poor example. I was trying to stress the differences between us." I winced as she stabbed my scalp with the wooden needle. "That hurt!"

"Sorry." Phebe set the needle and thread aside and began to braid the remaining section of my hair.

She was about as sorry as the recipient of an inheritance. I shifted my gaze to the looking brass to ensure she would not accidentally stab me again. "In truth," I confessed, "I know Ariston is capable and honorable. I am simply . . ." I shrugged. "I grew up in a certain world, and in that world, mistresses do not marry their servants."

Phebe tied off a braid. "Did Paulos not say the world is changing? And we are no longer slaves or free, but one in Yeshua?" She coiled the thick plait around my head, then began to stitch the braid in place. "You will have to make a decision. Ariston will soon arrive, and he will want an answer."

"I cannot answer until I know what to do."

"And how will you know?"

I blew out a breath. "Perhaps the Lord will tell me."

"If you do not know by now—"

"Please." I lifted my hand. "I need a few moments to listen."

Phebe pressed her lips together and continued stitching. I closed my eyes and focused on the decision at hand. What had other women done when they wanted to know if they should marry?

I considered the story of Ruth, which I learned while attending the synagogue. Ruth, a Gentile, had been instructed by her Jewish mother-in-law to visit a threshing floor and lie at the feet of the family's closest kinsman, a man called

Boaz. Ruth obeyed, creeping into place after the man had fallen asleep.

When Boaz woke in the night and found her lying beneath his blanket, he grasped her intention almost immediately. By sliding under his blanket, Ruth had symbolically placed herself under his protection. When he asked who she was, she replied, "I am Ruth, your handmaid. Spread the corner of your garment over your handmaid, for you are a *goel*." A kinsman.

Touched and impressed by her virtue and discretion, Boaz had promised to marry Ruth and sent her away with enough food for her household.

Ariston was not my kinsman, but I would be content to be under his protection. I would be content to love him as a brother in Christ. If we were married, he would honor me as Paulos instructed, serving me as Yeshua served His people. As I would serve him.

If our marriage could make it easier for us to find and rescue Sabina, was that not enough reason to become his wife?

"If you do not wish to marry Ariston," Phebe said, cutting into my thoughts, "perhaps I could. Then he could sleep in our room as *my* husband and keep both of us safe—"

"No," I said, surprised the word rose so easily to my lips. While I was not yet sure I should marry Ariston, I could not imagine anyone else doing so.

Phebe cut a dangling thread. "Finished. You look beautiful, Domina. Lovely enough for a wedding, if that is what you want."

She stepped back and clasped her hands, waiting for my response. But though she waited respectfully, I could not miss the yearning in her eyes. She did not want me to marry

Ariston because she loved him. Yet I was certain he did not love her or he would never have suggested marriage to me.

I stood and studied my reflection in the looking brass, tilting it to see from my head to my feet. My linen stola fell in long pleats to the floor, my palla of pale blue provided contrast to my dark hair, and my sandals revealed glimpses of shapely feet. I was not dressed like a bride, but I had not been thinking about marriage when we packed.

I lowered the looking brass and turned to Phebe. "Shall we go break our fast?"

As Phebe scurried to toss the last of our belongings into the trunk, I opened the chamber door. "Do not forget your knife," I called, glancing over my shoulder. "I saw it on the—"

I stepped through the doorway and lost my balance. My knees hit the floor first, rapidly followed by my forearms and forehead. Something—someone—lay beneath my legs.

"Domina!" Ariston sat up, his blanket falling from his shoulders. "Are you hurt?"

I rolled over, rubbing my elbows as I gaped at him in astonishment. "You slept *here*?"

He shrugged. "It seemed the best place."

And then, while I stammered in amazement, he placed his blanket over my bent knees, preserving my modesty. Just as Boaz had done for Ruth.

I had stumbled over my answer.

❖

As the first two stars of evening appeared in the night sky, signaling the end of Shabbat, Ariston and I went to the common room, where several travelers and local citizens were enjoying the evening meal.

206

Ariston seated me at a table and bent to scrutinize my face. "Are you certain you want to do this? You have a bump on your forehead, so you may not be thinking clearly."

"The bump is nothing. And I am certain."

"But if you truly do not wish to marry—"

"I am not delirious, Ariston, and I have had time to think. You are right. Traveling together will be safer and more circumspect if we are married."

"Is that the only reason you agreed?"

The eager expression in his eyes made the room begin to spin, so I looked away. "Of course not. You have good character, you have always seemed sincere in your devotion and gratitude, and you love the Lord."

"I only wish to serve you."

"So you have said." I clasped my hands together. "And now once again I will serve a husband. It may not be easy because I have been independent for some time. I have grown accustomed to making my own decisions. It will not be easy to give up my freedom."

A smile tugged at the corner of his lips. "Have you not already done that? Do you not call yourself a slave to Yeshua?"

I tilted my head, recognizing his point. I had surrendered my rights to Yeshua and yet every day I struggled to follow His will and not my own . . . "You are correct, of course. I surrender my will to Yeshua daily, but I still find it all too easy to rely on my own judgment."

"As do I, Domina. But since we are both learning what it means to be a slave to the Lord, perhaps we could do it together?" His eyes searched my face. "In any case, I would never want to change you."

"But being a wife is the opposite of being your *Domina*."

I lowered my gaze as my face heated. "A wife should serve her husband in all things, so I will do my best to fulfill that role . . . even if our marriage is in name only."

A small, strangled sound came from Ariston's throat, and I dared not look at him.

Fortunately, at that moment Phebe strode over. "I have found the witnesses, and they are ready."

I looked at Ariston. "If you are still willing, let us commence."

He held up a hand. "Wait for a moment."

I watched, bewildered, as he walked out of the common room. Had he changed his mind? Had he gone to change his tunic?

He returned a moment later with an old woman clinging to his arm. She wore the simple tunic of a slave, and when I saw the tenderness with which Ariston treated her, I knew who she was: Demetria, the slave who raised him.

I stood, and when Ariston introduced her, I caught her hands and held them. "May the one true God bless you," I said, hoping she could feel the sincerity in my words.

She pulled her hand from mine, then reached up to touch my face. "Beautiful," she said, looking at Ariston. "You have found a beautiful bride."

"You should sit." Ariston found a seat for Demetria and let her cling to his arm as she eased herself onto the bench. Once she was settled, he extended his hand to me, and together we walked to a corner where the three witnesses waited, one of them still nibbling on a roasted pigeon.

I drew a slow breath to still the stuttering of my heart. This felt a thousand times more awkward than my first wedding, but I could not improve the situation. I did not know if any of the witnesses were believers, but perhaps it did not matter. Our union did not depend on these men; it would be validated by our vows and our Lord Yeshua.

Something within my chest trembled when Ariston wrapped my hands in his.

"Where's the priest?" one of the witnesses shouted, slurring his words. "The sa-sacrifice?"

"There is no sacrifice," Ariston said, his brow lowering. "There will be no bloodshed tonight."

"No meat for the feast?" the man groused. "No invoking of the gods?"

"You are eating already," Ariston answered. "And as to the gods, only One matters."

He released my hands and raised his arms. "Father God," he prayed, his words ringing with an authority I had never heard in his voice, "Creator of the universe, witness this marriage today. Bless it and enable us to do your will as we two become one. I ask this in the name of Messiah Yeshua, our Lord."

The drunken witness stared, dumbfounded, as Ariston claimed my hands again. "Now," he said, his voice gentling as his lips curved into a smile, "let us proceed."

Ripples of shock spread from my chest, causing my fingers to tingle. I had never heard Ariston pray aloud. I knew he was a true follower of the Way—after Paulos visited, everyone in my household believed in Yeshua—but I did not know he had developed the confidence to pray in a roomful of idol worshipers.

I squeezed his hands. "*Ubi tu es Gaius, ego Gaia,*" I recited. *Where you are Gaius, I am Gaia.* "As Messiah is head of His community, so you shall be my head."

A faint line appeared between Ariston's brows as he felt his way through our improvisation.

"*Ubi tu es Gaia, ego Gaius,*" he said. "I will love you as Messiah loved His community. I will give myself for you and love you as I love myself . . . or better."

"I will respect you," I promised. "I will pray for you and the work of your hands. I will be your wife, your sister, and your friend."

"I will be everything you need," he answered. "And if I am not, you have only to ask, and I will do my best to serve you as Yeshua serves the ecclesia."

Nothing else needed to be said.

Smiling through tears—I could not tell if they were tears of joy or sorrow—Phebe bound our right hands with a length of silk ribbon. Then, as my heart stuttered, Ariston gently pressed his lips to mine.

"*Feliciter!* Congratulations!" the diners shouted, and Ariston leaned toward me. "Are you ready to depart?"

Unable to speak, I nodded.

"Let me see Demetria home and fetch the wagon, then I will return for you."

A moment later he was gone, leaving me with Phebe and a roomful of noisy travelers.

The witnesses went back to their tables; Phebe took my arm and led me to the vestibule where our trunk waited.

We would not enjoy a bridal bed, I would not be carried over a threshold, and we would receive no flowers or wedding gifts. I had enjoyed those things during my first marriage, and that union had been anything but blessed.

This one, however . . . could I hope for more?

Though my friends in Philippi would undoubtedly think

it bizarre for me to marry my servant, they had not looked into Ariston's eyes and glimpsed his steadfast commitment to serve and protect me.

I had. And I believed in him.

❖

We did not intend to travel far after our wedding, but Ariston thought it a good idea to put a few miles between us and Amphipolis. "We cannot be sure that the men who attacked us will not stop here and hear rumors about us," he said, lifting our trunk into the carpentum. "So we will ride until we find a safe place to pull off the road. We will rest and set out again at daybreak."

"Do you think—?"

"What?"

"Never mind." If I were still in charge, I would never have agreed to sleep along the highway, but I would not begin our marriage by breaking the vows I had just uttered.

The Via Egnatia was nearly deserted when we set out. The rising moon cast odd shadows across the silvered stones, and the well-rested mule clipped along at a steady pace. Phebe snored contentedly in the back, and Ariston and I sat behind the mule without speaking.

I could see nothing in the woods to our right or left, only a silvered sliver of sky. The moon traveled halfway across the heavens before he dared to look at me, then he snatched a quick breath. "You look tired, Dom . . ." He bit his lip. "We should probably stop to rest."

By the light of the moon, Ariston spotted a clearing not far from the road, so he guided the mule onto the grass, then unharnessed the beast and led it to a stream. Phebe was still sleeping when he returned, but I thought I should remain awake for my husband.

"Is the mule settled?" I asked, looking up as he crawled onto the wagon bed.

Ariston grunted as he sat near the front. "Why are you not asleep?"

I lowered my head, hoping the evening shadows would conceal my flush. "I thought I should check on you—to see that you are not overtired."

"I am fine."

"And I thought I should say good night." I patted an empty space on the wagon bed. "I have put down blankets so we can rest. There is another blanket to ward off the chill."

His gaze caught and held mine, but I could not read his expression in the darkness. I had no idea what he was thinking—indeed, I scarcely knew my own thoughts. But as I reclined on the pad of blankets, I did not know whether or not I wanted him to sleep beside me.

We had said our marriage would be one of form only, so I did not expect him to draw me into his arms. Perhaps he felt as awkward as I did; perhaps he still felt nothing but gratitude toward me. In time, he might grow fond, but surely I would be foolish to think he might love me . . .

Yet did Yeshua not say that two, once married, should become one flesh? Ariston might not want to consummate our marriage with Phebe sleeping inches away, but I could not deny that I trembled to think of his lips trailing over my skin. No man had touched me in over two years, and I had never expected to marry again. Yet here I was, newly wed to a good man, an *attractive* man, and one who already knew me better than my late husband had.

The boards creaked as Ariston shifted his position, yet he did not lie down. I thought he might be too embarrassed, so after a few minutes I lifted my head and saw him sitting at the front of the wagon, a moonlit silhouette with his injured leg extended, the other bent, and his head bowed as if he were dozing . . . or in prayer.

"You may sleep here," I called, patting the empty space. "I do not expect you to keep watch throughout the night. You will need your strength for the morrow."

He hesitated before finally stretching out beside me, his face only inches from mine. But though I felt the heat of his presence, I could not tell if his eyes were open or closed. I had no idea what he was thinking or if he was thinking at all.

After an awkward period of uncertainty, I closed my eyes and rolled over, turning my back to him. And though I only pretended to doze for at least an hour, I never heard his breathing relax to the slow and steady rhythm of a sleeper.

He might have remained awake all night, torn, as I was, between the desires of marriage and the façade we had carefully constructed.

Twenty-Five

To reach the enchantress, Hector realized, he would have to travel for several days, traversing Pella, Edessa, Florina, and Heraclea Lyncestis. In those cities he planned to make inquiries about a necromancer or priest who might be able to meet his needs, but unless he found one, he would press on and meet the enchantress of Lychnidos.

The journey might have been more enjoyable with a slave who could provide interesting or pleasant conversation, but the girl remained mostly silent and aloof as she rode behind him. She answered when he asked a direct question—"Are you hungry?" might elicit a nod— but she would not participate in a discussion. At first, her silence bothered him, then he remembered that no one purchased slaves for their fluency in speaking. Lucius had always been his conversational partner, and now the silence unnerved him.

Hector found himself regretting the fatal blow that had ended his comrade's life. He knew his own strength, and he should have known Lucius's skull could not withstand such a blow. He had reacted in anger because Lucius had sold the girl without his consent, but that offense was nothing compared to the resentment that had been simmering ever since Lucius announced his intention to leave. Lucius wanted a life apart from Hector; he had bought a house and was preparing to start a family . . . without his lifelong friend.

Hector swallowed the despair and released bitter laughter. How rich, the irony of it all! He had been upset because Lucius was leaving, and with one impulsive blow, he had forever rid himself of his friend.

That evening Hector camped in a wooded area only a stone's throw from the Via Egnatia. Wrapped in a thin blanket he had procured along the way, the girl fell asleep, her head resting on a moss-covered stone. Hector crouched beside her and studied her face, enigmatic even in repose.

What did she think of him? Perhaps she thought nothing; slaves were not supposed to think for themselves, but only for their masters. Perhaps she was simple-minded and rarely thought at all. Or perhaps the Jewish rabbi had not only excised the girl's gift of foretelling the future, but also her ability to utter lively speech.

He went back to his fire, intending to roast some grain. The girl seemed to like it.

For twenty years, he had sat beside fires like this one, warmed by the company of fellow soldiers. Men at arms shared a camaraderie that revolved around following orders, knowing one's place in the organization, and doing the job well. Bold, brash conversations peppered the crackle and roar of army campfires, their rhythm salted by profane oaths and seasoned with talk of women who had provided pleasure at the last encampment. The life was simple, one in which even an uneducated man could rise to prominence if he performed well and paid his gambling debts. The thirty-two men of Hector's turma knew they would never be officers or patricians, but it was a good livelihood for a man with no better prospects.

Hector broke a twig and tossed it onto the fire, then watched sparks ascend into the comforting darkness. Evenings like this reminded him of the night he and Lucius decided to join the army. Recognizing that Rome would one day rule the world, they had spent the next several weeks learning to properly wield a sword, a *lancea*, and the heavy Roman shield. They practiced the defensive formations that would keep their comrades safe and learned to flank an army on horseback, picking off enemy warriors who were foolish enough to break formation and rush willy-nilly into battle.

During peacetime, three times a month, the tribune ordered the cavalry and infantry to march out. The infantry, carrying their weapons and supplies, were commanded to march half a day's walk in one direction, then turn and march back to camp. The cavalry, fully armed and armored, covered the same distance but were required to practice pursuit and withdrawal not only on level ground but also in mountainous and difficult country. "No terrain," their commander reminded them, "should ever catch us unprepared."

After hearing how his homeland fell to Rome's Julius Caesar, Hector realized that the invaders had reinvented warfare. And though his ancestors might never understand his rationale, he had been pleased and proud to be part of the world's most formidable fighting force.

His first battle, which took place six months after his training ended, left him dry-mouthed with terror. He was careful not to show anxiety in front of his comrades, but one look at Lucius revealed that his friend was not eager to meet death, either.

Nevertheless, they did their duty, followed orders, and survived.

"Look on the ensign," their centurion had called, addressing the men before they charged into battle. He pointed to the banner emblazoned with the eagle of Rome. "When we march, we carry Rome's authority with us. When we fight, we fight with the authority of Rome. When we win, we further Rome's reach and power. And when we die, we die knowing the power and might of Rome will never cease."

Overcome by the memory, Hector blinked wetness from his eyes and looked away from the fire. He was thinking too much; he should sleep. He spread his cloak on the ground, pulled a bearskin over him, and stared at the tree canopy, his dagger only inches from his right hand. He had only to close his eyes . . .

A sharp sound woke him from a shallow doze. He sat up and spotted the girl sitting by the banked fire, her hands in her lap and her eyes wide. She was staring at something. He turned to see what had caught her attention. A snake slithered at the edge of the coals, moving toward the girl. She leaned forward and extended her arm as if she would grab the serpent. Did she not realize it would strike if threatened?

"Slave!" He threw his dagger and pinned the creature to the ground, its head only a handbreadth from the girl. As the reptile writhed and hissed, Hector drew his sword and lopped the head from its body, then kicked the head into the underbrush. The body, still squirming, would make a decent meal. He picked it up and held it high.

"Have you no sense?" he asked, glaring at her. "That was a deadly viper."

She did not answer but returned her gaze to the glowing embers.

He stared. The child was not deaf, so why didn't she react? "Do you *want* to die? Because I could grant your wish."

In answer, she went back to her resting place, lay down, and turned her back to him.

What should he do, beat her? He considered it but feared she would only grow more withdrawn. And she would doubtless bear scars when he presented her to the enchantress at Lychnidos. He shook his head and threw the snake onto the coals. He had planned to roast the body, but if the girl did not want to live, she would not want to eat.

❖

As he traveled from Odessa to Florina, Hector decided to provide his slave with a reason to live. After all, what would he benefit if he completed this arduous journey and then lost the girl to suicide? In at least one aspect, slaves were like soldiers—neither had power over their own lives, but both served because they wanted to survive. Well-trained and fortunate soldiers looked forward to retirement and citizenship; after years of service, hardworking slaves were frequently granted their freedom. But not every enslaved captive had the patience to endure. He had seen far too many kill themselves rather than be subjected to the slave market.

He did not want to lose the girl.

"I have been thinking about you," he said as they traveled through a quiet stretch of the Via Egnatia. "Last night, when you confronted the viper, I realized you may not know what awaits you if our venture is successful."

He glanced over his shoulder to see if the girl was listening. When her brow furrowed, he continued. "First, though you are young and unskilled, you will learn. Once this enchantress has restored your power, you will be famous and much sought after in Philippi. As an obedient slave, you will enable me to earn the wealth I need to build a racetrack, and once it is built, thousands will come to wager on the races."

He paused, hoping she had been impressed.

"At the racing complex, I will build a booth for you—not only a booth but also a comfortable apartment, perhaps large enough for you to have your own maid. You will no longer have to seek clients because they will come to you. You will have a quiet and prosperous life, if you do well and remain with me."

He waited and heard a faint whisper. "I would have done well with the woman who sells purple. She was going to love me like a daughter."

Hector scoffed. "Is that what she told you? And you believed her?"

When he turned, he saw that the girl's eyes had filled with tears. "She freed other slaves. She treats them like family."

He pulled on the reins, stopping the mare. "So she says. Did you speak to those slaves? Did you ask what would happen if they chose to leave her?"

The girl lowered her head. "What will happen to me . . . if this necromancer will not do what you want?"

He flinched, astonished by the question. "Why would she refuse? They say the enchantress has great power, so her abilities must come from the gods. Perhaps she will give you a more powerful spirit than you had before. Perhaps you will be able to summon fire from heaven or move stars with a flick of your fingers." Eager that she share his confidence, he tossed a smile over his shoulder. "Once my racetrack is finished, I may decide to give you a share of your earnings. You could buy anything you wanted—fine garments, pretty sandals, bright jewels. I could give you permission to marry, so you could have a husband and children. I would no longer require you to do menial labor because you would be far too valuable to waste on such tasks. When I travel, you could earn extra coin on the journey. You could visit places my other slaves will never even imagine. You could live a life beyond the reach of all other slaves."

He turned in the saddle, expecting a joyous response to his proposed largesse, but her face had emptied of all expression . . . and locked.

"Slave," he snapped. "Your master asked you a question."

A chill radiated from her thin frame. "You speak of things that might happen tomorrow," she said, her voice as cool as spring water. "But I may not live long enough to earn the coin you need. I could die of a fever on this journey. I could be killed by one of the men you send to lie with me."

He stiffened, offended that she doubted his ability to keep her safe. "I will protect you. Once you are restored, I will buy two slaves to guard you. Never again will I allow a man to touch you."

"You cannot stop a plague," she answered, "so how can you protect me? People like Paulos and Euodia are far stronger than you."

Against his will, anger rose in his chest. He had meant to encourage the girl, but how could he compete with a woman who offered freedom, the one thing he could not afford to give?

"If the Lydian woman is so strong, then why are you not with her at this moment?" He bit back an oath and gathered the reins. "I will never understand how you slaves can be so ungrateful. What a life you lead! No trials, no struggles, no need to worry about paying for shelter or food or clothing. Everything is given to you, and precious little is expected of you. You should be more grateful, and you should treat me with greater respect."

He kicked the mare, who set off at a slow walk.

"Be grateful or not, the choice is yours. But one thing is certain: I am your master, and I refuse to argue with a slave. If you want to keep your tongue, you will not speak for the rest of the day."

She did not.

Twenty-Six

Our vehicle was already rumbling across the road when I woke the next morning. Ariston sat in front, his posture relaxed as he scanned our surroundings and whistled tunelessly.

"If I had known," Phebe said, opening one eye to scowl at me, "that Ariston would begin to whistle once he married you, I would have protested the wedding."

Her good-natured jibe eased my guilt. I was now certain she had loved Ariston, but I was equally certain he did not love her. This marriage, odd as it was, had not interrupted a close and loving relationship.

"I did not know he whistled," I said, smoothing wrinkles from my stola.

"He didn't whistle in your presence because he cannot manage it properly." Phebe pushed herself into a sitting position. "But now that you must tolerate anything he does, our ears are destined to be tortured."

I rose to my knees and looked westward. We were among the first travelers on the highway, and I was surprised to see that mountains had arisen to our right. Soon we would arrive at Thessalonica.

I had Phebe refresh my hair, then pulled bread and cheese from a basket and shared it with Phebe and Ariston. I sat next to my husband, wearing what I hoped was a pleasant expression, and broke my fast while the landscape slid by.

Within an hour, we began to pass pedestrians taking their goods to the market. Some of them carried merchandise on their backs; others wheeled carts or guided a donkey. Paulos might have looked like some of these men as he walked to Thessalonica. I could almost see him—brown-haired, bearded, far shorter than Silas, and far faster. For every word Silas uttered, Paulos managed to say ten. For every step Silas took, Paulos took three, but Silas's steps were longer . . .

"We are following Paulos and his companions," I said, breaking the silence.

Ariston looked at me. "Aye?"

I nodded. "I remember the day they arrived in Philippi. They had made camp near the river and discovered me and my women the next morning. We had just begun the morning Kiddush for Shabbat when Paulos walked over and asked if he and his friends could join us. We welcomed them, but we had no idea who they were."

Ariston pulled the mule to the right to avoid a man who carried a heavy load on his shoulders. "Have you always worshiped with the Jews?"

I shook my head. "I tried to emulate what I had seen at the synagogue in Thyatira, though I did not understand what I was doing. But that morning I read the part of the Minchah for Shabbat that says, 'A redeemer shall come to Zion, and to those of Jacob who repent from willful sin.' Then Paulos asked if I knew who the Redeemer was."

Ariston smiled. "Did you know?"

I returned his smile. "I hesitated to answer. Paulos has piercing eyes, and I was a little afraid of him. I was not born a Jew, and even though I attended synagogue in Thyatira, I had not visited one in Philippi. I knew HaShem as the true God and Creator, master of the universe and ruler of the earth, but I knew nothing about the Jewish prophets."

"What did you tell him?"

I blew out a breath. "I gave him the answers others have given for years: the Redeemer was the Messiah. Paulos smiled and said, 'Yes! Do you know who the Messiah is?'" I laughed. "Of course I did not know. I looked at my ladies, hoping one of them might know the answer, but they were more confused than I. In Thyatira, the men at the synagogue had constantly debated all things concerning the Messiah—from where He would be born to what His purpose would be. So I looked at Paulos and said, 'I do not know. Do you?'"

My eyes misted with the memory. "And then he humbly placed his hands over his heart and said, 'I have met Him. His name is Yeshua, the Son of the living God.'"

I fell silent as the words washed over me, prickling my skin. Paulos had gone on to tell us the story of Yeshua—how He was born in Bethlehem, just as the prophets had predicted, and was persecuted even as an infant. He told us of Yeshua's ministry in Galilee and how He healed the sick and gave sight to the blind. Paulos told us that Yeshua raised several people from the dead, and on the third day after His crucifixion by the Romans, Yeshua resurrected himself, appearing first to a woman—a ripple of wonder moved through our group at *that* news—and then to the students who had traveled with Him.

My thoughts shifted to Ariston, who had not been part of

my household when we first met the emissary to the Gentiles. "Paulos told us, 'Yeshua is the Messiah. Put your trust in Him and you will be saved—you and your household.' And that was the day I believed." I looked at Ariston, who listened intently. "What Paulos said answered all the arguments I had heard in the synagogue. The Messiah was everything the Scriptures said He would be, yet few of those men recognized the truth. But my ladies did. Ten of them believed that morning, including Syntyche. We have worked together ever since."

A tremor touched Ariston's lips. "I have always wondered," he said, "how you came to believe in Yeshua. I could not understand why a woman like you had Jews living in her home."

I laughed again. "Paulos was the one who suggested I needed a steward. When I said I would look for a man at the slave market, he told me to hurry because the Lord would show me the one He had chosen for me."

Ariston cut a glance from me to the road. "Is that how it happened? The Lord told you to buy me?"

"He did not tell me in words. But still, I knew." I shook my head. "At the time, I had no idea I was buying a husband."

Ariston threw back his head and released a peal of laughter. I smiled, uncertain how to interpret his mirth, and pressed on. "When you arrived, Paulos's time with us was nearly over. Still, I am glad you were able to meet him and that you also believed in Yeshua."

"Who also set me free," he whispered, his eyes shining. "So how did the ecclesia find its way to your home?"

"After that first morning, I told Paulos and Silas that if they judged me to be faithful to the Lord, they should stay at my house. By the time the sun set that Shabbat, Phebe and Dione had believed in Yeshua, as well." I turned to better see my husband. "Do you remember the day you met Yeshua?"

"How could I forget?"

"I have never doubted you, but this morning, when you prayed . . ."

He lifted a brow.

"I was amazed. You prayed like Paulos. Your faith did not seem, well, immature."

His mouth twisted. "And you were surprised?"

"I was, for you have not followed Yeshua nearly as long as others who do not seem as mature."

His mouth relaxed. "I have been studying the Greek Torah. The Jewish prophets wrote of Yeshua on many occasions."

"Yet when I attended the synagogue in Thyatira, they never spoke of Him. Of Messiah, yes, but not of Yeshua."

"Perhaps they were blind."

"What do you mean?"

"It is possible, Domina, to live with something and not see it."

"Such as?"

A hint of merriment shone in his eyes. "Consider it a riddle. When you discover the answer, let me know."

I blew out an irritated breath. I had not married him to be teased.

"And," Ariston continued, apparently oblivious to the shift in my mood, "since we are married, I believe I should refer to you by name. May I call you Euodia?"

The suggestion startled me. He was correct, of course, but never had my name been on his lips nor, before last night, had his lips been on mine. But he had kissed me, as was his right as my husband. He had the right to speak my name, as well.

"You may call me whatever you like," I answered, lifting my chin. "Though it may take me a while to grow accustomed to the change."

❖

The sun had traveled halfway down the western sky by the time we arrived at Thessalonica. The sheer size of the city left Phebe and me agape with astonishment.

"Welcome to the capital of Macedonia," Ariston murmured as we drove through the city gate. "Home to dozens of temples, hundreds of priests, and scores of politicians. The governor of Macedonia lives here, too." He cast me a curious look. "It was this governor who commissioned the purple cloak, yes? Have you met him?"

"I have not," I answered. "He sent Polydorus, his aide, with the deposit and details."

Ariston nodded. "You should be complimented that the man came all the way to Philippi to seek your work. Perhaps you should thank him while we are here or send a message to say the work is going well."

"*If* it is," I said. "I pray Syntyche is making progress, but I cannot know for certain."

"I will add my prayers to yours," he said. "Try not to worry. If the Lord sent you on this mission, He will take care of the work you left behind." Ariston guided the mule to the side of the road. "Let us find a suitable inn on the outskirts of the city. I would rather not venture into its depths."

I peered at a mountain of bleached stone structures. "Lest we be swallowed alive?"

"Exactly," Ariston replied. "I have never seen so many people in one place."

After finding accommodation for the mule, Ariston inquired about a nearby taberna. We were directed to an establishment not far from the stable. While Ariston spoke to the taberna's owner, I wandered over to the fire, where a woman was stirring an iron pot. The aroma of roasting meat and vegetables made my stomach growl.

Ariston joined me a moment later. "A private room with dinner," he said, his cheeks glowing unnaturally, "is available for five assarii."

I blinked in confusion, then realized the cause of his embarrassment. What husband had to come to his wife for coin? My first inclination was to give him the five assarii, but then I realized I would be failing in my promise to make him husband and lord. Reluctantly, I sat on a bench and began pulling stitches from the hem of my cloak.

"Do not remove all of them," he whispered, moving closer so that no one could see what I was doing. "We would be wise to keep several coins in reserve."

He took a handful of assarii and went back to the owner while I assured myself all was well. I would have to trust him with everything I owned, including the profit from my business.

If I did not—if I *could* not—I had made a terrible mistake.

❖

The taberna offered dinner in its common room, furnished not with dining couches but with long wooden tables and benches.

"Not a very comfortable arrangement," Phebe remarked.

"But a plentiful spread," Ariston countered, leading the way to a table. "And it smells delicious, so let us eat."

The room was about half filled, so I accepted Ariston's suggestion that we eat before going to our chamber. A trio of slaves trudged to-and-fro, bringing bowls of stew, platters of meat, and fruit trays from the kitchen. We sat and helped ourselves from dishes already on the table. I had to admit the food looked good; the fare was far from common and featured roasted boar, numerous urchins and snails—a pity they did not extract the dye before boiling them—as well as cold clams and oysters for dessert.

"Everything looks delicious," Ariston said, picking up a ball of cheese that had been rolled in sesame seeds. "But this cook could not be better than Dione."

"I wonder how she is doing without us." Phebe reached for a pomegranate. "She must be bored, cooking only for herself."

"She is probably having a good rest." I smiled, imagining our cook with her feet up. "Or maybe she is cooking for Syntyche and her family. Dione is not the sort to sit and do nothing."

"Speaking of Syntyche"—Ariston's eyes shifted from the feast to me—"how do you suppose she is doing with that cloak? Should she be buying more wool now?"

I nodded and picked up a roasted chicken leg. "She should. She will need more coin, of course, but I told her to sell some things from the house—"

"There is no need for that." Ariston leaned toward me. "You are my wife, so what is mine is yours. I have money in my chamber, and she is welcome to it."

I caught my breath. Though I had paid Ariston wages for

over a year, I had no idea how he spent his income. I assumed he spent it as he earned it; most men liked to gamble or have a meal in a tavern now and then. Or did he have coins stuffed in his mattress?

"You have coin?" I asked.

"I do. And I would freely give it to Syntyche, but how can I when we are miles apart?"

I turned to Phebe because I could not think coherently when I looked at Ariston. Her face lit with a brilliant smile. "We are in Thessalonica," she said, triumph in her voice, "and Polydorus is in the same city."

"So?"

"Polydorus works for the governor, which means he has access to the cursus publicus. Go to his office, explain your need, and write Syntyche a letter. Have Polydorus dispatch it via the imperial mail, and Syntyche should receive it within two days."

I squeezed Ariston's arm. "Do you think it would work?"

"An inspired suggestion, surely." He grinned. "You should meet with Polydorus again, if only to assure him the work is going well."

"But do you have enough coin to make a difference? I do not know how much you can offer—"

"Everything," he said. "Every assárion you have paid me lies in my chamber, and all of it is yours. What would I spend it on? You have supplied my food, my bed, my shelter—everything I need."

"Many slaves save their wages to buy their freedom," Phebe said. "But you have already freed us. Ariston is right, so you can have my wages, too. I have not saved every denarius, but every bit will help, no?"

Tears filled my eyes. "You are both too generous," I said, my voice breaking. "I know it will be enough to buy the wool we need. Syntyche will be so relieved to know she will not have to scratch and scrape to buy our supplies."

"Then only one thing remains," Ariston said, reaching for his cup. "Tomorrow we will go to the governor's palace and find Polydorus. The sooner we send the letter, the sooner Syntyche will be able to finish the work."

I pressed my fingertips to my lips, overcome with gratitude. I would have thanked him again, but I did not trust my voice.

❖

I had never beheld a city quite like Thessalonica. In what I assumed was the merchants' quarter, buildings crowded cheek by jowl together, a continual line of shops with open doorways and colorful canopies to welcome anyone with coin in hand. Beyond the merchants stood several *insulae* with the lower floors given over to more shops and the upper floors reserved for residents. The multistory buildings, literal islands edged by four streets, rose seven or eight stories over the shops, bathhouses, and theaters. Here the daily life of Thessalonians was on full display. On wooden balconies I saw women shaving their husbands, doing their laundry, and occasionally dumping their chamber pots. Smoke streamed from the few windows, along with the scents of coal and roasting meat.

As I had seen in every city, the lower walls were decorated with graffiti. *I admire you, wall, for not having collapsed at having to carry the tedious scribblings of so many writers* appeared in several variations, along with political advertisements: *I ask that you elect Lucius Popidius Ampliatus and Lucius Vedius Nummianus aediles.*

Chie, another author had written, *I hope your hemorrhoids rub together so much they hurt worse than ever before!* Beneath this quote, perhaps the aforementioned Chie responded: *Samius: go hang yourself!*

On the outside of a cheap inn, I read: *We have wet the bed. I admit, we were wrong, my host. If you ask 'why?' There was no chamber pot.*

I caught Phebe's eye and smiled. "At least our taberna is properly furnished."

She giggled. "No need to wet the bed."

After wandering for over an hour through the twisting streets of Thessalonica, we found ourselves outside the imposing palace of Publius Memmius Regulus, prefect of Macedonia and Achaia. I had never seen a more amazing building. Across from the imposing temple of Jupiter, the Roman building blazed with color: red columns upheld the peristyle, blue eagles on golden disks decorated the base of each column, and the decorative details on the huge doors had been overlaid with gold. Phebe, Ariston, and I were awestruck, then Ariston reminded us of our purpose—not to gawk at the power and wealth of Rome but to find one public servant.

We crossed a tiled threshold and entered a spacious hall, traversed by dozens of men in white tunics, some of them trimmed with purple—red-purple, I noted, and not the royal purple produced by my ladies. Ariston approached a man who stood behind a lectern and asked where we might find Polydorus. The fellow, who was busy scanning documents, pointed down a corridor. "That way," the man said. "You'll find him in the governor's office."

I gulped at this news. "Is the governor—?"

"Gone," the man said, already looking at the next document. "He's in Rome, so Polydorus works in his office."

Reassured that we would not have to ask a personal favor of the governor, we walked down the corridor until we came to a pair of imposing doors. Two guards stood outside, and when we inquired of Polydorus, one of them glared down his nose at us. "Who asks to see him?"

"Euodia of Philippi," Ariston answered, lifting his chin. "She has business with Polydorus of a most urgent matter."

The guard stepped inside and returned a moment later. "You may enter."

The man behind the desk blushed to see me and hurried forward, extending both hands. "Euodia! May the gods protect you, but please tell me you do not bring bad news. The prefect is counting on that cloak arriving here by autumn—"

"I do not bring bad news," I hastened to assure him. "In fact, the news is good. I have found the softest wool imaginable, shorn from protected yearlings, and very expensive. The work continues on schedule, but I was called away to deal with some personal business regarding a slave."

Polydorus frowned and crossed his arms. "An escaped slave? Shall I send guards to help you search?"

"Not exactly." I forced a smile. "I did not come here to enlist your help with that matter, but with another. I need to send a letter to Syntyche, my assistant in Philippi, so she can procure more of this special wool. We thought you might be able to help us send the message via the imperial post. The sooner she receives it, the more certain I am that the cloak will be completed on time."

"Ah." Polydorus nodded and moved behind the desk. "That would be no trouble at all. Who is your city magistrate? I will need to address it to him so he can deliver it."

"Albanus Marinus," said Ariston, stepping forward. "He will not have to read the letter . . . or will he?"

Polydorus, who had pulled out parchment and a reed pen, pulled a face. "Is he the type to break a sealed message?"

Ariston and I glanced at each other. "Possibly," Ariston said.

"Then I shall write a sealed letter and place it in a sealed pouch." Polydorus dipped his pen in ink. "Dictate, dear lady, whenever you are ready."

I gave him a nervous smile—I had never dictated a letter before. "Dearest Syntyche," I began, "Greetings and blessings to you. We are well and think of you often, especially as you work on the cloak for Memmius—"

"How about 'our marvelous and esteemed prefect Memmius'?" Polydorus arched a brow. "That would be better."

I nodded. ". . . as you work on the cloak for our marvelous and esteemed prefect Memmius. I am aware that you may be short of funds to buy the halo hair required, so please visit my villa and avail yourself of funds belonging to Ariston and Phebe. You will find Ariston's coin . . ." I glanced at him. "Where is it?"

"In an empty vase in the corner of my chamber," he said, shrugging. "Best place I could think of to hide it."

I sighed and looked at Polydorus. "Did you get that?"

". . . in a vase in the corner of his chamber," Polydorus said, his pen scratching the parchment. He looked up. "And?"

"And you may find Phebe's coin . . ." I looked at her. "Where?"

She blushed. "At the bottom of my trunk, wrapped in a square of linen."

I looked at Polydorus. "What she said."

He continued writing. "Anything else?"

"Yes. Please know you are in our prayers. I wish I were there with you, but searching for a lost soul is more important, no? Give my love to our co-workers and be assured that your mother was safely delivered to her home in Amphipolis. In the grace of our Lord, I am your servant. Euodia."

Polydorus's stylus flew over the parchment as his lips shaped the words I'd spoken. Finally, he held the parchment aloft, skimmed it, and smiled. "I can send this out with the next rider."

"Thank you!"

He held up a hand. "If you will answer one question."

I hesitated, not knowing what he had in mind. "Go ahead."

"Are you one of those who follow that Judean?"

I knew I should be cautious, but I could not help but smile. "If you mean Yeshua of Nazareth, yes, I am."

"Interesting." Polydorus threw a handful of sand on the wet ink, then rolled up the parchment and sealed it with wax and his ring. "You promise the cloak will be ready on time," he said, placing the letter into a leather pouch.

"I promise to do my best," I answered. "If I have to weave the thing myself, I will have it done by autumn."

"Then may the gods preserve you." He stood, formally ending our interview, and we left the palace.

"I am glad that is done," I said, hurrying to exit the building. "At least we will no longer have to worry about the work in Philippi."

"The hardest work still lies ahead of us," Ariston said,

his smile flattening. "And the time to renew our search for Hector begins now."

We inquired after Hector in several shops, at a mansio, and outside the temples of Jupiter and Caesar, but either no one had seen him or no one wanted to speak to us. Finally, we headed back to the taberna and dropped into empty places at the common dining table. Like a heavy blanket, a profound weariness settled over me. I stared at a tray of sausages, dormice, and fruit and felt absolutely no appetite.

Ariston, however, was able to eat, and so was Phebe. They ate quietly, clearly aware of my despairing mood, and then Ariston wiped his hands and leaned toward me. "I am going back out," he said. "There are places I can go where a virtuous woman should not. And it may be that Hector is known in those places. You and Phebe should get some rest. I will return before morning."

He left, and Phebe and I went upstairs to our chamber. Once there, I slipped out of my stola and crawled into the elaborate bed. A few minutes later, Phebe sighed and settled on the couch.

Overcome by exhaustion, I fell into a deep sleep. I was dreaming of my garden in Thyatira when unexpected sounds intruded into my dream—the creak of a leather hinge and the soft slap of a sandal against a tile floor.

I opened my eyes, as wide awake as if someone had punched me. I had not been dreaming of doors or floors, but of playing with my daughter. I lifted my head and saw nothing amiss in the shadowed room, so I closed my eyes and then heard the undeniable creak of my trunk.

Phebe and I were not alone. Had Ariston returned?

I looked toward the door. Thin rays of moonlight streamed from the edges of the window blind, allowing me to see the door, still closed and barred. The blind, however, hung askew, and a man's shadow played over Phebe's sleeping face.

I sat up and screamed. A shadowy figure leapt toward me, a sweaty hand clapped over my mouth, and something sharp edged my throat. I heard another scream—Phebe's—and a rough voice snarled in my ear: "By Jove, shut your mouth or die!"

Realizing I had little to lose—what thief would proceed if I kept screaming? —I bit on a finger and screamed again. The door swung open, the sturdy bar breaking beneath a sharp assault. I saw another shadowed figure, a big man, barrel into the room, and at the sight of him, the intruder released me and jumped out the window.

Ariston lunged in my direction. "Domina! Are you hurt?"

I pressed my hand to my throat and felt wetness. "I-I may be."

"Phebe, light!"

With trembling hands Phebe lit the lamp and brought it closer while Ariston peered at my throat. I glanced at my trembling fingertips—they were tipped with blood, and a drop had fallen to the bodice of my under tunic.

Fury burned in Ariston's eyes. "You *are* hurt!"

"I am not much hurt," I said, touching my throat again. "The cut is not deep."

With a complete disregard for propriety, Ariston sat on the edge of my bed and examined my neck more closely. "You are right, the cut is not deep, but the blade may have been rusty. Phebe, bring a wet cloth so we can clean the wound. We must know how deep the cut is."

I lifted my hand. "There is no need to make a fuss. If the cut was severe, we would be awash in—"

Ariston gave me a stiff smile. "Domina, you cannot see the injury. I will decide what to do."

I snapped my mouth shut and watched as Phebe handed a wet cloth to Ariston, who proceeded to gently swab my throat.

When he was satisfied I was not at death's door, he stood and looked out the window. "The intruder is gone," he called, "but I could probably find him. Someone must have noticed a man leaping from the upper story." He shook his head. "It is my fault. I thought the second floor would be safer, but as long as there are trees to climb . . ."

I blew out a breath. "Do not blame yourself. Think of your own injuries, which are far worse than mine. The thief is surely cowering in a corner somewhere and is bleeding, as well."

Ariston's brows arched. "What?"

"I bit him. He did not leave here totally unscathed."

Ariston stared and then burst out laughing. "You *bit* him?"

"And my lips still taste of him. Phebe, will you bring me a cup of water?"

Ariston covered his mouth, silently laughing as Phebe brought water. I drank, then moistened my fingertips and ran them over my lips to clean them.

By the time Aniston stopped laughing, his eyes had begun to smolder.

"Let me remind you of our purpose in this place," I told him. "We came to find Sabina."

He flushed. "Right."

"And I thought you were going to call me by my name."

The tip of his nose went pink as he gave me an abashed smile. "Did I not?"

"You called me Domina, and I am no longer your mistress. I am your wife."

"Of that," he said, his chest heaving, "I am well aware."

He looked at me, his eyes shimmering with twin reflections of the oil lamp, and I could not read his expression. Had affection spurred the slight smile on his lips, or was he thinking he had made the biggest mistake of his life?

I lowered my gaze as he took a deep, shuddering breath. "Are you certain you are well? An attack can leave a person jittery, frightened, or even ill—"

"Do I appear frightened or ill?" I looked him in the eye, determined to prove my words. "I have been through worse than this. When I say I am well, I am."

He leaned forward to give my throat a final scrutiny, then seemed to realize his face was perilously close to mine. "Forgive me," he said, pulling away.

I gave him a tight smile and tried to ignore the pulsing knot that had formed behind my breastbone. "You have not offended me. You are my husband." *And I never asked for a marriage in name only.*

Silence stretched between us and I found myself studying his strong profile. He made no attempt to hide that he was examining me as well, but then Phebe broke the silence.

"I thought the scoundrel would murder both of us," she said, fanning her chest with great enthusiasm. "I did not hear anything until you screamed, and then I saw him upon you—"

"We were not harmed," I reminded her, looking past Ariston. "Now, we must get some rest. We have had more than enough excitement for one night."

"Wait." Ariston gestured to the bed. "Phebe, sleep with your mistress. You will be good company for each other while I continue guarding the door."

I stared, tongue-tied, as Phebe gratefully left the couch and came toward my bed. Did my husband not want to even sleep *near* me?

I sighed and slid over to make room.

❖

When Phebe and I returned from dinner, I glanced out the window and saw that a brilliant sunset had burnished the western sky. "No news from Ariston yet," I murmured. "I do not want to worry, but it has been nearly a full day."

"This is a huge city," Phebe said. "Surely he has not had time to do a thorough search."

"I suppose you are right." I lifted the blind and peered into the streets below. Our second-floor chamber offered a view of a busy thoroughfare, but I did not see Ariston. "Where would he have gone?"

Phebe shrugged. "He could have gone anywhere. But do not be concerned. Earlier, I walked to the stable to fetch my cloak from the trunk. The carpentum and mule were still there, so he has not abandoned us."

I drew a breath, about to say I did not think he would leave us, though the thought *had* entered my mind. A less trustworthy man might have married me, taken the wagon, and left us, but not Ariston.

So where had he gone? I pasted on a calm smile and asked

Phebe to go downstairs to see if he had returned, even briefly. Perhaps he had come back to ask the innkeeper for directions or to get something to eat.

As Phebe left the chamber, I leaned forward with my elbows on the windowsill. Beyond the shops near our taberna, several insulae rose in the distance. I had heard horror stories about such buildings in Rome. The residents, mostly the working poor and freedmen, paid for the convenience of city life by risking their lives. The wooden structures were prone to burn and collapse because residents cooked and warmed themselves over open braziers. Not only did insula dwellers contend with fire, but all water had to be hauled from city fountains and carried up several flights of stairs. Those who had seen the insulae of Rome reported that the people who lived in the highest chambers suffered the most—from small rooms, poor ventilation, and leaky roofs.

I suddenly felt very grateful for my cozy villa by the river. I endured damp air, occasionally wicked winds, and frequent floods, but at least I did not have to haul water up eight flights of stairs.

From the window I could also see the port for which the ancient city was famous. Fishing boats and cargo ships lined the harbor while the docks teemed with life, even at this late hour. Lanterns glowed aboard ships anchored offshore, and for an instant I wondered if Ariston had found his way to one of them.

Then the door opened, and he strode into the room with Phebe trailing behind him. "I am sorry," he said, unfastening the brooch that held his cloak in place. "But while I was making inquiries about Hector, I discovered a group of brothers."

"Believers?"

He nodded. "For three weeks after leaving Philippi, Paulos taught in the synagogue here, but then the unbelieving Jews forced him out. He did not leave the city, but stayed for months, living with the family of a man called Jason." He grinned. "They say Paulos worked as a tentmaker while he lived here. Tonight I met several men who believed in Yeshua during that time, and they have formed an ecclesia."

My heart warmed at the news. "Paulos's work has borne even more fruit. Amazing."

"Indeed." Ariston sank onto a bench and unlaced his sandals. "The brothers said many God-fearing Greeks had believed, as did several Jews, some of whom were quite prominent. But the other Jews were jealous, so they gathered troublemakers from the marketplace, incited a mob, and stormed Jason's house, intending to drag Paulos and Silas into the street. When they could not find them, they brought Jason and the other believers to the city officials and accused them of acting against Caesar's decrees by proclaiming Yeshua as king."

"Did they beat Jason?" I asked. Despite my desire to stay strong, my voice trembled. If the same situation had taken place in Philippi, I would have been dragged out of my house, along with Phebe, Ariston, and Dione.

Ariston must have seen my fear because he gently shook his head. "The authorities allowed Jason to post bond and guarantee Paulos's departure from the city. So that same night, the brothers sent Paulos, Silas, and Timothy to Berea."

Phebe sank to the couch and groaned. "I do not know why Paulos continues to preach. He risks his life every time he opens his mouth."

"Why would you fear for him when he does not fear for himself?" I blew out a breath. "I often wonder if I would have the same kind of courage when faced with opposition. I am not sure I would." I looked up at Ariston, grateful for the good report. "I am glad you met other believers. And it is good to know Paulos is safe in Berea."

"He is no longer there," Ariston said. "The Jews in Berea received him, but they did not believe until after they had spent hours searching the Scriptures to test his claims. Afterward many of them accepted the truth, along with numerous Greeks. But the troublemakers from Thessalonica went to Berea and incited people there, so the brothers sent Paulos to Athens by boat. Silas and Timothy remained in Berea to teach those whose hearts burned to know the truth."

"Silas and Timothy." I nodded, remembering Paulos's tall companion and the likable young man who had accompanied them in Philippi. "Are they still in Berea? Could we—?"

"They recently joined Paulos in Athens. And I am sorry, but that is all the brothers could tell me. Still, they pray for the emissaries every day and were quick to offer their assistance when they learned we had come from Philippi." A dimple appeared in his cheek. "Apparently, Paulos told them about the Lydian woman who started an ecclesia in her home."

I pressed my hand to my chest, at once pleased and embarrassed. "Well, I will pray for them, too. It is good to know we are not alone." I then remembered my duties as a wife. "You must be starving. Would you like me to order dinner for you?"

His eyes softened. "I ate with the brothers. I need nothing else."

"All right. So, we still need to find Hector."

Ariston nodded. "I will continue the search tomorrow morning." He chuckled. "In truth, I did not expect to locate him in a single day. Over two hundred thousand people live within the walls of this city, and every day hundreds come and go from the highway or the sea. But if Hector is asking for a necromancer, someone will recall seeing him."

"I can help, too." I turned to Phebe. "I will need to dress and do my hair tomorrow because I will find the fullers' collegium and attend the midday meeting. I will ask if anyone has heard about Hector or knows a necromancer. I am certain I can find someone."

An awkward silence descended, then Ariston braced his hands on his knees. "If there is nothing else tonight . . ."

"We should go to bed." I glanced at my trunk. "Phebe will help me—"

"I need to stretch my legs," Ariston interrupted, standing. "I will probably not return until you are abed, so I will sleep on the couch. Let your maid sleep by your side so I will not disturb you when I return."

I blinked, surprised—and a bit disappointed—by his tact.

"Very well." I gave him a stiff nod. "Good night, Ariston."

"Rest well, Euodia." He gave me a fleeting smile and left.

❖

I woke early, sat up, and saw Ariston's sleeping form on the couch. I would not have been surprised to learn that he had slept at the stable, but he probably wanted to protect us. Had he chosen the couch to preserve my modesty, or did he really wish our union to be only an imitation of a marriage?

Shafts of sunlight pierced the ancient window blind, and

a dancing sunbeam landed on Ariston's face. It played over his chin and cheek, then landed upon his eye, which promptly opened. I sank back and drew the blanket to my chin, as embarrassed as if I had been caught peering through a keyhole.

The floor creaked as Ariston stood, then I heard water splashing in the basin. He was probably washing his face, but I would not sit up until he had gone.

An inner voice chided me. Ariston was my second husband, so why was I behaving like a virgin bride? Furthermore, he had been my servant for months; we were far from strangers. Yet I had not known him as a husband, a title implying intimacies we had not experienced. I did not want to explore them when we shared a room with my handmaid.

After I heard the door close, I elbowed Phebe. "Time to rise," I told her, my voice sharper than I intended. "I need you to do my hair and bring something to break my fast. For a meeting of the fullers' collegium, I must dress appropriately."

Phebe yawned and pulled herself out of bed, stumbling to my trunk. As she took out combs and thread, I fastened my palla over one shoulder, walked to the window, and raised the blind. I looked down at the street and saw Ariston buying bread and cheese from a merchant.

A smile twisted the corner of my mouth. As my husband, he could have commanded me to procure his food, but he had chosen to let me sleep . . . as if I could.

I ducked behind the wall when Ariston turned and looked toward our window. Had he seen me? Probably not or he would have called out a greeting. When I looked again, he had turned away, so I could watch without being observed. A pair of young women walked by, their colorful veils fluttering, and turned to stare at him with pure feminine admiration. Yes, Ariston was extraordinarily attractive . . . so why had he wanted to marry me?

I shook the unfathomable question from my head and considered the day ahead. I had not thought of going to the fullers in Amphipolis, but I would be more likely to hear news of Hector in Thessalonica. Anyone who owned fine garments visited a fuller regularly because no one could properly clean garments at home. While fullers tended to be despised by the wealthy—likely because they used urine to whiten togas—they were necessary, and the fullers realized their power. They cleaned and repaired togas, pleated the stolas of wealthy matrons, and dyed the colorful pallas that adorned every woman of consequence in any Roman city.

As Phebe helped with my morning ablutions, I prayed about my visit to the collegium. Since Thessalonica was both a major trade center and the capital of Macedonia, I expected the garment workers to be powerful and knowledgeable.

As a dyer, I had joined the fullers' collegium in Thyatira, and even that small city felt the fullers' influence. When the city magistrates instituted a tax on urine one summer, the fullers went on strike. After wearing smelly clothing for one unusually warm season, the city leaders repealed the tax, and the fullers were again free to remove urine from the public toilets and collection pots outside wealthy homes.

As a teenager, my mother urged me to apprentice with a woman who sold purple goods, so I learned the trade in my youth. By the time of my marriage, I had advanced to the position of laborer, and through the collegium I learned that the Thyatiran method of dyeing, which depended on the madder root as its source of color, produced a red-purple, not nearly as prized as the deep purple produced by the murex snail. But since the snails could only be found in sea-water, those who lived inland had no choice but to master the dye made from plants.

The guild proved invaluable as I perfected my skill, and by the time I achieved the rank of master, I was bored with roots and eager to learn about royal purple. I begged my husband for permission to journey to Smyrna, where I could learn how to produce the dye from snails. He agreed, albeit reluctantly, because he knew my knowledge would increase our income and standing in the community.

In search of knowledge and royal purple, I spent three weeks away from home, reveling in my first journey and the joy of discovery. Those three weeks, during which I learned my most valuable skills, were among the happiest in my life. They stood in stark contrast to the days following, because when I returned home, my world fell apart.

❖

My trip to Smyrna would not have occurred if a woman in the collegium at Thyatira had not written letters to introduce me to Eleni, a woman who had mastered Tyrian purple. Weeks passed before I heard any response, then I received my answer: yes, I could visit. She would be happy to teach me the art of creating royal purple.

Such was the power of dedicated women with similar goals. I thanked the members of my collegium, bid farewell to my husband and precious daughter, and undertook the three-day journey to Smyrna. Because it was not safe for any woman to travel alone, my husband insisted I join another group of travelers as soon as possible, so I fell in with a group of actors on their way to Ephesus. They were skilled with the art of mime, a new form of acting, and delighted me on our long walk south.

When I arrived in Smyrna, I gratefully breathed in the scent of salt water and hastened to the shore. There I found Eleni's women wading along the waterline. I must have been a sight, windblown and dusty, but Eleni came out of the water and greeted me with a warm embrace. "Welcome," she said, her dark eyes sinking into nets of crinkles as she smiled. "I am happy to teach you, but I must know—where do you intend to find sea snails in Thyatira?"

I stammered in embarrassment, then confessed that my husband was an importer. "I was hoping he could buy snails in a coastal market and bring them home."

Eleni tipped her head back and released a laugh that echoed the chattering sea gulls. "My dear," she said once she caught her breath, "your husband would have to buy ten thousand snails for you to produce enough dye for a single garment. This work is only suitable for those who live near the sea."

My heart sank, but I would not be dissuaded. "I will learn anyway," I said, my voice overly bright in my own ears, "and teach others. Perhaps some of the women of my collegium will one day live near the sea. Or perhaps we can learn something from your techniques."

Eleni grinned, her smile dazzling against her olive skin. "Then let us begin."

She bade me drop my traveling bag and remove my sandals. I did and followed her into the shallows near the docks. "There," she said, pointing to the rocks near the base of the wooden piers. "We are searching for rock snails, and they live among those stones. They eat clams and oysters, so you may find one attached to a shell. They are not easy to spot, but with practice you will gain a sense of where they will hide. Ask the gods to show you their hiding places, and you will be rewarded."

I gave her a sidelong glance. "Do you pray to a special god?"

"Oceanus," she answered, her dark eyes already probing the waters. "I leave an offering on his altar every morning."

I walked beside Eleni, the water chilling my warm skin as we searched the rocks and sand. I startled when small sea creatures skittered away at our approach, but Eleni paid them no mind. Behind us, a long line of women carried baskets on their hips and occasionally dropped shells into them.

I shouted when I spotted my first snail. Eleni grinned in approval and added it to her basket. In that moment I thought the gods had given me a sign. Perhaps I had a gift for finding snails, a gift that would raise my status in my own collegium.

But that night I felt as though I had aged two years in one afternoon. My back ached from bending, the sun had burned my arms and legs, and my feet had shriveled from hours in the water. Adding to my misery was the knowledge that I found only one snail.

Even so, I persevered. The next day I spotted several, and within a week I was harvesting as many as Eleni's regular workers.

Over the next week, she taught me how to crack the shells and extract the mucus containing the precious dye. The mucus was dried in the sun, then crushed.

"How did anyone discover the connection between this slime and dye?" I asked Eleni, amazed that deep purple could come from a colorless blob.

Eleni chuckled. "They say Melqart, the patron god of Tyre, had a mistress who owned a dog. As Melqart and his mistress walked along the beach one day, the dog bit a sea snail. A few moments later, the dog's mouth had turned purple. Melqart's mistress asked for a tunic of the same color, and the dyeing of purple began."

I smiled, not certain I believed the story, but it was no stranger than other stories about the deities that ruled our lives.

Over the following days, I watched Eleni add seawater to a pot of crushed flakes and boil the mixture for three days. After the pungent liquid had cooled, she called me over. "Watch this," she said. "It's a miracle of the gods."

She grabbed a handful of clean fleece and dipped it into the pot. Once the wool had been thoroughly saturated, she pulled it out and squeezed the water from it. As I watched, the white wool shifted to the color of the sky, then deepened to a rich purple.

"It *is* a miracle," I whispered. "How did you learn this?"

"A master dyer taught me," she said, "just as I am teaching you."

I ran my fingers over the damp wool and marveled that none of the color came off on my hands. "And this color will not fade?"

"Never," she said. "The Jews have a particular purpose for the blue dye. Their God commands that men wear blue fringes on their garments. To make blue, we let the wool remain in the water only a short time. The longer we leave it in the pot, the deeper the color becomes."

I remained with Eleni another week, practicing each stage of the process. By the end of the third week, I was able to predict the amount of time necessary to create blue, violet, and purple. I felt reasonably sure I could produce a purple to match Eleni's.

I envisioned earning a commission from a city official or even the provincial governor. With my newfound knowledge, I dreamed of traveling to the sea and owning a business that provided imperial purple garments. The Romans were certainly fond of the color—equestrians, wealthy citizens of a high rank—wore a thin purple band above the hem of their togas, while Senators wore a broad band of the same hue. But as I embraced Eleni and thanked her for her kindness, I had to admit I could not see an order for purple coming from Thyatira.

"You never know what might happen," she said, smiling. "Your husband travels, does he not? Perhaps you will travel with him to a port, and you can collect shells for your own use. The dried flakes will remain potent until boiled."

I traveled home with hope in my heart and a small bag of dried flakes—a gift worthy of an emperor—in my bag. Eleni had been more than generous. I decided to wait for the perfect project, then I would use the flakes to create a purple unlike any Thyatira had ever seen.

Twenty-Seven

I dreaded wandering through Thessalonica's maze of twisting streets, but the owner of the taberna had given me good directions. I found the fullers' collegium in a midsized building halfway between the shore and the temple of Jupiter.

Two women glanced at my purple veil and eyed me with open curiosity. "Purple," the tallest woman remarked, her brow rising. "How can there be a dyer of purple we do not know?"

"I am from Philippi," I said. "I am visiting your city."

"Ah." The woman smiled, probably in relief. "Welcome, sister. You are a member of the fullers' collegium there?"

"We do not yet have one, but I used to belong to the group in Thyatira. I look forward to meeting new sisters."

She gestured toward an inner door, and I thanked her with a nod. At the center of the interior room, an altar stood beneath a statue of Abundantia, the divine personification of abundance and prosperity. The women who dropped small gifts at her altar wore vibrant white stolas and colorful pallas; some wore intricate sandals of dyed leather. More women arrived for the traditional midday meal, and every woman who entered paused before the goddess to drop an offering at her feet.

I waited near the door, wearing what I hoped was a pleasant expression. If my plan were to work, I would need to befriend someone and inquire after Hector and Sabina. I walked forward, too, but my conscience smote me as I approached the statue. I could not give an offering to a false goddess, yet these women would not understand if I did not leave the customary offering before taking a seat. What should I do?

In a flash of inspiration, I pulled a skein of purple thread from my bag and handed it to the young woman behind me. As she stared in confusion, I said, "In gratitude to Messiah Yeshua, my Lord, I give you this gift. May the Lord use it to your benefit." I smiled and chose a seat at a nearby table.

The woman to whom I had given the skein dropped onto the dining couch next to me. "I am Irene," she said, her eyes wide, "and I have never heard of your God. Who is he?"

Surely there was never a more heaven-sent opportunity.

"He dwells in the heavenlies," I said, helping myself to bread on a nearby tray. "Yet He can be found anywhere on earth."

"Has he a temple nearby?"

"His Father's Temple is in Jerusalem, but His temple"—I patted my breastbone—"is here."

Irene's brows slanted in a frown. "How odd. What part of your life does he control?"

"All of it." I dipped a piece of bread into a bowl of olive oil. "His Father controls the weather and the hearts of kings. He controls the earth and the seasons, the sea and the shore." I smiled, grateful that the Spirit had led me to this woman. "And the Son directs my path, while His Spirit gives me wisdom."

Irene leaned back, blinking in bafflement. "He is not a god of the Greeks, then."

"Nor of most Romans," I added. "He is the only God of the Judeans, and His Temple holds no image of Him. But His Son came to earth and walked among us, so all who saw Him saw God in flesh."

The woman's eyes appeared to be in danger of falling out of her face. "Truly? Did you see him?"

"I was not so fortunate. But I have met people who knew Him and are spreading the word about His deeds."

Irene caught the sleeve of a woman walking by. "Olympias, sit and listen to this sister. She comes from—" she paused and tilted her head—"I have forgotten."

"Philippi." I smiled at the newcomer. "My name is Euodia, though some call me Lydia because I was born in that province."

Olympias sat, one brow arching. "What brings you to Thessalonica?"

"I am glad you asked." I leaned closer. "Before I left Philippi, I purchased a slave, intending to teach her our trade. But one of her former owners went to the city authorities and demanded to have her back. Because we had no receipt of sale, I was forced to surrender the girl. Now this man Hector Hostilius—a hard and brutal fellow—is traveling the Via Egnatia, and I am trying to find him."

Irene frowned. "Why not simply buy another slave?"

How could this woman understand? Sabina was not an ordinary slave; she was the girl Paulos had freed from a demon, yet her salvation was not complete. To become *truly* free, she needed to understand the power—and the love—that had broken the unclean spirit's hold on her.

"I have grown attached to the girl," I said. "I made promises, and I intend to keep them."

The two women looked at each other, then Irene turned to me. "I do not know how we can help," she said. "We do not often deal with men other than our husbands."

"The man who took her is large and quite memorable," I said. "He is a former soldier, and I have heard he is searching for a necromancer."

Irene pressed her hand to her chest. "If we hear of him, what should we do?"

"Send word to me, please. I am staying at a taberna not far from here—the one with the bright blue columns. It is important that I find the girl before she is lost to me."

The women nodded. "We will spread the word."

"Thank you."

"Now," Irene said, taking a stalk of grapes from the fruit tray, "tell us more about this God who walked with men."

❖

When I returned to the taberna, I found Ariston in our chamber with Phebe. Both sat in silence, their faces glazed with despair.

"What?" I asked, my heart contracting. "What has happened?"

Ariston glanced at Phebe, who nodded.

"I was at the city gate," he said, slowly turning toward me, "speaking with some of the town elders when a man walked over. He asked if I was looking for someone—I think he wanted to sell me a woman—and I told him about Hector. He said he remembered Hector Hostilius, having been of service to him a few days ago."

I looked from Ariston to Phebe, but she would not meet my gaze. "What sort of service did he provide?"

Ariston moistened his lips. "He buried the man's slave."

I stared into the space where Ariston's words had landed. They made no sense and seemed out of place in this sunlit chamber. Sabina had not been in the best condition when I last saw her, but would Hector actually *kill* her?

"What did that man do?"

When Ariston's face revealed nothing, I turned to Phebe. "Speak."

"I do not know anything," she wailed, tears spilling from her eyes. "All I know, I heard from Ariston."

I sat on the end of the bed and looked at my husband. "Tell me," I said, steeling my voice. "Tell me exactly what this man told you."

Ariston sighed. "I would do anything to give you good news. But the man said he had buried Hector's young slave outside the city."

"A girl? Are you sure he was talking about Sabina?"

"He described Hector perfectly and said he traveled with only one slave, a girl of about twelve years."

"Why did she die? Was she wounded? Did that brute strike her?"

Ariston's features tightened. "He did not say, and I did not have the heart to ask. I did not want to be the one to give you distressing details."

His transparency shot straight to my heart. He meant

every word and berating him for bad news was not going to soften the blow. I lifted my arm, signaling that I did not want to hear more, and buried my face in my hands.

Where were you, Lord? Why did Paulos free her from evil if you intended her to die? Could you not have saved her?

An hour before, I had felt clear inspiration from the Spirit; in that moment I felt nothing. No answer to my heart's question, no comfort, no assurance . . .

Perhaps the fault was mine. After all, my neglect had killed my daughter, my marriage, and finally my husband. Perhaps HaShem intended for me to be alone like Paulos, so I could invest my life in spreading the Gospel instead of attempting to love and be loved. Perhaps I was never meant to be a mother or a beloved wife . . .

Leaving Philippi might have been the biggest mistake of my life.

Twenty-Eight

I did not fall asleep easily. I had no appetite at dinner, so Phebe went down and brought back a tray for herself and Ariston. I did not eat, but sat at the window, staring out at the sky and regretting my decision to follow Sabina.

If we were not pursuing Hector, would he have been gentler with her? Would he have taken better care of her health? I did not know how or why she died, but I could not help but feel that things would be different had I minded my own affairs and not become involved in her life.

Ariston must have been feeling the same guilt, for although Phebe tried to make light conversation, he rarely responded and only picked at the food on the tray. From the corner of my eye, I saw him glance at me from time to time. Though I wanted to give him a reassuring smile, I could not. The weight of responsibility was too heavy, and it lay on my shoulders alone.

When sunset spread itself like a silk scarf over the horizon, I announced that I would go to bed. Ariston took this as his cue to depart. Phebe came over and released my hair, then undraped my silk palla. I stepped out of my stola, which she carefully folded so as not to disturb the pleats.

Wearing my under tunic, I slipped beneath the blanket on the narrow bed. "Will you sleep now?" I asked.

"Later," Phebe said, glancing toward the window. "I should take the tray downstairs."

I closed my eyes. When I opened them again, the room was dark, lit only by a single flame from the oil lamp. I heard soft breathing coming from the space next to me and knew Phebe had crept into bed. I sat up and looked at the couch against the wall and could not see anyone. Ariston was either gone or sleeping in the hallway.

I was about to lie down again when I heard the soft whisper of my name. "Euodia?"

I peered into the darkness and saw a nebulous form on the couch. As I watched, the shape moved toward the faint bands of moonlight coming from the torn blind. I recognized the slight frame—Sabina.

The realization sent a tickling finger down my spine and elicited a shudder. I had to be dreaming. Sabina was dead; had we not heard as much from the man who had buried her?

"Euodia?" I could see her features clearly now, along with lines of heartsickness and weariness on her narrow face. "Do not give up on me, Domina. I need you. You promised me freedom."

I opened my mouth to speak, but words would not come. How could I speak to a spirit? Sabina lay somewhere in the earth outside these walls, and only HaShem knew what had become of her soul.

"Please," the shadowy figure said again, retreating. "Do not give up. I am waiting for you."

Prodded by a courage I did not feel, I reached into the darkness . . . and felt nothing. Shivering, I sank back to the bed and closed my eyes, troubled by a dozen questions and mired in uncertainty.

"I will not give up," I whispered into the night. "As HaShem gives me strength, I will continue to search."

❖

As bright sunlight slid into the room, I sat up and looked around. Phebe lay beside me, her face blank and her arms flung over her head. Ariston lay on the couch, his long legs hanging off its end.

My nighttime visitor must have been a dream. The vision had felt as real as the blanket beneath my hands, yet I could not see, hear, or sense any lingering proof of Sabina's presence.

I rose and pulled my stola from the trunk, then slipped it over my head. I had finished pinning the palla into place when Phebe sat up, her face a study in surprise. "You dressed yourself?"

I nodded. "We need to go out this morning as soon as possible. Can you do my hair quickly? The style need not be elaborate."

Phebe stumbled out of bed and found the comb; within minutes she had smoothed my hair into place. No elaborate curls today, no layers. We had no time.

I stood, walked over to the couch, and loudly cleared my throat.

Ariston's eyes fluttered and opened. "What?" He sat up and looked around. "What is happening?"

A hot tear rolled over my cheek, and I swiped it away,

resolved not to cry in front of my friends. "Where," I asked, my voice breaking, "did he bury her?"

Ariston frowned. "What?"

"The young man who buried Sabina. Where did he bury her?"

Ariston blew out a breath. "He did not say."

"I would like to pray over her grave and know she has been properly laid to rest. I beg you to take me to this young man, so that I may discover everything he knows."

Ariston bent to strap on his sandals. "We will go," he said, glancing at me, "as soon as I have had some water. I am parched with thirst; all night I dreamt of deserts and blazing suns."

"I dreamt of Sabina," I said, "and she begged me not to leave her."

Ariston accepted a cup of water from Phebe and extended his hand. "Shall we go?"

We walked for at least half an hour, Ariston holding tight to my hand and leading me through the waking city. Throngs filled the streets, slaves hurrying to the market to purchase the household's daily food, merchants heading to their shops, worshipers going to the temple to offer a morning sacrifice. I hoped the young man Ariston mentioned was an early riser.

My husband's broad shoulders cut a clean path for me to follow, and he frequently glanced behind to make sure his pace was not too fast for my shorter legs.

The sun had just topped the mountains when we reached the entrance to the city. Inside the gate, a group of young men had gathered, several already throwing dice against the wall.

Ariston pointed at a youth dressed in a short woven tunic. "You there—we spoke yesterday, do you remember?"

The man looked from Ariston's face to mine. "Aye, we did."

"Tell my wife what you shared with me."

"About the Roman soldier?" The young man glanced at his friends, a couple of whom were snickering behind their hands, then looked at me. "I did a job for Hector the soldier. I buried his slave."

"Was she young?" I asked. "A brown-haired girl about so high?" I held my hand at Sabina's height.

The young man nodded.

"C-could you tell how she died? *Why* she died?"

He shook his head. "I could not tell, and did not ask."

I wiped a tear away. "Take us to her grave, please. We would like to pray for her."

The youth's gaze flashed toward Ariston, then lowered. Behind him, some of his friends laughed aloud, and I suspected their humor had nothing to do with gambling.

I took Ariston's arm and quietly pinched it. "Will you lead us to the place?"

The young man lowered his head. "In truth, lady, I do not remember where I buried the girl. I found a spot, dug a hole, and put her in it."

"Truly?" My mind was working on an entirely new set of questions that had nothing to do with Sabina. This young man, obviously poor, had been gambling and so recently obtained some coin. Not enough to buy a new tunic or a decent pair of shoes, but only enough to join a game of dice. His friends' mirth indicated some conspiracy to which they alone were privy, and his forgetfulness seemed odd in one so young.

"Perhaps," I said, sharpening my tone, "you have heard of my colleague Polydorus. He is an assistant to the prefect."

The young man's head lifted. "I have heard of him."

"Good, because I consider him a friend. Suppose I ask him if he knows anything about a slave being buried—without cremation—outside a proper necropolis. He might also be interested to know *who* placed this innocent child in the ground—"

The youth lifted his hands. "The soldier, Hector, asked me to look for a woman in purple with two servants. I saw you come through the gate with him"—he pointed to Ariston—"and caught him yesterday. Hector told me to say that I buried the girl."

"So you did not bury her?"

"How could I with her still standing beside her master? It is not right to bury someone still breathing."

I nodded. "You lied, then."

"He paid me two drachmas," the youth said, his tone defensive. "That's more than I can earn in a good month."

Ariston took a step closer. "What happened to the girl?"

The man flushed. "How am I to know? Last time I saw her, she was on a horse, clinging like a tick to her master's back."

I turned to Ariston, a cry of relief breaking from my lips. Sabina still lived.

❖

Phebe and I were dining in the taberna's common area when I heard someone call my name. I looked up to see a young woman in a slave's tunic, searching the room.

I lifted my hand and caught her attention. "I am Euodia from Philippi."

The woman hurried forward, her cheeks flushing. "I serve my mistress Irene, who met you at the collegium."

"I remember," I said. "Have you had dinner?"

She blinked. "Do not mind me. My mistress would have you know that her husband *did* encounter the man called Hector Hostilius near the port. My lady's husband said the older man was gambling with a younger fellow. He heard Hector say he would soon be traveling to Lychnidos."

Lychnidos? I searched my memory for the name and came up with nothing. "Did Hector have a slave with him? A girl of about ten or eleven?"

"Yes, my master said Hector traveled alone but for his slave. He thought it odd that a man like Hector would travel with a girl and not a manservant."

I looked at Phebe. "Thessalonica is so large, I thought Hector would find a necromancer here. But, praise be to the Lord, he did not." I turned back to the slave. "How long ago did your master see this man?"

She closed her eyes. "I think it was several days ago."

"Not yesterday or the day before?"

"No."

"Thank you." I lifted the hem of my cloak and discreetly plucked out a bronze coin. Then, because I could not help noticing the way she surreptitiously studied our food, I made room for her on my dining couch. "Please, sit. Phebe and I cannot eat everything on these trays."

The slave bit her lip, visibly wavering, then shook her head. "Thank you, but my mistress would beat me if I took such liberty."

I caught her hand and pressed the bronze coin into it. "Then take this."

I feared she would throw it onto the table, but she kept it, hurrying away before I could say anything else.

Phebe turned to me with wide eyes. "That could have been me," she said, her face a shade paler than it had been a moment before. "If you had not given me freedom and honest work, I would be in that young woman's position—afraid to speak, afraid to eat, afraid even to sit with a free woman."

"If I had not met Paulos—" I caught Phebe's hand and squeezed it—"I would have been just like that slave's mistress."

Lost in the silence of deep thought, we finished our dinner and went upstairs.

❖

Ariston did not return until the end of the day, which made me wonder if he was attempting to avoid spending time with me. He had spent more time in my company when we were servant and mistress.

But I had more important things to consider at that moment. "What news have you?" I asked.

"Hector was in Thessalonica," he said, washing his hands at the basin, "but he has departed for Lychnidos."

I did not have the heart to tell him I had already learned as much. "Why would he go all the way to Lychnidos when Thessalonica is almost certain to have many who claim to be necromancers?"

Ariston sat across from us, his gaze bouncing from my face to Phebe's. "Lychnidos is a journey of three or four days, but Hector is a soldier, so distance means little to him. He could be going to the slave market there."

"Every city has a slave market. Why does he not go to Pella or Edessa?"

"Because Lychnidos has the largest market in Macedonia," Ariston said, rubbing the stubble at his chin. "He must want to visit that market for a reason. He either wishes to sell his slave for the highest possible price or he plans to buy another." A flush crept up his throat. "He may wish to buy a male."

"Why would he go all the way to Lychnidos to buy a manservant?"

Ariston looked uncomfortable and remained silent, but Phebe whispered the answer. "For the purpose of breeding."

I blinked in astonishment. How could the Romans, who prided themselves on their noble civilization, be so base? I had come to see slavery as abominable in all its forms, but it seemed especially heinous when it involved children. Though many Roman families kept slave children as pets, when those innocents were no longer adorable and big-eyed, they were either sold, set to menial tasks, or used for sexual pleasure.

I would not wish that life on anyone. And if Hector planned to eventually use Sabina like a broodmare, perhaps in the hope of producing a child with the gift of divination . . .

Shuddering, I reached across the space between us and caught Ariston's hand. "If Hector is going all the way to Lychnidos," I said, "we should hurry. Perhaps HaShem will allow us to catch up with him on the road."

"Perhaps," said Ariston, "but since we have not done so thus far, HaShem may expect us to meet Hector at the slave market."

"Or not meet him at all," Phebe interjected. "He could be a danger to us."

I closed my eyes and prayed she was wrong.

❖

We left Thessalonica the next afternoon, driving the mule westward on the Via Egnatia. Nearly a week had passed since our encounter with thieves on the road, so Ariston insisted on driving. "My wounds are nearly healed," he told me, taking the reins from my hands. "I do not need your help, but I would not mind your company."

"Very well," I said and remained at his side. His words, however lightly spoken, brought me a great deal of pleasure.

We rode without speaking for a long while, our thoughts broken only by Phebe's gentle snoring and the garbled conversations of travelers we passed. I broke the silence by nudging Ariston's arm. "Since we are husband and wife," I said, my tone dry, "suppose you tell me about your childhood. I know so little about your history."

The corner of his mouth drooped. "Are you certain you want to know? Mine was not a prosperous beginning."

"Tell me everything you can remember. We will be riding for days yet."

He drew a deep breath and shifted his weight. "I have been told I was the son of a slave woman in Amphipolis and my mother died giving birth to me. When the other slaves placed me at my master's feet, he did not pick me up, so I was not acknowledged as his son. When the slaves asked what they should do with me, he told them to put me in the street where I could provide a meal for hungry dogs."

I could not repress a shudder. No wonder Ariston did not like to speak of his childhood. "Who was your father?" I asked.

"I do not know his name. I know only that he was the head of a household."

I nodded; the story was a familiar one. "How did you learn of this?"

His eyes misted. "Demetria—you will remember her from Amphipolis—lived in a nearby villa and rescued me before I came to harm. She asked her mistress if she might rear me. Her mistress was taken with the idea and agreed to let Demetria care for me." He shrugged. "Apparently, I was quite spoiled by everyone in the family. I have few memories of those years, but I do remember the mistress dressing me in fine clothes, oiling my hair, and having me sit on her lap. She engaged a tutor, who taught me to read and write Latin and Greek. She called me her precious darling and covered my face with kisses every time I sang or danced for her."

I smiled. Considering Ariston's present good looks, he must have been a beautiful boy.

He looked away, flushing, and cleared his throat before speaking again. "Demetria kept close watch over me, probably because she knew my mistress's habits. When I began to sprout a beard, Demetria realized that the mistress had begun to entertain inappropriate thoughts about me. The mistress would not have thought her plans unseemly, but Demetria wanted to protect me and feared I would be used and then cast off.

"So she went to the steward and asked him to obtain the master's permission to sell me to anyone who would make a reasonable offer. I do not know why the dominus agreed to do so, but he did. Demetria slipped me out of the house and led me to my new master, a traveling merchant." Ariston smiled. "That is why I have traveled so many places and seen so many things."

"You are a true man of the world," I said. "Was this master kind to you?"

"As masters go, he was good. I learned many things from him—how to negotiate a bargain, how to change the wheel on a wagon, how to describe worthless goods so they appealed to a buyer. I had only one complaint." He pushed a hank of hair away from his right earlobe, which, I realized, had been pierced and stretched out of proportion. "Because he worried I would escape, every night he fastened one end of a chain to the wagon and the other end to my earlobe, then he tied my hands. Every morning he would free me, and we worked together. But though we shared almost every experience, I was never allowed to forget that I was property and he my owner."

My heart swelled with sympathy as I looked at his misshapen ear. "How long did you stay with that man?"

"Until he died. He stopped breathing one night, and I did not realize what had happened until he failed to release me the next morning. So I remained on the ground for hours, hands tied and ear chained to the wagon. I tried chewing through the rope around my hands and even thought about ripping the chain from my ear. I prayed to every god I knew. The merchant had been fond of Diana, so I cried out to her, but she did not answer."

"How did you free yourself?"

He drew a deep breath. "We had pulled off a main road and camped under the trees. I thought I was destined to die in those woods, but that night another man followed my master's example and pulled his wagon not far from ours.

He heard my cries, released me, and gave me a choice. I could try to escape or be killed or I could become his property." He glanced at me. "What choice did I have? I was only about twenty and five years and desperate for food and water. So I agreed to become his slave and traveled with him to Iconium, where he trained gladiators."

My stomach clenched at the thought of the scars on his arms and legs. "Do *not* tell me you fought in the arena?"

"Despite my size, I did not." A rueful smile split his face. "My master often said he was tempted to let me fight, yet he could not afford to lose me. I did my job well. So long as I remained indispensable to my master, I did not have to fight as a gladiator."

I closed my eyes, imagining Ariston in the frenzied atmosphere of an arena. While I had never attended such a contest, I had heard stories that made my skin crawl. "How did you endure such a place?"

He chuckled softly. "When one is a slave, it is better to cooperate than die. My master was old, so he kept me busy doing all the things he used to do: unloading new slaves for training, cooking their meals, buying supplies. I raked the bloody sand in the arena and buried those who died in training. I came to pity the gladiators. Though they were celebrated and spoiled when they were victorious, they were quickly forgotten after their deaths. The crowd was fickle, and though the men of Iconium were not as wealthy as patricians from Rome and Thessalonica, they lavished gifts on the contestants. Highborn women would pay handsomely to be serviced by the fighters, and I was often ordered to make arrangements for such visits."

He threw me a quick glance. "I hope I am not embarrassing you. I know you are a virtuous woman."

I scoffed. "You forget—I have been following Yeshua only a year. Before that, I followed HaShem, but when I lived in Thyatira, I was as lost as the women who visited your gladiators. Though Greek, I was brought up by parents who adored all things Roman. My father lorded his authority over all of us—my mother, my two brothers, and me."

Ariston stretched his injured leg. "Now I must know something of *your* life. Will you tell me more about your family?"

"But you have not finished. You were working for the arena . . ."

"There is not much more to tell. My master died. His son was going to take me and the remaining gladiators to the slave market in Lychnidos, but then he fell ill on the journey and left us at the market in Philippi. That is where you found me." He smiled. "See? My life did not truly begin until I met you. Now I would like to know more about my wife."

"My history is not as interesting as yours." I swallowed as a knot rose in my throat. "I was born to Roman citizens in Thyatira. I was fortunate to be educated—my father was determined that all his children learn to read and write—and when I was seventeen, my parents betrothed me to Lysander Cassius. I married, and a year later we had a daughter, Cassia Gaia."

Ariston remained silent a moment, then cast a glance in my direction. "Were you happy?"

My thoughts came to an abrupt halt. *Was* I? I thought I was, but I was restless. I kept searching for something I lacked . . .

"I was not unhappy. My husband ran an import business and traveled frequently, leaving me at home to care for Cassia. I did not mind because I loved being a mother. We had no other children, but I do not think Lysander cared. More than anything else he craved status, and he was well on his way to achieving his dream."

Ariston made a sound deep in his throat, a noise I interpreted as encouragement to continue.

"I was working with other dyers at that time," I said, "and Cassia, young as she was, worked with me. When I was offered an opportunity to learn about Tyrian purple, I asked Lysander if I could travel to Smyrna. He recognized an opportunity to increase our wealth and agreed, but he would not allow Cassia to travel with me. I went to Smyrna, where I learned how to create the royal dye—" I swallowed, trying to dislodge the lump in my throat—"and after three weeks, I returned home."

Our villa, which usually reverberated with Cassia's laughter, had been silent and still when I returned from Smyrna. The elderly doorkeeper greeted me in the vestibule and took my bag and cloak but did not flash his customary smile. "Where is everyone?" I asked, a flicker of apprehension tingling my spine.

He bowed his head. "Dominus is with the physician in Cassia's chamber."

My uneasiness shifted to stark fear. "Is she ill?"

"Yes, Domina. Your little daughter has been sick for the past several days."

I flew to my daughter's side. My sweet girl, only ten years old, lay like one dead, her eyes closed, her hands crossed over her chest. A violent rash had inflamed her pale skin.

I sank to my knees and clung to Lysander's arm. "What is this?"

He looked at the physician, whom I recognized as the Greek freedman we had summoned on other occasions. "It is a fever, my lady," he said, bowing. "The red spots were small at first, but they have spread—undoubtedly a reaction to the elecampane I administered to help with her digestion."

I pressed my hand to Cassia's forehead. Despite her pallor, her skin felt as hot as oven bricks.

"If the herb made her worse, why did you give it to her?"

Lysander shot me a warning look, but the doctor remained calm. "She could not eat, my lady. She could keep no food in her stomach, and the pain in her throat made it impossible to swallow."

I drew a ragged breath and turned to my husband. "Have you made an offering to Asclepius?"

"Of course."

"Have you prayed?"

"I have done nothing *but* pray and pay for sacrifices." Lysander turned to the doctor. "Is there nothing else you can do?"

The physician shook his head. "Some would say she should be bled to balance the humors. I have never seen any benefit in bleeding a patient, but if you wish—"

"Bleed her," Lysander commanded. "Perhaps the fever will flow out with the blood."

The doctor opened his bag, removed a sharp fleam, and held it in the flame of the oil lamp above Cassia's bed. "As you wish."

While I watched, he lifted Cassia's limp arm and sliced into the blue vein at the crease of her elbow. He did the same with the other arm, then felt for a pulse at her neck and made another cut. As blood flowed at all three incisions, he picked up a cup, collected blood from the wound at her neck, and examined it. "I do not see any evidence of poison," he said, "but often we cannot see an imbalance of blood, phlegm, or bile."

Distressed by the sight of our dying daughter, Lysander left the room. I remained, nauseated by the coppery scent of blood, while I held Cassia's hand and prayed to Asclepius, Minerva, Jupiter, any and all gods who might listen.

After an hour, Cassia's hand grew cold. When her chest ceased to rise, the physician positioned a looking brass over her nose, held it a moment, then tilted the brass for my inspection. "It pains me to tell you, mistress," he said, "but your daughter has drawn her last breath."

I rose, racked by guilt and shattered from the unexpected calamity. Longing for Lysander, I took a step toward the door, but then my legs turned to water and I fell onto the polished tiles. A brown hair, long and curled, lay only inches from my outstretched hand. Cassia's.

I should have been home with my daughter. I should have cared for her myself. If I had been with her instead of in Smyrna, I would have noticed her rash and felt the first flush of fever. I would have sent for the physician sooner, and I might have saved her life.

I, the woman who had given Cassia life, had utterly failed her.

❖

When I finished telling the story of my greatest failure, Ariston looked at me, his eyes gleaming with unshed tears. "I am truly sorry," he said. "How did you survive such a loss?"

"I think HaShem saved me, even then." I looked at my

trembling hands. "I did not know what to do. But I am a dyer, so I took the bag of purple Eleni had given me and dyed one of Cassia's tunics." A hot defiant tear trickled over my cheek. "We buried our child in a purple tunic unlike any other. Lysander and I began our time of mourning, but within two days he became ill with fever and red spots. The physician would not let me care for him but bled him immediately. He died shortly thereafter."

I halted, unable to utter another word. Ariston remained quiet, his eyes on the road, and in the back of the wagon, Phebe suddenly stopped snoring.

"Do you still mourn for your husband?" Ariston finally asked. "Do you still hold affection for him?"

I waited until I could speak with a strong voice. "I grieved as a wife should, no more and no less. The day before he died, Lysander made it clear he wanted nothing more to do with me. He blamed me for Cassia's death and said I should have been home to care for her. I could not disagree with him, so after we buried our daughter, I made plans to leave, knowing he would soon divorce me."

"But—"

"Death intervened. After I buried my husband, I knew I could not remain in Thyatira. My neighbors blamed me for killing my family, and I blamed myself. Sometimes . . . even though I know the Lord loves me, I still castigate myself. Until a few days ago, I had decided to be like Paulos and remain unmarried so I could devote my life to serving the ecclesia."

"But how could you hold yourself responsible for Cassia's death? You were not home when your daughter took ill."

"And that is why I am to blame. Our friends said I cursed

my house with plague and deliberately went away so I would not become sick. I did not have the energy to argue with them, so I sold what I could, bought a wagon and mule, and left Lydia for Macedonia, where I thought I would be able to live in peace. I bought my villa, and every morning I walked to the riverbank and searched for snails after the tide had come in. I know the people of Philippi thought me odd at first, and I could not blame them. Some of them probably still do."

I searched Ariston's features, wondering if my story had changed his feelings about our marriage, but his face remained inscrutable.

"So?" I asked, bracing for the worst. "Do you now regret marrying me? Some people in Thyatira still believe I am a curse."

His gaze moved into mine as he smiled. "I could never believe that, my Lydian woman. Not at all."

Twenty-Nine

A week after leaving Thessalonica, Hector spied the city of Heraclea Lyncestis through a break in the tree line. He kicked the mare, urging her to pick up her pace, and soon caught up to a man leading a donkey. The donkey trudged beneath a pair of bulging saddle baskets and brayed with every step.

"Salve," Hector called, lifting his hand. "Are you by chance traveling to Lychnidos?"

The man grinned, displaying a blackened front tooth. "Nay. I live in Lyncestis."

Hector pointed to the donkey. "You have picked up many supplies."

"I have picked up enough food for my ten children, with none to spare." His eyes narrowed. "If you are planning to rob an elderly man, I should warn you that I am armed."

Hector chuckled. "Though it would be easy for me to take everything you have, I will refrain, old man. I seek information, not food."

The old man squinted. "What do you want to know?"

"Perhaps you have heard about the enchantress in Lychnidos? They say she is quite powerful."

"I have heard the same."

"Have you ever seen her?"

The man recoiled. "*See* her? I would not dare. My gods are jealous . . . and so is my wife."

"Perhaps you have heard others speak of her. I have heard she can make the lame walk and give sight to the blind."

The man wagged his hoary head. "I hear that Caesar is a god, but how can such a thing be proven? Emperors die like other men."

"True. But surely people would not talk about this woman if she did not have the power to amaze."

The man snorted. "People often say things that are not true. But go to Lychnidos if you wish, and if you have enough coin, you may find the miracle you seek." He paused, then asked, "Is your child sick?"

Hector frowned, then realized the old man had noticed the slave. She lay against his back like a bag of grain, most likely sleeping.

"She is my slave. We have been traveling many days."

"She is starving. Her arms are like sticks." The man's voice brimmed with disapproval. "Even a slave deserves a decent meal."

Hector shrugged, weary of the conversation. "She gets enough."

The old man's mouth flattened in a grim line. "Only a fool does not care for his property. If you must have a slave—"

"Do *you* have slaves?"

"Nay. Cannot afford them."

"Then you know nothing. A man with an overabundance of opinions should keep his mouth shut."

"But she is a person, a body and soul," he went on, ignoring the warning in Hector's tone. "Give food for her body and care for her soul. Does she have a mother?"

"Not in my house." Hector turned to leave. "Jupiter grant you a safe journey, old man." He spurred the mare forward.

He had encountered disapproval on a thousand previous occasions, especially in the army, but the old man's scraggly beard and lined face transported him back to his childhood. Growing up in a poor village, the townspeople and even his family considered Hector dull and slothful until a hot, fateful day in his ninth summer when a stallion escaped from a holding pen at the town center. Everyone, including grown men, trembled with trepidation as the animal cleared the streets, then stood pawing and snorting at anyone who dared approach.

When three men tried to trap the animal with a net, the stallion tossed its head and bounced in nervous excitement, then set off at a gallop. All those along the main road scattered like rabbits—all except Hector, who was determined to stop the beast.

Moving with great speed, he climbed atop a wooden barrel, waited until the horse approached, and launched himself at the stallion's neck. The gods must have been with Hector because his hands caught hold of its mane, while his leg landed across its broad back.

Using his voice, Hector guided the panting beast back to its holding pen in the town center. Somehow he had managed to calm the horse.

After that day, no one spoke of him as dull. He became Hector the Horseman, and the community's respect spawned a confidence that carried him into the Roman army and enabled him to survive it.

He could easily dismiss an old farmer's disapproval, especially since the man's reproach had centered on his treatment of a lowly slave. Still, though the old man meant nothing to him, the image of his frowning face remained with Hector long into the night.

❖

Hector could not determine how the old man had cursed him, but two days later he was convinced the peasant had ruined his venture. The girl did not wake when he called, but instead lay on the ground, either asleep or nearly dead.

"Girl." He nudged her with his boot. "Rise and fold your blanket. We are nearing our destination."

She did not move.

Hector squatted by her side and peered at the tangled hair covering most of her face. When he pushed it away, he saw that she had gone pale, save for two unnaturally bright spots on her cheeks. His pulse quickened, but then he quickly realized she still lived. Death did not paint the cheeks of its victims in rosy hues.

He felt her forehead. Despite the pallor of her flesh, her skin radiated heat. He should seek out a physician. Emperor Claudius had recently decreed that if a master abandoned a sick slave, that slave would be automatically freed. Hector had done too much and come too far to lose the girl now.

"By the crud between Jupiter's toes," he muttered, scooping her up, "this slave is no end of trouble."

Her dry lips moved as he carried her to the mare, yet she did not open her eyes. He draped her over the saddle and covered her with a blanket, then took the horse's reins and started walking. If the gods were with him, he might encounter a physician on the road and save himself the expense of hiring one in Heraclea Lyncestis.

He did not encounter any pedestrians while traveling on foot, but several vehicles and riders passed him. Every time he was overtaken, he called out for a physician. No one replied. Then, just before midday, he saw a large group of men approaching from the west, all of them walking briskly. He had not seen such enthusiasm since his training days.

"Salve!" he called. "Is any among you a physician?"

The men looked at each other, then one of them stepped forward. This one appeared to be Greek, judging from his simple tunic and cloak. A smile flashed in the midst of the man's heavy beard. "I am a healer," he said and pointed at the girl. "Do you seek help for her?"

"She is only a slave," Hector said, guiding the mare to the side of the road. "But I would hate to lose my investment."

The physician murmured something to his companions, then joined Hector. "Good of you to be so concerned. Let me see if I can help."

Hector pulled the girl from the saddle and lowered her to a patch of grass on the roadside. The physician bent and listened to her breathing, then laid his hand against her forehead.

"She has ague," he announced. "She needs water, and lots of it." The physician lifted her arm and pressed his fingers to a spot near her wrist. "Her heart is weakening, as is her body." He studied her arm more closely, pinched the skin, and gave Hector a sharp look. "How long since this girl has eaten?"

"She ate yesterday." Hector lifted his chin. "A perfectly adequate meal, considering her position."

The physician's brows drew together in a frown. "This child is starving. I do not know what you have been feeding her, but she needs more meat, more plant foods, more bread. Her flesh is hanging from her bones."

Hector crossed his arms. "You forget her status."

"'A righteous person cares for the life of his animal, yet even the compassion of the wicked is cruel,'" the physician said, looking up at Hector. "Have you not heard that saying?"

Hector gritted his teeth. "Sounds like something a Jew would say."

"Aye, it does, for it comes from the Torah." The physician lifted one of the girl's hands and held it between his own. "Have mercy on her. Treat her as though she were your child, not your possession. I have seen men feed dogs better than this."

Those men had never been part of the Roman army. Hector struggled to tamp down his rising anger. He had called for a physician to save his future, not to receive a lecture on the proper feeding of a slave.

"I have no children," he snapped, "and care nothing for them. I am a soldier."

"Where are your comrades?"

"Dead or retired."

"Consider this: did Rome allow you to march on an empty stomach?"

"Often."

The physician shrugged. "I am certain your superiors would never let you starve—Rome would want to protect its investment. When you were short on supplies, you were allowed to eat wild game, were you not?"

Hector did not answer.

The physician stood and brushed dead leaves from his tunic. "You have two choices. Either give food and clean water to this girl at once or hand her over to me so I can care for her."

Hector squinted at the man. "When will you return her?"

"Never." A smile lifted the corner of the physician's mouth. "I will grant her freedom."

"By Poseidon's foul breath," Hector shot back, "has the world turned upside down? No! I will not surrender my property to anyone."

"Then you must give her food, water, and time to regain her strength or she will die." The physician looked at the girl again, then adjusted his cloak. "If you find yourself in Corinth, ask for the physician called Luke. I would like to know this girl has recovered."

"I am not going to Corinth." Hector was relieved to know their paths would not cross again. Something about the doctor reminded him of the disapproving old man.

He was stepping forward, about to put the girl back on the horse, when the physician thrust out an arm, blocking his path. Hector drew back, ready to land a blow, but the physician knelt by the girl's side and placed his hands on her head. He uttered a prayer in a hoarse whisper, remaining so long on his knees that Hector wondered if the man had gone into a trance.

Finally, the physician lifted his head. "God go with you."

"You worship a patient god," Hector grumbled, lifting the girl. "Did you have to tell your god the entire story?"

"My God already knew this child's story . . . as well as yours. I prayed for both of you."

Hector turned to place the girl on the horse. When he looked back, the physician had been swallowed up by his enthusiastic friends, who were once again moving eastward.

❖

Though everything in Hector resisted the idea of obeying a Greek physician, after entering Heraclea Lyncestis, he found the nearest mansio and reserved a bed. He placed the girl on the straw mattress and brought her a hearty bowl of stew. He had the owner's wife fetch a pitcher of chilled honey water, and every time the girl's lashes fluttered, he ordered her to eat or drink.

"We can go no farther until you improve," he said, feeling resentful and out of sorts. "I will not suffer the chiding of other men because you are not the image of health. And I refuse to have you stand before the enchantress and faint."

The girl ate and drank, but not much. Hector paid the owner's wife to watch over the sleeping slave, then went out to survey the city. Heraclea Lyncestis could boast of no major temples, but he found several shrines dedicated to Heracles, son of Zeus, and Alcmene, granddaughter of Perseus. He purchased incense at a perfumer's shop, lit it, and left it at a shrine, confident that Heracles—known to the Romans as Hercules—would answer his prayers and heal the girl.

Heraclea Lyncestis appeared to owe its existence to travelers on the Via Egnatia. Hector counted ten inns within walking distance of the road, five stables, a bathhouse, two public toilets, and a small theater. A central market allowed travelers to exchange their goods for other necessities, and in one booth several women offered slabs of hog, deer, and rabbit.

Hector purchased some dried venison and chewed a piece as he walked through the marketplace. The meat would serve as supper for him and the girl and should increase their strength and stamina. About this, he realized, the physician was right. If the girl was going to stand before Magaere the enchantress, she would need strength to endure whatever the woman demanded. If she did not have the required vigor, or if Magaere proved to be a fraud, the slave market awaited.

But why should he sell her? The laws of nature dictated that what had once been possessed could be regained. If a man lost a horse through gambling, he could win it back. If he lost a denarius on the road, he could search until he found it again. Even if it was picked up by a ruffian, the original owner could always find the ruffian, beat him soundly, and re-claim his lost property.

No, he would not sell the girl, not yet. If Magaere proved to be powerless, or if the girl refused to cooperate, he would continue on his journey. He would go to Rome, the center of power. He might seek an audience with Claudius himself or ask to speak to the emperor's priest. He would not give up until he had exhausted every avenue.

He put the dried meat in his tunic, then purchased a basket of dates, a surprisingly expensive pair of lemons, and a small pot of honey. Convinced he had done more than he should for a slave, he walked back to the mansio.

The girl would eat, drink, and grow stronger if he had to feed her himself.

After three days of sipping honey water and nibbling on bits of venison, the girl's fever broke. She woke with a raging thirst and the appetite of a whale, so Hector went to the mansio's common room and took what he could from the trays. When he returned, the girl was sitting cross-legged on the floor, an expectant look on her face.

"Here." He handed her a pomegranate, a bowl of gruel, and a plate of figs, then pulled the remaining dried venison from his tunic. "This will have to do until the owner's wife prepares dinner."

She lifted a fig and bit into it, then closed her eyes as if it were the most wonderful food on earth. "Is there water?" she mumbled.

"I will get it." He walked away, abruptly realizing that the master had become the servant. The situation galled him, but it would not continue. Today they would leave for Lychnidos, and soon he would take her to see the enchantress. If his effort failed, they would press forward to the coast.

But today would be the last day he would feed her. Tomorrow, their roles would return to what the gods had decreed them to be.

❖

Reclining on a dining couch in a Lychnidos mansio, Hector picked out the best bits of the roasted chicken and vegetables on a platter. The cook brought out another tray loaded with toasted grain, barley cakes, and olive relish. Hector grinned, winked at the slave, and took several barley cakes for himself.

Another man strolled in, sat on an adjacent couch, and murmured a vague greeting before focusing on the food.

As Hector ate, he studied the man. The fellow had the look of a soldier—big, muscular, and fit—but his spotless linen tunic and the gold rings on his fingers implied wealth beyond that of most retired legionaries. Furthermore, most soldiers were a sociable lot at mealtime, yet this man seemed intent on remaining silent.

When Hector had eaten his fill, he poured honey water into a crystal goblet and looked across the space between them. "Well met," he said. "Have you come far?"

The man smacked his lips and tossed a chicken bone onto the floor. "I live outside the city."

"You know the area well?"

The man swallowed a bite of barley cake. "Of course."

"In truth, I was hoping you could tell me about the enchantress called Magaere."

The man's mouth curved in an expression that bore little resemblance to a smile. "You have not yet been to see her?"

"I have just arrived and have not had time to explore the city."

The man snapped his fingers at a slave, who hurried forward and filled his goblet with red wine. "You should not miss Magaere. She performs every fifth day at sunset. You can see her at the amphitheater near her home."

"I have heard as much. This theater is near the lake, yes?"

"That is right."

"How can I find this place? And how can I arrange to speak with her in private?"

The man grabbed another piece of chicken from the tray and narrowed his gaze. "Are you certain you want to?"

Hector chuckled. "I would not have journeyed this far if I did not wish to meet the woman."

"I have met her," the man said, frowning. "I wish I had not."

"Did her performance disappoint you?"

He scoffed. "Her performance is worthy of Caesar's praise. But I married her, then later left her. That woman cares for no one but herself."

Hector shifted his gaze to the colorful mural on the wall, not certain how to proceed. "I am not looking for a wife," he finally said, "but I am interested in her gifts. They say she wields power from the gods. Would you agree?"

The man leaned forward, his eyes crackling with dark fire. "Yes, she has powers. Some of her so-called miracles do not last through the night, but she is quite convincing in the moment."

"That is what I want—to be convinced her powers are real."

"What good is power if the woman has no heart? If you *do* find a way to speak to her, ask her what she did with her baby. *Our* baby."

Hector could see that his companion had lost all objectivity. Still, it would not hurt to better understand the woman he sought. "I am sorry, friend, but what baby do you speak of?"

"She tried to use our child as a sacrifice." The man looked away as his hand curled into a fist, his eyes gleaming. "She was going to bargain with our baby's blood, but I would not allow it."

Hector felt a disturbing quake in his confidence. He had witnessed the sacrifice of hundreds of sheep and oxen, yet who would sacrifice an infant? No one thought it wrong to expose a child to the weather or to wild animals, for such children would only be an inconvenience. But to deliberately sacrifice a child, especially one who was loved by its father . . .

"You saved the baby?"

"Saved her from Magaere's blade, at least for a while. Then I had to leave and could not take the child with me. May the gods help any man who loves that woman. She is darkness itself, and she devours souls for sport."

"I do not want to love her; I only wish to speak with her." Hector leaned forward. "Please, I need directions."

The man crossed his arms, a vein in his forehead swelling. "Your blood be on your own hands, then. Anyone can give you directions. To see the enchantress perform, you must leave the city and walk the southern path that leads to the lake. When you near the water's edge, turn east and follow the track through the woods. It is well-worn; you cannot miss it. You will come to a small building at a fork in the road. If you see candles in a tall candlestand, Magaere will perform at dusk. Take the southern fork. The other path leads to the woman's house, and you do not want to go there."

"Thank you." Hector sat back, satisfied.

The man frowned. "I am curious—why do you seek the enchantress?"

Hector propped his arm on the curved back of the dining couch. "It is a simple matter. I wish to present her with an offer."

"What could you offer her?"

"I have a young slave. She had the gift of divination when I bought her, but her gift was stolen by a troublemaking rabbi. I will pay Magaere to restore it."

"How could a rabbi steal a gift from the gods?"

Hector shrugged. "Some questions can only be answered by the gods, friend. So be well and thank you for your help."

"Be careful," the man warned as Hector stood. "The price Magaere most often demands is not coin, but blood."

Thirty

After six days, which included a day to observe Shabbat, we finally arrived in Lychnidos. The city was not nearly as large as Thessalonica, but we found a serviceable taberna and reserved a chamber. While Ariston drove the carpentum to the stable, I threw open the shutters and gazed out on the city.

Like Thessalonica and Amphipolis, Lychnidos had been erected on the slope of a mountain, but this slope ended at a large lake. Much of the land around the lake had been cleared, and from my elevated window I could see several large villas, probably the summer homes of wealthy Macedonian merchants or Roman senators.

A swath of forest lay between us and the lake, though our immediate surroundings were distinctly urban. Buildings near the highway were well-tended, while farther up the mountain I spotted a dozen mud-brick houses with walls sloping into ruin. The narrow streets around us were tight with foot traffic and clotted with pushcarts.

On the building directly across from us, someone had written, *Oppius, you are a clown, a thief, and a cheap crook.* Beneath it, another hand had scrawled, *Lucius wrote this.*

Several shops stood within walking distance of the taberna—a baker, tanner, smithy, and a stall that sold votives and images of the gods. Nothing truly unusual caught my eye, save for the large oval structure in the center of the city.

My heart sank. Without being told, I knew I had to be looking at Lychnidos's infamous slave market.

I turned from the window and sat next to Phebe. "See anything interesting?" she asked.

I sighed. "The lake, the shops, and the slave market. Let us hope Hector has not already taken Sabina to that terrible place."

Though we had looked for Hector on our journey, we saw no sign of him on the road. After Ariston and I discussed the matter, we decided not to inquire about him, lest another traveler alert him to our presence. Three times he had tried to stop us from following him, and I did not want him to make another attempt.

I gave Phebe a tired smile. "On the morrow we will begin our search for Sabina. I have been praying we will find her quickly."

"And that she will be returned to us without argument," Phebe added. "But knowing the history of our adversary, I do not think our prayer will be granted."

"Do not doubt the Lord's power," I chided her. "If we remain faithful, He will be faithful, as well."

I reached for a pillow and leaned against the arm of the couch. I was weary of traveling and more than ready to take Sabina home to Philippi. "Hold on," I whispered, hoping she could somehow hear me. "We are coming."

Ariston entered our chamber a few hours later, and from the sharp scent on his clothing, I knew where he had been. "You have been loitering in a tavern."

"I went to make quiet inquiries about the slave market. The Lord must have sent an angel to guide me."

"An angel guided you to a tavern?"

His mouth split into a wide grin. "Who do you think I saw there?"

I caught my breath. "Hector?"

"He was drinking at a table with others. All retired soldiers, from the look of them."

"Did you see—?"

"Sabina was there, too, poor child, sitting at Hector's feet. Everyone in the place was eating and drinking, but Hector provided her with nothing but crumbs from his dinner."

"Did you speak to him?"

"No." He gave me a warning look. "We must make a plan before we confront him. I fear we will have only one opportunity to win Sabina's release."

I pressed my hand to my mouth, overcome with sudden revulsion. Before she was freed from the unclean spirit, Sabina had been valued, well-fed, and secure in Hector's household, despite her low status. Now she was an empty vessel, which Hector was endeavoring to fill with evil . . .

"So, what *is* the plan?" Phebe rose from the couch. "Shall we follow them? Hector does not know me, so if you want me to spy on them—"

"I do not think spying will help," Ariston said. "I was hoping we could lure Sabina away in the middle of the night, but that will be nearly impossible if she sleeps beside Hector's bed. If he believes we are still following, he may chain her so she cannot escape."

"What then?" I folded my arms. "We have not come all this way to fail."

"Let me think." Ariston tented his fingers. "We know Hector wants to restore her unclean spirit through a necromancer. Why then did he come here instead of finding a purveyor of the black arts in Thessalonica or one of the other cities?"

I shrugged. "We might have received incorrect information. What if he brought her here to sell her?"

Ariston blew out a breath. "How much coin remains?"

I fingered the hem of my cloak. We had spent quite a sum on meals and lodging, but I still had fifty denarii hidden in my hem.

"If Hector sells her, I do not think she will bring a high price," Ariston said. "She is nothing but skin and bones."

"Then we must use what we have to win the auction." I lifted my chin. "Tomorrow we will rise early and be among the first to enter the slave market. We will pay whatever is required and then nurse her back to health."

"We will redeem her." Ariston squeezed my right hand. "We will buy back the girl who was meant to be free."

❖

I dreamed that night of Cassia. I entered a large room filled with laughing girls, but Cassia lay on a bier, as pale and weak as the last time I saw her alive. She looked up at me, her brown eyes filling with tears, and whispered, "Help me, Mama . . ."

I woke as if a hand had slapped me from sleep. The dream was not as vivid as my dream about Sabina, but the vision was charged with the same sense of urgency. I sat up in the shadows, gasping, and spotted gray light at the base of the door. Dawn had crept up on us.

Moving carefully to avoid waking Ariston, who slept on the couch, I washed my face and shook Phebe awake. "We must not make Ariston wait for us," I told her. "Help me into my stola and get dressed so we can be ready to leave when he is."

By the time Ariston awoke, Phebe and I were dressed and ready to go. He blinked at us and pointed to the door. "I will join you downstairs in a moment."

Phebe and I went to the common room, where the owner's wife had set out honey water, almond cakes, and a bowl of honey-baked figs. We were washing down the overbaked cakes when Ariston waved for our attention.

"Shall we go?" he asked, waiting by the door.

A few moments later, we were on our way to the slave market. I walked quickly, eager to see Sabina again, and could not help marveling at the almost jovial atmosphere that energized the crowd around us. I heard the speech of several different peoples—Greek, Hebrew, Aramaic, Latin, and a few tongues I did not recognize.

Once inside the oval, open-roofed structure, I realized that even the slave market in Thessalonica could not compare to this. A wooden stage, presently unoccupied, had been built at the north end of the oval. A large metal cage stood at each side—one filled with men of all ages, another occupied by women and girls. Each enclosure held at least thirty slaves, but I found it difficult to estimate their number because guards in dark tunics stood outside the bars, occasionally prodding the slaves with blunted spears to keep them moving.

I walked to the women's cage and studied the women, who walked in a slow circle. Some seemed resigned to their fate, while others appeared hopeful. A few would be purchased for their beauty; the rest would never see the inside of a villa but would be consigned to work in the kitchen or at the family farm. One woman carried a baby on her hip, and I prayed they would not be separated. A woman with white hair carefully navigated the circle with a cane, and I prayed she would be purchased by an understanding master.

I searched for Sabina but did not see her. I waved for Ariston's attention. "Are these all the women to be sold today?" I asked when he joined me. "Or will they bring others once these have been auctioned?"

He shook his head. "I do not know how this market operates."

After about half an hour, the crowd cheered when the auctioneer climbed onto the stage and introduced himself. I barely heard his patter because I kept thinking about the women in the enclosure. Would that I had enough wealth to free them all! Then they would not have to serve masters, but could rule themselves . . .

No. A hard, cold truth swept over me in a sobering wave. Everyone served someone, whether or not they wanted to. Even me. I had never been an earthly slave, but I had been enslaved to the darkness of false gods. Like most of the others within this stone oval, I had made offerings to Jupiter, Minerva, Venus, Isis, and Osiris. In Thyatira, I once visited the temple of Caesar and offered my favorite goat as a sacrifice, begging the divine Caesar to bring love to my marriage. When I was expecting, my husband purchased a lamb and asked Jupiter for a son.

Lysander served success and lusted after wealth. Eleni, the woman from Smyrna, served Oceanus. In the name of Rome, Claudius, our emperor, served his own legacy. Hector, our adversary, served himself.

But Paulos, Silas, even young Timothy served Yeshua, Son of the living God. Now I served Him, too, as did Ariston, Phebe, and Syntyche.

Everything in life depended on whom you chose to serve . . .

I girded myself with resolve, knowing that Sabina desperately needed to hear about the Savior. I did not know how or where she was, but if Hector succeeded in his plans, she would soon be serving another master or whatever spirit inhabited her. We had to find her. We had to show her how she could exchange slavery to darkness for slavery to a loving Lord.

Phebe and I stood arm in arm, hoping that Sabina would soon be brought out. The auctioneer began with the men, so we waited as patiently as possible as the men's cage emptied. Then the auctioneer called up mixed couples, men and women to be sold together. An obviously wealthy patrician, probably visiting Lychnidos on holiday, purchased five men and five women. "To serve at his vacation house most likely," Phebe whispered, "or for breeding. Wealthy patricians often want slave couples for their farms. Children bring more hands to do the work."

My heart broke with every sale. But as much as I wanted to buy all of them, I had come for Sabina alone. I would wait for her and pray for the others.

My mind drifted back to the afternoon Paulos commended me for granting freedom to Phebe and Dione. "We *live in a fallen world,"* he had told me. *"And until Yeshua returns, we are to honor one another with no sign of partiality. For we are slaves of Messiah, doing God's will from the soul. So we serve with a positive attitude, as to the Lord and not to men—knowing that whatever good each one does, this he will receive back from the Lord, whether slave or free."*

"Euodia?"

Ariston's voice snapped me out of my reverie. "Yes?"

He jerked his thumb toward the empty stage. "No women remain."

Suddenly limp with weariness, I clutched Phebe's hand and told Ariston we were going to visit the toilets. I had heard that exceptionally attractive, young, or gifted slaves were often held in reserve for private sales to wealthy clients. Perhaps Sabina was one of them.

Phebe and I went to the toilets, but instead of returning directly to the arena, I pulled her toward a curtained area at the back of the stage. Not knowing what lay beyond, I gathered my courage and parted the curtains.

I stared into a soiled and empty enclosure. It had once been occupied, but now all that remained was human excrement.

Phebe grimaced and held her nose. "Can we leave?"

"Yes," I said, trying not to gag from the stench. "Sabina is not here."

❖

Ariston, Phebe, and I were sharing a platter of dried fish and vegetables in the taberna's common room when an idea occurred to me. "What if the report from Hector's cook was correct?" I asked. "What if he brought Sabina to Lychnidos to receive another unclean spirit?"

Ariston's earnest expression dissolved into bewilderment. "Do you believe such a thing is possible?"

"Sabina did not receive salvation simply because Paulos cast out the unclean spirit. If we do not prevent Hector from handing her over to a necromancer, she will be even harder to reach. She could be filled with more spirits than before."

Ariston lifted his head. "Why Lychnidos? What does this city have that others do not?"

I shrugged. "It has a huge slave market. It has a large lake with wealthy people living around it." I racked my brain, trying to think of a connection between wealth and necromancy.

We sat, nibbling at our food, and Phebe suddenly looked up. "Yesterday," she said, her eyes widening, "I was walking down the street and saw a puppet show."

I made a face. "Most of them are terribly bawdy."

"This one," she went on, "was about a woman called Magaere. She was the most powerful enchantress in Macedonia, and she could give answers to anyone who sought her advice. She put a curse on a puppet man, and then a puppet woman . . ." She stared at us, her eyes round. "Do you not see? I thought the story was an invention, but what if it is true?"

I looked at Ariston, whose lips had drawn into a tight smile. "If this enchantress is so well-known that they immortalize her in puppet shows—"

"Do you think Hector has asked this woman to cast a spell on Sabina? Are we too late?"

"If he came to Lychnidos to ask this thing of this Magaere, he would not be likely to linger once the deed was accomplished." A muscle flexed in Ariston's jaw. "Since he is still here, he has not yet been successful." He turned to Phebe. "How do we find this woman?"

"According to the puppet, she appears every few days at an amphitheater by the lake. Her performance begins at sunset."

I looked at Ariston. "Is there such an amphitheater?"

"We will ask the innkeeper," he said, rising. "And if the story is true, we will leave well before sunset."

❖

The thought of seeking an enchantress—a witch in any language—rattled my conscience, but I did not intend to seek the woman's advice. I was going for only one reason—to find Sabina.

Ariston talked to the owner of the taberna and learned that Lychnidos was indeed home to the famous enchantress. He called for me and Phebe, then we set out to find her.

As we threaded our way through the crowded streets, I prayed this venture would be more successful than our outing to the slave market. We had wasted an entire morning when we could have been searching for Sabina.

As the setting sun stretched glowing tendrils across the sky, Ariston picked up a torch from a vendor, knowing we would soon need one. We made our way through the winding streets and found a flagstone road that led to the lake. We walked for some distance through the woods until finally we spied the silver shimmer of water.

"Look." Ariston pointed to a stone building between two branches of a fork in the road. A tall iron candleholder stood outside the building with candles burning in protective copper shields. "The innkeeper said to look for this building. If the candlestand is outside, we take the southern fork to Magaere's theater."

We followed the road toward the lake, and I took Phebe's arm as darkness rose with every step and slid up the trees. In the distance, I spotted bright cones of light and a stone structure—the torchlit amphitheater.

Scores of people had already seated themselves by the time we arrived, so we followed their example. While we waited, I studied the stage, which featured only a black table with two iron candlestands on its surface. What sort of performance did this woman give? Did she have a talent for lighting candles?

When nearly all the seats had been filled, servants snuffed the torches along the perimeter, leaving only the moon and the candles to light the center of the stage. Wearing a silver stola with extravagant pleating, the enchantress emerged from darkness, her arms extended, her head thrown back as if she were communing with the stars. Her crimson palla draped like shining plumage over her arms and shoulders, folding like a bird's wings when she crossed her arms and lowered her head.

As the crowd applauded, she walked to the center of the stage and looked out at the audience. I might have been imagining it, but I had the distinct impression she looked directly at me and was surprised to find me in her theater.

I shook my head, amazed at my own audacity. The woman did not know me at all.

"Welcome," she said, dark promise in her smooth voice. "You have come here seeking wisdom, light, and truth. If you will offer something in return, I am happy to provide all three."

A big-bellied man in a spotless toga stood and lifted a bag of coins. A slave at the end of his row promptly ran over to take the bag. After glancing at its contents, the slave nodded at Magaere.

She extended an arm in a graceful gesture. "Your question, sir?"

"My wife is expecting a child. Will it be the son I desire?"

Magaere closed her eyes, shuddered slightly, and spoke in an unnatural voice that raised the hairs on my arms. "If the child is a son, he will bring you great sorrow." Her lips moved, but I suspected the voice was not hers. "If it is a girl, she will bring wealth and delight. Which would you have?"

The expectant father bit his lip, then snatched a breath. "I would have a son."

"Because you have freely decided to taste sorrow," the indwelling spirit said, "grief will visit you after the birth of your child, be it son *or* daughter."

The audience emitted a collective gasp as the father sat, stone-faced.

Magaere shuddered again, then spoke in her own voice. "Prepare yourself, friend. Do not let grief catch you unaware."

Ariston leaned toward me and whispered, "The unclean spirit does not know anything about the child."

"It is not God," I agreed. "It confuses by speaking in riddles."

Despite the prediction of disaster, the expectant father threw a handful of additional coins onto the stage, and Magaere's slaves hurried to gather them.

Another man stood and asked if his wife was faithful. After her slaves collected his coin, Magaere closed her eyes, and a high nasally voice answered, "Your wife speaks three languages . . . and cannot say *no* in any of them."

I sank lower, horrified and bewildered by the woman's performance. Nearly every wealthy Roman woman spoke Greek, Latin, and a smattering of Aramaic, but the crude joke had blinded everyone to the obvious. The unclean spirit did not know the truth, yet it did know the sort of man it was addressing.

I propped my chin on my hand and leaned forward, determined to understand what I was witnessing. Sabina was the only person I knew who had been freed from an unclean spirit, and the unfolding of that event had stunned me. Watching Magaere, I had to wonder how many demons were working within her?

I turned to Ariston. "If only Paulos were here . . ."

On and on the questions came—about the future, the dead, and the gods. The voices inside Magaere claimed to know the future, have frequent conversations with the dead, and be on good terms with the immortal gods. While I listened, stunned by the blind faith of those who offered Magaere coin, Ariston scanned the audience. Finally, he touched my arm and nodded toward the front. "There they are," he said, his voice rumbling in my ear. "Hector and Sabina are standing near the front."

I followed the direction of his gaze and spotted them. Hector Hostilius stood in a line that had formed to the right of the stage. Like Ariston, I assumed Sabina was the veiled girl standing next to him.

"What do you think he will do?" I asked. "This woman has worked no miracles tonight. Will he challenge her to summon—"

"I do not know," Ariston replied. "But if that is his plan, we should work our way toward him. I cannot stand the thought of that woman touching Sabina."

Ariston, Phebe, and I stood and shuffled past the people seated in our row, then stood against the wall with several others.

After several more minutes, Magaere said she was weary and needed to rest. Anyone whose question had not been answered could return for the next performance.

I watched in stupefaction as the cheering audience rained gold and silver onto the stage. While Magaere's slaves gathered the coins, she turned to leave.

By then Ariston and I were close enough to hear Hector's shout. "Honored lady!" he called, his voice booming through the abating applause. "May I have a private audience?"

Magaere turned, gave him a quick glance, and gestured to one of her slaves. The man hurried toward Hector.

Then, while we watched, Magaere whirled and disappeared, her crimson palla enveloping her thin frame and then falling to the stone floor, empty.

Thirty-One

The young male slave stood at the edge of the stage with an expectant air.

"What?" Hector snapped, irritated because Magaere had not answered him directly. "Will she see me or not?"

"For five drachmas, she will." The boy put out his hand. "If you pay, I will take you to her."

The woman demanded a high price, but she was his best hope. She had the same power—indeed, the same sort of voice—the girl had once possessed.

Hector pressed the required amount into the boy's palm and followed him down a set of stairs, his hand tight around the silent girl's wrist. The boy led him through the woods and to the stone hut at the fork in the road. The three-pronged candlestick still stood outside, its candles valiantly pushing back the darkness.

"In there." The slave pointed to the door. "She waits inside."

Hector opened the door and entered, dragging along the reluctant girl.

Magaere was wiping cosmetics from her face when she

caught his gaze in her looking brass. "Why did you not ask your question in front of the others?" she asked, her brows rising like a pair of dark ravens. "Why did you seek a private audience?"

"Honored lady." He bowed as deeply as his stiff joints would allow. "I was most impressed with your abilities. But I was not surprised by your gifts, because this girl, my slave, once possessed a gift equal to yours. She was able to see things others could not, and she knew things others could never know. But she has lost her gift, and I have come to ask you to restore it."

Magaere swiveled, gave Hector a disdainful look, then turned her attention to the child who huddled on the floor. "She looks ill," the woman said, her voice as cold as mountain water. "If she is so gifted, why have you not taken better care of her?"

"Why should I pamper a slave who no longer brings a profit? Long gone are the days when I had coin to spare. Now I must account for every copper, and my expenses are high. We have traveled many miles to find someone with your abilities. I begged the gods for direction, and they led me to you."

Sighing, Magaere left her dressing table and knelt before the girl. Hector held his breath as she lifted the slave's chin and pushed away her hair to reveal the girl's face.

"A pretty thing," she said, studying the slave. "You have been foolish to neglect her."

He thought she would say something else, but instead the woman blinked and her shapely lips parted. Something moved in her eyes as she turned the girl's head and lifted the hair behind the slave's ear.

When Magaere looked at him again, her eyes brimmed with disturbing shadows. "How did you know?" she whispered, her voice rough. "Who told you?"

"Told me *what*?"

"Do you not see it?" She lifted the girl's hair again and pointed to a mark on the slave's flesh, just behind her ear. Hector looked and saw a birthmark that bore a slight resemblance to a heart.

Magaere rose and backed away. "Where did you find her?"

His mind whirled at her response. "At a slave market in Thessalonica, but why should it matter?"

"When—*when* did you find her?"

His eyes narrowed. "Two years ago. Why?"

Quietly muttering, Magaere returned to her dressing table and took another swipe at her face. Then her gaze swiveled to the girl and remained there.

Hector crossed his arms. "Will you help her or not?"

"What do you call her?" The witch's voice had grown hoarse.

"I call her *slave*."

"What is her name?"

"My partner bought her . . ." He searched his memory. "Rabine? No, Sabine."

Magaere leaned forward, her loose hair hiding her countenance. Hector did not know what to make of this odd response, but who was he to question such a woman?

She lifted her head again, her face sheened with perspiration. "The gods have an odd sense of humor. I set her free, and yet she returns. Do the gods plan on taking what I received in the exchange?"

Hector shrugged to hide his confusion. "You know the gods better than I. But if you can—"

"Her name," Magaere said, staring past him, "is Sabina. Ten years ago, she was born in this room. In agony I bore her, and in relief I promised her to the gods if they would grant me the powers I sought." She clutched her throat and looked at the slave by the door. "Water. I need water."

As the boy hurried to pour water from a pitcher, Hector rubbed his jaw. Her words had kindled something in his memory, but the spark did not ignite. What did she mean? And why did he feel as though he had heard this before today?

Magaere drained the cup, then a cold, congested expression settled on her face. "So I surrendered her, the gods blessed me with untold gifts, and now they have sent her back to me." She looked at him, a flicker of fear in her eyes. "Is this my day of reckoning?"

Hector stared in utter astonishment. The woman was speaking nonsense; perhaps she had gone mad. He could not believe that such a powerful and wealthy woman could have given birth to anyone, let alone this slip of a slave.

He stepped forward, determined to fulfill his mission no matter what the woman's mental state. "Lady, I have come a long way on this girl's behalf. I do not care about her origin; I only want her powers restored. If the gods gave you powers, then they must be able to grant them to this slave, as well."

Magaere's eyes raked his face, then hardened. "First, we must give this child food and water. Then we will see if she is strong enough to bear the will of the gods."

Magaere's slave stared at his mistress, clearly puzzled. "Well?" Hector asked. The boy sprang into action, pouring another cup of water and bringing it to Hector.

"I will fetch bread," the slave said, bobbing in an abbreviated bow. "One moment."

The girl raised her head and drank. Magaere moved closer, bending as if to study the girl. When she lowered her cup, she met the necromancer's gaze . . . and Magaere shuddered.

Hector felt a lurch in his composure. "What?"

Magaere shook her head. "This girl may have been a seer once, but she will never be again."

"How can you be sure?"

"My voices . . . sense something. She has been chosen."

"By whom? And for what purpose?"

"I can have nothing to do with her." Magaere took another step back and pointed to the door. "Take her and go."

"But I paid five drachmas!"

"Have you not seen enough? Leave me or I will summon my guards."

"I have not received satisfaction!"

"Perhaps," the enchantress hissed, "you are not meant to be satisfied."

Hector growled, but though the woman's eyes had gone large and brilliant with anxiety, she did not fear him. She feared whatever had chosen the girl.

Frustrated beyond endurance, Hector grabbed his slave's arm and pulled her through the doorway.

Thirty-Two

Ariston, Phebe, and I were about to reach the fork in the road when Hector and Sabina spilled through the doorway of the stone building. I halted in mid-stride, my heart constricting, but Hector did not seem to see us. A servant slammed the door behind the soldier, leaving us alone with the man we had been seeking.

So many miles. So many problems. Because of this one man.

Ariston must have read my mind.

"Hector Hostilius!" Ariston's voice, rumbling with righteous anger, echoed under the dark sky. "May God be praised for leading us to you. We want Sabina. My lady paid for her freedom, so the girl rightfully belongs to us."

Hector turned, regarding us with a remarkable expression of malignity, but his grip on Sabina slackened. The poor child fell to the ground, and only by the sternest of self-admonishments was I able to stop myself from running forward and pulling her into my arms.

Hector, who had squinted at Ariston, transferred his burning gaze to me. "I have cursed you," he said, a dark smile quirking the corner of his mouth. "Apparently I will have to curse you again before the gods are persuaded to destroy you."

"Curse me all you like." I lifted my chin. "Your curses are powerless against those who are defended by the Almighty God."

"You should consider your own well-being," Ariston said, squaring his shoulders, "before you curse my wife. I will also defend her, though it cost me my last breath."

"Your wife?" A flicker of mirth crossed Hector's face. "The Lydian woman has married a slave?"

"I am a freedman. And happy to have found so virtuous a wife."

"So you say." Hector shifted, his right hand moving to the hilt of his sword. "But she attempted to take my slave, and that is not a virtuous act."

"A sale was legally concluded," I said, raising my voice. "Ariston negotiated with your partner, so Sabina belongs with us."

Hector regarded Ariston with narrowed eyes. "This matter has been settled by the city magistrate. You have no proof of any sale."

"I am a witness," Ariston answered. "And my wife confirms my testimony. Every man and woman in Philippi knows the strength of Euodia's character. She does not lie."

Hector spat on the ground. "All women lie. Including that one."

My cheeks burned, but I would not argue with a fool.

"If you will not give Sabina to us," Ariston said, "then let us purchase her freedom."

"Do you jest?" Hector grinned. "This girl is worthless—

not even her own mother wants her. I was thinking about drowning her in the lake, but if there is coin to be made . . ." He tilted his head as if mentally calculating. "You may purchase her for fifty talents."

The number stole my breath. Fifty talents was more than I would earn in a dozen lifetimes. No one, save a senator or the emperor himself, could pay such a price, especially for a young female slave.

"Do not be ridiculous," Ariston answered. "The price of a half-starved slave is ten denarii at best."

"She is worth more than that." I stepped forward. "She is worth everything to those who love her, but I cannot pay fifty talents. Perhaps I can pay in purple."

Hector's grin widened. "Now who is being ridiculous? This girl is the daughter of Magaere, the famous enchantress of Lychnidos. She will be worth a fortune in Rome. I may sell her to the emperor."

Ariston's features hardened, yet I did not want him to fight. "We are not leaving." I took another step toward our adversary. "I purchased the girl and promised to give her freedom. She is rightfully mine and rightfully free."

Hector drew his sword. "I thought you had learned your lesson. I have named my price and you will not pay. I have urged peace, but you refuse to depart. If you remain here, I can only assume you intend to rob me. Be warned—with my life I will defend what is mine."

My blood chilled as Ariston glanced around. He had no sword, no blade, nothing but brute strength and courage. But as panic gripped my heart, Sabina pushed herself up, sprinted toward the building, and grabbed the tall candlestand. She dropped it at Ariston's feet, then ran into my arms.

As I drew her close, Ariston picked up the candlestand and thrust the three-pronged end at Hector.

"We are not leaving without her," he said, bracing for a blow.

My heart leapt to my throat as Hector assumed a fighting stance. His blade flashed in the moonlight, Sabina whimpered, and Phebe's hand went to her throat.

How could this be what HaShem intended?

◈

Hector charged toward Ariston, his sword gleaming, and Ariston lifted the candlestand to block the blow. I pressed Sabina's head to my shoulder, not wanting her to witness such violence. But I could not look away from the two men who would decide her future within the next few moments. Guilt avalanched over me—Ariston would not be fighting if not for me—yet at the same time I felt profoundly grateful that the Lord had sent me a champion. He might not be as skilled as Hector, but he was courageous, strong, and younger than the soldier . . .

Hector and Ariston moved along an invisible track, Hector steadily holding his sword at the level of Ariston's neck as Ariston held the candlestand, ready to block each blow. How had the situation come to this? Ariston was a steward, not a warrior, and he did not have a proper weapon. I looked around, searching for something to improve Ariston's odds. I saw nothing but Magaere's slave, who opened the door, peered out, and quickly retreated.

"Yeshua, have mercy!" Phebe whimpered. "What can we do?"

"We can pray," I told her, struggling to contain my desperation. "We can pray that Yeshua will strengthen Ariston, and HaShem will provide justice."

I looked down at Sabina, who trembled in my arms. "This will soon be over," I said, my voice breaking. "As soon as it is finished, Lord willing, we will take you home."

I spoke with a confidence I did not feel, but my words were a prayer, frantically lifted from a sincere heart. We had come so far, cared so deeply, and risked so much for this girl's soul . . . had we truly been following the Lord's will, or had I forced my own desires onto the situation?

Hector's sword whirled and flashed, occasionally throwing sparks as steel clashed against iron. I winced with every blow and cried aloud when a strike from Hector split the candlestand. Ariston stared, then gripped the upper half with both hands, pointing the prongs at his opponent.

I gaped at him, suddenly realizing that Ariston was more capable than I had imagined. He thrust and parried with surprising agility and grace, moving more quickly than his more experienced opponent. And though the three candleholders were topped with sharp flanges, Ariston did not attempt to stab Hector but seemed content to defend and dance, parry and whirl away.

Hector's eyes gleamed beneath his perspiring forehead. At one point he feinted, tricking Ariston into lunging with the heavy candlestand. The resulting imbalance caused Ariston to slip and fall to one knee. Then Hector pivoted, and momentum carried his blade toward Ariston's throat. I screamed, certain my husband's head was about to be separated from his body, but Ariston must have anticipated the blow. He ducked, but barely, and the sword grazed the top of his scalp.

Clinging to Sabina, I whispered a frantic prayer. "Lord Yeshua, help him!"

When I opened my eyes again, I saw that both men had grown weary. Perspiration streamed from their faces, but Hector was panting, expending more effort each time he swung his sword. The dance of death had slowed, and finally Hector swung and missed. Ariston swatted the lowered blade with the candlestand, and Hector's gladius landed in the dirt.

I released Sabina and ran forward to claim it. What next? Should I keep it or give it to Ariston?

I did not have to decide, for at that moment Hector toppled into the sand, face-first. For a moment, I thought he had died, but then he turned his head and inhaled a rasping breath.

Ariston gulped air, too, but he stepped forward and knelt on one knee. "We are taking the girl," he stated, wiping sweat from his face. "Let this be the end of the strife between us."

Hector did not answer. I tossed his sword into the bushes and ran to Sabina. After placing a kiss on her forehead, I left her with Phebe and went to check on Ariston.

Before I could reach him, a bellow broke the silence. Time seemed to slow as I spun around and saw Hector rise, the broken candlestand in his hand. He drew his arm back and threw the shaft, which flew in a graceful arc and struck between Ariston's shoulder blades. He turned, his face twisting, and fell while Phebe screamed. I ran to him, my pulse pounding in my ears.

In some dim recess of my mind—one not occupied with concern for Ariston—I wondered if Phebe still loved him. I saw that she was not watching Ariston. Instead, her wide eyes were focused on something else, and when I followed her gaze, I saw the reason for her alarm. Magaere had come out of the building and grabbed Hector's hair with her left hand while her right hand ran a blade across his throat.

Before I could look away, Hector toppled sideways, staring at Magaere as he fell. Then the enchantress of Lychnidos dropped her blade and walked toward Sabina with outstretched hands, her eyes glittering and her chin high. She studied the girl, then turned and met my horrified gaze.

"The girl's tormentor is dead." Voices came from Magaere's throat, a river of inhuman sound. "And despite your prayers to the Almighty, the girl will soon die."

I stood like a statue, terrified and unmoving, but Ariston's groan snapped me out of my stupor. He was trying to push himself upright.

"Did you hear us?" Magaere's voices streamed in a deafening roar. "The girl is as good as dead."

I closed my eyes. *Lord, help me. Help us!*

Refusing to listen to the unclean spirits, I moved behind Ariston, gripped his shoulders, and struggled to support him.

"DID YOU HEAR US?"

"I will not argue with you," I said, staring into her eyes. "In the name of Yeshua, Son of the living God, I rebuke you. You do not know the future, for you are not God. You do not hold power over life and death, HaShem does. You have no power over that girl. She has been chosen, and your defeat will be complete when Yeshua sets her free."

Magaere's eyes rolled back in her head, then she dropped to the sand.

Ariston relaxed, the weight of his shoulders falling onto my arms. A Sabbath stillness enveloped us, broken only by the sound of Phebe's whimpering.

"Are you all right?" I asked Ariston.

A faint smile flickered across his face. "I have felt worse. But I *would* like to finish this on my feet."

"Phebe," I called. "I need your help."

She wrung her hands. "What should we do? Have we killed that woman?"

"We have done nothing to her. Please, I need help."

When she did not respond, I glanced over to see what was keeping her. Magaere was now standing, her eyes trained in my direction. "You surprise me," she said, her voice as normal as mine. "You wield your power so easily."

I drew a deep breath and shook off the fear that threatened to leave me speechless. "I have no power," I said. "The power you speak of comes from Yeshua."

Without another word, Magaere lifted a brow, then smiled and returned to her house.

I looked at Ariston, about to ask for his thoughts, then heard Phebe's startled cry, "Domina! She's running away!"

I turned and saw Sabina sprinting toward the lake.

❖

I ran after Sabina, my heart pounding painfully in my chest. I did not know what had spooked her, but it could have been anything—the sight of blood, the fight, or seeing two injured men on the ground. Hector was dead. I thought she would be relieved to know he would trouble her no longer, but what if she had developed some sympathetic affection for her master? I knew nothing about what had happened on the long road to this lake, but I had heard about slaves who developed affection for their masters because belonging to someone was better than belonging to no one.

"Sabina!" Breathless, I struggled to call her name. "Sabina, stop!"

I ran as fast as I could, dodging bushes and hollows and fallen trees. I could see the moonlit lake in the distance, but it seemed so far away. After cresting a rocky hill, I realized why. This side of the lake was not bordered by a gentle shore, but by a steep cliff. Sabina was nearing the edge, so surely she realized the danger awaiting her only a few steps away.

"Sabina, wait! I am coming!"

She turned, saw me, and held up her hand as if to ward me off. But I kept running, determined to calm her.

Before I could take another step, she disappeared.

Terror lodged in my throat, making it impossible to speak. I stumbled to the edge and looked down, expecting to see water and rocks below. Instead, I saw Sabina clinging to a sapling that had managed to grow from the side of the moss-covered rocks.

My heart resumed beating, but at double speed. "Sabina!" I dropped to the ground and slid forward, my palla fluttering in the wind. I ignored the rough rocks scraping against my chest and tried not to think about the distance to the water. "Give me your hand, sweetheart." I forced a smile and thrust my arm toward her. "Catch my hand and I will lift you."

Clinging to the branch, Sabina shook her head. "No," she said, tears streaming over her pale cheeks. "I have already cost you too much. You should not have cared for me. I have brought you nothing but trouble. Let me go so you can return to your home." She lowered her head. "I should have died the day I was born."

"I do not believe that." I clenched my jaw. "I will *not* let you go, nor will I leave you. I promised to give you freedom, and with HaShem's blessing I will keep my word."

"I am cursed," she wailed, finally meeting my gaze. "I was born from that evil woman's womb, so how could I ever be good? How could any good come from my life?"

"Through the power of Yeshua, Paulos freed you from an unclean spirit," I reminded her. I inched forward on the rock, placing my feet behind a fallen tree. "Yeshua loves you, and He has called you by name. Answer Him, Sabina. He wants you to serve Him."

She shook her head. "I deserve to die. If I had never been born, Ariston would not be dead. I know you love him."

Some random thought struggled to be born, but I could not chase it because I had to focus on Sabina. "That is not true, dear one. Ariston is not dead, only injured. And he wants you to live."

I slid as far forward as I dared, but the rational part of my brain assured me I could never pull her to safety. Even if by some miracle I could reach her, I did not have the strength to lift another person, even a child.

What had made me imagine I could save her? I had not saved Cassia, my own daughter. I had not been able to save Lysander. I had failed them both, and I was about to fail Sabina.

"Forgive me." My chin trembled as I struggled to find a way to say farewell. "I know I promised to free you, but I cannot if you will not reach out to me."

Tears flooded my eyes when she pried one hand from the tree and stretched her arm, even her fingers, as high as she could. Why had I told her to reach out? She had weakened her grip on the little tree, her salvation, and reached out in faith. Yet how could she trust me when I was doomed to fail? I could not lift her, and I should not have promised that I would. I should have left her alone. I should never have invited Ariston and Phebe on this journey, and I made a colossal mistake when I married a man I did not deserve . . .

A pair of strong hands encircled my waist.

"You cannot reach her unless I slide you forward," Ariston said, his voice near my ear. "I will not drop you."

"But—" My voice broke. "I cannot lift her, Ariston. I am not strong enough. I have never been strong."

"All you have to do, Euodia, is *hold* her. Will you do that?"

I was willing, but could I?

Though the thought of suspending even more of my body over the edge made my stomach shrivel, I nodded. I held my breath as Ariston pushed me into the cool breeze rising from the lake. My legs rose as I reached out, coming closer to Sabina, until finally our fingertips touched. "Farther," I gasped, realizing I had absolutely no control over the situation. If Ariston tired, if his wounds pained him, or if he lost his footing, I would fall and take Sabina with me.

Then I felt him on my back. He was *sitting* on me, his weight anchoring me to the earth while I dangled in empty space and reached for Sabina . . .

At last I caught her hands.

"Pull," Phebe shouted. "Euodia has her!"

While my heart throbbed, my muscles strained, and my hands grew slippery with sweat, Ariston dragged me across the rock, scraping my legs and ripping my stola, but lifting Sabina from the abyss. Phebe came running as Sabina appeared at the cliff's edge and helped haul the girl onto solid ground.

The four of us lay near the edge, struggling to catch our breath as we stared into the starlit sky.

When I could finally speak, I turned my head and saw Ariston lying next to me. "We should get you," I rasped, "to a doctor."

He moved his chin in a barely discernible nod. "Whatever you think best, wife."

❖

I was relieved to find Ariston still breathing when we reached our taberna. Phebe went for bandages and clean water while I helped Ariston to the bed and examined his wounds. Three punctures marked his back, yet the cuts were not deep. Hector's sword had licked the top of his head, but I could see no damage other than a faint scratch.

I did not realize the extent of my own injuries until Phebe pointed them out. "Euodia, you are bleeding."

She pointed to my arms. I lifted them and saw long scratches on the underside of both. My legs were doubtless marred in the same fashion, and a glance in the looking brass revealed similar abrasions on my chest.

Phebe shook her head. "That stola will never be made right again. I suggest we cut it up and use it for pillow covers."

I sighed. "You are probably right."

I looked at Sabina, who lay on the couch, a ball of stunned silence. At Phebe's request, she had run to the innkeeper to inquire after a physician, and now the doctor worked on Ariston's wounded back. Sabina had not spoken since.

When the physician finished, I paid him, then Phebe, Sabina, and I stood and stared at the silent figure in the bed.

"I think," I whispered, carefully choosing my words, "we should take another room so he can sleep undisturbed."

Phebe lifted a brow. "You are his wife. Would you be separated from the man who needs you?"

"The woman makes a valid point." I flinched when Ariston's voice rumbled in the quiet. He lifted his head and smiled. "Let Phebe tend to Sabina. I would like to sleep next to my wife."

My cheeks burned as I met his gaze. "You have proven yourself a man of character, strength, and courage, and you deserve a good night's rest. We would not have Sabina with us if you had not been around to rescue her."

He cleared his throat. "I would have jumped into the lake after her if you had wished it. By now you should know I would do anything for you."

"No need for lake jumping," I answered, sitting on the edge of his bed. I gave him a coy smile. "But if you wish me to stay with you tonight, I suppose it is the least a wife can do."

<hr />

When Phebe and Sabina had gone, I sat cross-legged on the bed and turned to face my husband. Adopting a severe tone, I attempted to scold him. "You frightened me," I said. "And you surprised me. You are a steward, so how did you manage to hold your ground against a seasoned soldier?"

His mouth curved in a smile. "Did I not mention that I served a man who ran a ludus?"

"Yes, but you kept his accounts and ran errands."

"That is true." His smile diminished slightly. "But he also used me to train his gladiators. Their job was to punish me in the arena; mine was to survive through defensive maneuvers. I learned my lessons quickly."

My heart rose to my throat. "When you stumbled, I thought you would be mortally wounded. And in that instant, I knew I could not bear to lose you." My hand crept to his chest and settled against the skin above the blanket. I had not seen his bare chest before, never had an opportunity to notice the many scars.

"I am not sure what married love is, Ariston. My parents' marriage was arranged, and they operated more like partners than friends. My first marriage was also arranged, and I saw little of my husband because he was so often away from home." I swallowed hard, struggling to compose my riotous thoughts. "Since believing in Yeshua, I have learned that love means valuing someone else above yourself, so I have loved you, Phebe, Paulos, Sabina, and many other believing brothers and sisters. But now I sense a new kind of love in my heart, one that yearns to place you above all other men. Because you have done so much for me, I want to give you everything I am and have and ever will have. I want to—"

"Euodia?"

"Yes?"

"There is a time for talk. This is not that time."

His mouth closed upon mine, and my foolish thoughts scattered as my lips and arms and hands sought the man HaShem had sent to be my husband.

Thirty-Three

The next morning, I startled when a loud knock roused me from sleep. Ariston's arms tightened around me, so I soothed him with a quick kiss. "I am sure it is only Phebe," I whispered. "Go back to sleep while I see what she needs."

I pulled on my chemise, then opened the door and frowned. An unfamiliar woman stood in the hallway, but after seeing me, she lifted her veil. Magaere.

"May I come in?" she asked, her voice low.

Too stunned to protest, I opened the door, and she entered the room, barely glancing at the man in my bed.

"I wanted you to know," she said, looking directly into my eyes, "that Hector Hostilius is gone, so you need not worry about him. No one will ever know what happened last night—at least they will not hear the story from my household."

I felt an instinctive stab of fear at her first words, supposing that Hector had somehow survived all I had seen. Then I realized she was referring to his mortal remains.

"The body—?"

"Has disappeared." A faint smile lifted the corners of her mouth. "As to the girl . . ."

I lifted my chin in a flash of defensiveness. I did not know if Hector had spoken the truth when he said Magaere was Sabina's mother, but if she had come to take Sabina away—

"She is free," I said. "I have promised to grant her freedom, and I will see to her manumission today. She will belong to no one but herself."

Beneath the sharp features of Magaere's impassive face, I saw a trace of movement, as if a silent spring was threatening to break through. "Good," she said, looking away. "I was never suited for motherhood. After the birth I told my servant to sacrifice the child as an offering to the gods, but apparently the gods had other plans."

"One God did," I said, smiling. "He is called HaShem."

Though her statement would ordinarily have made my blood run cold, the evidence of HaShem's intervention could not be denied, even by the enchantress of Lychnidos.

"I was curious." Magaere tilted her head. "Hector said the girl once had a spirit of divination. Is that true?"

I gave her a reluctant nod. "It is. She made her masters a great deal of coin until Paulos cast out the unclean spirit."

"And who is Paulos?"

Tell her.

The Voice was unmistakable, so HaShem was still at work. "Paulos is an emissary of the Most High God. He is currently in Corinth, teaching about Yeshua, the Son of HaShem."

"Corinth." Magaere sighed. "I have not visited that city in years. Perhaps it is time for a journey."

"If God wills," I said, "you should go."

Magaere's brow arched. "You would send me to this man? Do you not fear for him?"

"Not at all." I crossed my arms. "I fear for you if you do *not* go to see him."

The door creaked, and I looked past Magaere. Phebe and Sabina stood in the doorway, both wide-eyed at the sight of the necromancer.

"Come in," I urged them. "Magaere is going to Corinth. She may even meet Paulos."

Phebe's eyes widened further, while Sabina's countenance remained troubled.

"I will detain you no longer," Magaere said, turning toward the door. She stepped forward, then paused beside Sabina. "I gave birth to you," she said, "but the gods have given you another mother, one who loves you far better than I did. Honor her, child."

Without another word, the enchantress left us.

<hr />

We remained in Lychnidos while Ariston's wounds healed. Though he complained because we would not let him rise from his bed, I rather enjoyed having him at my side. No longer was he running through the city, listening for rumors of Hector or visiting gambling dens and taverns hoping for a glimpse of the man.

While Ariston rested, I fulfilled my promise to Sabina. I summoned the proper officials, who met us in the taberna's common room, and there a scribe wrote out Sabina's manumission papers, which were signed by witnesses and a city magistrate.

The magistrate touched Sabina with a rod, the *vindicta*,

and pronounced her a free woman. As a final gesture, he placed a felt cap, the *pileus*, upon her head, covering her short hair.

"Now you are free," I told her, blinking away tears as she took the documents. "You may go anywhere you choose, though I hope you will stay with me. You will always have a chamber in my home and a place in my heart."

Sabina wept and threw her arms around me, then embraced Phebe, the startled magistrate, and the scribe.

As she hurried upstairs to show her papers to Ariston, Phebe caught my arm. "If you will wait a moment—"

I stopped and gestured to an empty table. We sat, and I waited, curious as to what Phebe had on her mind.

"I have given a certain matter much thought and prayer," she said, lowering her voice, "and I have decided not to accompany you on the return to Philippi."

"What?"

She spread her hands. "You may not have noticed, Euodia, but for months I fancied myself in love with Ariston. I do not think anyone noticed my feelings, including Ariston, but I cannot deny them. But since he is now a fulfilled and happily married man"—she smiled, probably at the blush searing my cheeks—"I think it best that I remain single to better serve Yeshua. That is what Paulos urged some of us to do, is it not? To be unmarried as he was?"

My thoughts scampered like wild rabbits. In truth, I had noticed Phebe's infatuation with Ariston; everyone had. But clearly, HaShem had other plans for her, and Phebe had accepted His will.

"I love you, sister," I said, taking her hand. "And we will all miss you. But you will be a bright emissary for Yeshua wherever you go." I smiled. "Have you decided where you are going?"

"Corinth," she said. "Since Paulos is there, I thought I would see if he could use my help. He may need it if Magaere seeks him out."

"Go with God." I squeezed her hand. "And write to us. We will be eager to hear of the work you are doing in that city."

We stood, I linked my arm through hers, and together we went upstairs to join the rest of our family.

<hr />

A week after our encounter with Hector, Ariston and I were back in the carpentum, riding side by side as we followed the Via Egnatia toward Philippi. Sabina napped in the back, content, happy, and with a little more flesh on her bones.

She had blossomed since her rescue. Throughout the week of Ariston's recovery, we had shared everything we knew about Yeshua, the power of the Most High God, and His love for His creation. "That includes *all* people," I reminded her. "Not the Jews only, but also those who are not Jewish. Paulos says our window to accept God's salvation will be open until HaShem's plan for the Gentiles is complete, and then all of Israel will be saved."

I glanced back to make sure she was comfortable, then slipped my hand over Ariston's strong arm and luxuriated in his presence. So much had happened since we left Philippi. We had begun the journey as strangers, but now I felt as though I had spent a lifetime knowing and loving the man who was my husband.

What had Sabina said while she dangled from that cliff? *"I know how you love him."*

Perhaps I did love him then, but I would never have admitted it. I would have admitted needing him, admiring him, caring for him as a believing brother, and being concerned for him . . .

If that was not love, what was?

I looked up at him and smiled.

He arched a brow. "What?"

"When we began this journey," I said, "you gave me a riddle. Something about living with a thing and being blind."

"Ah." His smile deepened. "I said, 'It is possible to live with something and not see it.'"

"Will you never explain what it means?"

His brows rose again. "You do not understand? Even now?"

"If I understood, I would not ask."

He sighed. "I have always loved you, Euodia. On the day we met, I recognized you as a woman of great worth."

"Phebe loved you," I said. "She told me as much before she left us."

He shook his head. "Phebe did not know me, but you did. When you saw me in the slave market, I think you understood the sort of man I was, and that is why you bought me. And"—his tone lightened—"I would like to think that is why you married me."

I squeezed his arm and smiled. "Perhaps you are right. Or perhaps the Spirit whispered to me. In any case, I have no regrets. I would choose you again and again and again."

Ariston did not answer, but slipped his arm around me, kissing me again and again and again on the road back to Philippi.

Author's Note

In my historical novels, especially those featuring biblical characters, I strive to remain true to the Scriptures and history. Readers frequently mention that they appreciate knowing how much of a novel is fiction, so let me anticipate and answer a few general questions about the story and the history behind it.

Q. Why would you think the "Lydia" mentioned in Acts 16 is actually named Euodia?

A. Scripture tells us that Paul (*Paul* is English, *Saul/ Sha'ul* is Hebrew, and the Gentiles of his day would have known him as *Paulos*) met Lydia in Philippi, but her hometown was Thyatira, a city located in the Roman province of Lydia. When this "seller of purple" moved to Philippi, it follows that the Philippians might have called her "the Lydian woman" and then shortened it to "Lydia." As a general rule in ancient days, most people were born, lived, and died in the same town, so this woman would have been considered an outsider.

Still unconvinced? Scripture tells us that Lydia was the first convert in Philippi (and in Europe!), and Paul established the Philippian *ecclesia* in her home. This woman was baptized and became an active member of the fledgling community of believers. Paul and his companions lived with her in her home for some time.

Since she was a pillar of the Philippian church, why doesn't Paul mention her in his letter to the Philippians? He mentions Euodia, Syntyche, and Clement, who might have been the Philippian jailer mentioned in Acts 16:31.

I suppose it's *possible* Lydia died between Paul's visit to Philippi and his letter to the Philippian church, but I suspect Lydia was alive and well and named Euodia. As to her squabble with Syntyche (Philippians 4:2), well, when we reach heaven, we can ask what they were fussing about.

Had Lydia/Euodia been attending a synagogue before she met Paul? Yes. Jews used the phrase "God-fearer" (your translation may use another term) to describe Gentiles who believed in HaShem ("The Name" of God, which was too holy to speak). Even during a time when most people worshiped false gods and idols, the Holy Spirit drew Gentiles and put them in situations where they could hear about Jehovah and the coming Messiah. Acts 16:14 tells us "The Lord opened her [Lydia's] heart to respond to what Paul was saying." The phrase "God-fearer" is used of other Gentiles in Acts 13:16, 26; 17:17; and 18:7.

The slave girl with the spirit of divination is not named in Scripture, nor does the Bible tell us what happened to her after her deliverance. I am certain, however, that believers in the Philippi ecclesia must have tried to reach her with the Gospel . . . which led me to write this story.

Paul traveled to Philippi on his second missionary journey, described in Acts 16–20, which took place around AD 50. This story is set in AD 51 when Paul was working in Corinth. He spent over eighteen months in that city where he met Priscilla and Aquila.

And that community, Lord willing, is where the next novel in this series will take place.

Q. About Lydia's purple, what color was it exactly?

A. No one is sure, as clothing does not usually survive the passage of time. Roman purple varied in hue, "encompassing shades of pink, red, rose and scarlet referred to in the ancient ideology as red-purple," writes David Graves of Liberty University. "In Pliny's opinion, the best purple was the color of congealed blood that is 'blackish at first glance but gleaming when held up to the light.'" Graves concludes that the dyeing process has been found to be "somewhat of an enigma."

To my way of thinking, a purple that is blackish at first sight is very dark, not reddish. But since purple is a combination of red and blue, I'm sure there are a thousand variations in tone.

If you study a map of Philippi, you will see that the city is not located on the sea, but on a river that flows from north to south. Neapolis, a city south of Philippi, is located on the coast. The only way I could have Lydia harvesting sea snails was to theorize that more than two thousand years ago, the river at Philippi flowed all the way to Neapolis, so the coastal tides deposited creatures in what would have been brackish water. It is a fictional invention that is, I believe, at least possible. It's also possible that Lydia hired people in Neapolis to harvest snails and bring the living creatures to Philippi.

If you're interested in natural dyes, check out Graves's excellent article. You'll find the link in the list of references at the end of the book.

Q. What is a *palla*?

A. A palla is the Roman version of the Greek himation—a rectangular piece of fabric used for many purposes, but mainly as a useful addition to a woman's main garment—a girl's short tunic or the long stola of a married woman. The most common way to wear a palla was over one shoulder, draped across the back, beneath the opposite arm, and joined to the starting corner at the front. It could also be tied around the hips or used to cover the hair (a convention expected of modest women). The palla could be made of wool, linen, or silk. Wealthy women opted for expensive fabrics and vibrant colors; poorer women wore pallas made of sturdier stuff.

The typical Roman woman wore undergarments that wrapped around the breasts and loins (probably long strips of linen), an under tunic, a tunic or stola, and a palla. In harsh weather, she may have also worn a cloak, though a palla often sufficed in chilly weather.

Q. Are your descriptions of pagan worship accurate? They seem terribly gory.

A. Yes. We who are accustomed to organized church services may find it hard to imagine that pagan worship could be bloody, violent, and even sexual, but it often was. Our moral code is largely based on Judeo-Christian values, and the idea of equality under the law was foreign to ancient Romans. Life was precious, but the head of a household's right to control his family was even more sacrosanct. A father could kill his slave, his child, or his wife, and no one would fault him for it.

Some aspects of Roman life were admirable, others less so. The Romans valued faithfulness, piety to the household gods, and one's duty to the Republic. They believed duty to Rome was more important than love for family. They saw themselves as peacekeepers, even as they waged war across the known world. If you were not a Roman citizen, you were, by default, a slave or a "barbarian."

We have inherited much from the Romans, from their virtues and their vices. Consider the blood sports of the arena where gladiators executed slaves and accused criminals at the whim of a cheering crowd. The violence may be abhorrent to you, but ask yourself this—how often have you watched a movie and thrilled when the hero finally destroyed the villain? That frisson of satisfaction also enthused the crowds in Roman arenas. People in the twenty-first century are not so different from the people who lived in first-century Rome.

Q. *"Phebe's hands trembled as she sewed the curls above my forehead into place."* Mind explaining that?

A. Hairbrushes had not been invented in the first century, and neither had bobby pins. Heated curling irons were common (though none of them had plugs!), and combs were plentiful.

Roman women were fond of elaborate hairstyles, with curls and braids and hair piled high upon the head. Since hairspray had yet to be invented, a regal lady's handmaid would literally "sew" the braids and curls into place with thread designed to match the lady's hair color. Wealthy women also owned wigs, which were permanently sewn into whatever style the lady preferred.

Q. The women in the story use a *looking brass*? Were there no mirrors then?

A. Glass mirrors did exist by the first century, but they were small, of terrible quality, and extremely expensive. Most reflective surfaces were polished metal or stone.

Q. Euodia visited a fuller's collegia or guild. What's a fuller?

A. The fullers were professional launderers. Since few families had indoor plumbing (it was rare even in the first century, though the wealthy *did* have heated bathroom floors), most people had no way to wash their clothing or take a bath. Hence the need for public bathhouses, public toilets (and home chamber pots), and fullers. Fullers used urine to bleach clothing, and while society tended to look down on them, these launderers were among the highest-paid people in any city. Everyone who wanted clean clothing had to visit the ancient version of a laundry. Fullers also offered pleating for the stolas of married women, the "felting" of garments to make them waterproof, and the dyeing of fabrics and shoes.

Incidentally, fullers are mentioned in the Bible. We find a reference to their work in Mark 9:2–3, but most modern translations don't use the phrase. What the verse literally says is this: "And after six days doth Jesus take Peter, and James, and John, and bringeth them up to a high mount by themselves, alone, and he was transfigured before them, and his garments became glittering, white exceedingly, as snow, so as a fuller upon the earth is not able to whiten [them]" (Young's Literal Translation). Malachi 3:2 speaks of "fuller's soap," and 2 Kings 18:17, Isaiah 7:3, and Isaiah 36:2 refer to a "fuller's field" where laundry was cleaned and dried in the sun.

Q. Why don't you use the word *church* in the novel?

A. The word *church* was not introduced until the thir-
teenth century and did not become imbued with its
present meaning after the publication of the King
James Bible in 1611. When it was first used, the word
church referred to a building people worshiped in, not
a gathering of believers. The people of the first century and for generations afterward would have spoken of the *ecclesia*, the "called-out assembly." They
placed the emphasis on the *people*, not the building.

Q. Did the Romans invent the modern mile?

A. Not quite. The Roman mile measures only .92 of a
modern mile. For the Romans, a *mille passus* was
literally 1,000 paces. In 29 BC Agrippa standardized
the measurement to 5,000 Roman feet, but no one is
quite sure how long a Roman foot was. People have
gone so far as to measure the feet on extant Roman
statues, but those measurements, though similar, are
not uniform. I believe it's safe to say that a Roman
mile was a wee bit shorter than the modern version.

Q. Is a curse tablet an actual thing?

A. Yes. Called *defixiones*, curse tablets were sheets of
lead or stone on which someone could write out a
curse on an enemy. These curse tablets were then buried in a place where they could not be disturbed, and
the practice continued until AD 5. Hundreds of them

have been found in and around Rome, as well as in Roman Britain.

The Romans were a superstitious lot and truly believed their gods would act on their behalf. Lest you think the idea is only for primitive people, not so long ago I read an article about the St. Joseph statues some people bury with an ancient prayer or incantation to speed the sale of their houses. One act may be more malicious than the other, but the belief and practice are the same.

The Bible has never endorsed putting one's faith in anything or anyone other than God.

Q. The Scriptures say the slave girl had a "spirit of divination." Could the unclean spirit within her really tell the future? Do demons have that ability?

A. In short, no. Consider Isaiah 8:19–20: "When they say to you: 'Consult the mediums and necromancers who chirp and mutter,' shouldn't a people seek their God? Should a people consult the dead on behalf of the living? To Torah and to the testimony! If they do not speak according to this word, it is because they have no light."

Unclean spirits have no light. They are not omniscient, omnipresent, or omnipotent because they are not God. They cannot see the future; they can only guess or make ambiguous statements in an attempt to confuse or flatter those who seek them. Modern-day astrologers do the same thing.

Most people come under the influence of demons

when they flirt with the occult or other dark forces, opening a door to supernatural entities. That is why the Bible warns us not to have *anything* to do with fortune-telling, astrology, witchcraft, or mind-altering drugs. We are at war with real supernatural forces (Ephesians 6:12). My story is built on the theory that Sabina became demonized because her mother offered her to demons shortly after birth, and the Bible tells us that demons are associated with false gods (Deuteronomy 32:16–17; Psalm 106:36–38).

Galatians 5:19–21 tells us: "Now the deeds of the flesh are clear: sexual immorality, impurity, indecency, idolatry, witchcraft, hostility, strife, jealousy, rage, selfish ambition, dissension, factions, envy, drunkenness, carousing, and things like these. I am warning you, just as I warned you before, that those who do such things will not inherit God's kingdom."

References

Achtemeier, Paul J. *Harper's Bible Dictionary*. New York: Harper & Row and Society of Biblical Literature, 1985.

Baker, William H. "Acts." *Evangelical Commentary on the Bible*. Vol. 3. Grand Rapids, MI: Baker Book House, 1995.

Betz, Hans Dieter. "Paul (Person)." Ed. David Noel Freedman. *The Anchor Yale Bible Dictionary*, 1992.

Cartwright, Mark. "Lydia." https://www.britannica.com/place/Lydia -ancient-region-Anatolia, April 3, 2016. Accessed April 4, 2022.

Devine, Aaron, and Karelynne Gerber Ayayo. "Lydia of Thyatira." Ed. John D. Barry et al. *The Lexham Bible Dictionary*. Bellingham, WA: Lexham Press, 2016.

Dockery, David S., ed. *Holman Bible Handbook*. Nashville, TN: Holman Bible Publishers, 1992.

Gangel, Kenneth O. *Acts*. Vol. 5. Nashville, TN: Broadman & Holman Publishers, 1998.

Graves, David Elton. "What is the Madder with Lydia's Purple? A Reexamination of the Purpurarii in Thyatira and Philippi." https:// www.researchgate.net/publication/321241274_What_is_the_Madd er_with_Lydia's_Purple_A_Reexamination_of_the_Purpurarii _in_Thyatira_and_Philippi. January 2017. Accessed July 25, 2022.

"Guilds from the Ancient to Medieval Worlds." https://brewminate

.com/guilds-from-the-ancient-to-medieval-worlds/, June 18, 2020. Accessed April 6, 2022.

Hartog, Paul A. "Philippi." Ed. John D. Barry et al. *The Lexham Bible Dictionary*, 2016.

Hawthorne, Gerald F. "Philippians." *Word Biblical Commentary*. Vol. 43. Dallas: Word, Incorporated, 2004.

Heiser, Michael S. *Demons: What the Bible Really Says about the Powers of Darkness*. Bellingham, WA: Lexham Press, 2020.

Jamieson, Robert, A. R. Fausset, and David Brown. *Commentary Critical and Explanatory on the Whole Bible*. Vol. 1. Oak Harbor, WA: Logos Research Systems, Inc., 1997.

Johnston, Harold Whetstone. *The Private Life of the Romans*. Northbrook, IL: Scott, Foresman and Company, 1903.

Marks, Joshua J. "The Fullers of Ancient Rome." *World History Encyclopedia*. https://www.worldhistory.org/article/46/the-fullers-of-ancient-rome/references, July 14, 2021. Accessed June 27, 2021.

McGee, J. Vernon. *Thru the Bible Commentary*. Vol. 5. Nashville, TN: Thomas Nelson Publishers, 1997.

McVean, Ada. "Measles: The Plague that Ruined Rome." https://www.mcgill.ca/oss/article/did-you-know-history/measles-plague-ruined-rome. June 27, 2018. Accessed April 8, 2022.

Ogilvie, Lloyd J. *Acts*. Vol. 28. Nashville, TN: Thomas Nelson Publishers, 1983.

Packer, J. I., Merrill Chapin Tenney, and William White Jr. *Nelson's Illustrated Manners and Customs of the Bible*. Nashville, TN: Thomas Nelson Publishers, 1997.

Polhill, John B. *Acts*. Vol. 26. Nashville, TN: Broadman & Holman Publishers, 1992.

Richards, Larry. *Every Man in the Bible*. Nashville, TN: Thomas Nelson Publishers, 1999.

Roberts, Ronald D. "Philip V." Ed. John D. Barry et al. *The Lexham Bible Dictionary*, 2016.

Robertson, A. T. *Word Pictures in the New Testament*. Nashville, TN: Broadman Press, 1933.

Smith, William. *Smith's Bible Dictionary*. Peabody, MA: Hendrickson Publishers, 1986.

Stern, David H. *Jewish New Testament Commentary: A Companion Volume to the Jewish New Testament.* Clarksville, MD: Jewish New Testament Publications, 1996.

Talbert, Andrew R. "Thessalonica." Ed. John D. Barry et al. *The Lexham Bible Dictionary*, 2016.

Thames, Norwood E. III. "Weights and Measures." Ed. John D. Barry et al. *The Lexham Bible Dictionary*, 2016.

Vincent, Marvin Richardson. *Word Studies in the New Testament.* Vol. 1. New York: Charles Scribner's Sons, 1887.

Wentz, Lazarus. "Amphipolis." Ed. John D. Barry et al. *The Lexham Bible Dictionary*, 2016.

"What is the Meaning and Origin of the Word 'Church'?" https://www.gotquestions.org/meaning-of-church.html, accessed June 22, 2022.

Wilson, Mark. "The Roman Road System around the Mediterranean (Acts 8:26; 20:1–3; 23:23–33; 28:13–16; Romans 15:19)." *Lexham Geographic Commentary on Acts through Revelation.* Ed. Barry J. Beitzel, Jessica Parks, and Doug Mangum. Bellingham, WA: Lexham Press, 2019.

Wineland, John D. "Amphipolis (Place)." Ed. David Noel Freedman. *The Anchor Yale Bible Dictionary*, 1992.

Youngblood, Ronald F., F. F. Bruce, and R. K. Harrison, *Nelson's New Illustrated Bible Dictionary.* Nashville, TN: Thomas Nelson Publishers, 1995.

Angela Hunt has published more than 150 books, with sales exceeding five million copies worldwide. She's the *New York Times* bestselling author of *The Tale of Three Trees*, *The Note*, and *The Nativity Story*. Angela's novels have won or been nominated for several prestigious industry awards, such as the RITA Award, the Christy Award, the ECPA Christian Book Award, and the HOLT Medallion Award. Romantic Times Book Club presented her with a Lifetime Achievement Award in 2006. She holds doctorates in Biblical Studies and in Theology. Angela and her husband live in Florida, along with their mastiffs and chickens. For a complete list of the author's books, visit angelahuntbooks.com.

Sign Up for Angela's Newsletter

Keep up to date with Angela's latest news on book releases and events by signing up for her email list at the link below.

FOLLOW ANGELA ON SOCIAL MEDIA

Angela Hunt, novelist

AngelaHuntBooks.com

More from Angela Hunt

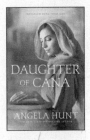

When a wedding guest tells Tasmin to have the servants fill the pitchers with water, she reluctantly obeys and is amazed when it turns into the finest wine ever tasted in Cana. But when her twin brother, Thomas, impulsively chooses to follow the Teacher from Nazareth, she decides to follow the group and do whatever she must to bring her brother home.

Daughter of Cana
Jerusalem Road #1

When her husband is thrown into debtor's prison, Pheodora—sister of Yeshua of Nazareth—pins her hopes on the birth of two spotless goats to sell for the upcoming Yom Kippur sacrifice so that she can provide for her daughters and survive. Calling on her wits, her family, and her God, can she trust that He will hear and help a lowly shepherd's wife?

The Shepherd's Wife
Jerusalem Road #2

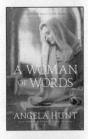

Asked by Mary to record stories of Yeshua while the eyewitnesses are still alive, Matthew, a disciple, reluctantly agrees. But the longer they work together, the more difficult their task becomes as they face threats and opposition. And when Matthew works to save his people, he realizes that the job he hesitantly accepted may be his God-given destiny.

A Woman of Words
Jerusalem Road #3

After moving to Jerusalem, Aya expects to be bored in her role as wife to a Torah student but finds herself fascinated by her husband's studies. And when her brother Sha'ul makes a life-altering decision, she is faced with a troubling question: How can she remain true to all she's been taught since infancy and still love her blasphemous brother?

The Apostle's Sister
Jerusalem Road #4

⬥ BETHANYHOUSE

 Bethany House Fiction   @bethanyhousefiction   @bethany_house   @bethanyhousefiction

 Free exclusive resources for your book group at bethanyhouseopenbook.com

Sign up for our fiction newsletter today at bethanyhouse.com